# FALLEN ANGEL, PART 5

## A MAFIA ROMANCE

### TRACIE PODGER

Jeanette
Thank you so much for your friendship!
Tracie

Fallen Angel, Part 5
A Mafia Romance
By
Tracie Podger

# CONTRIBUTORS

Cover designed by Margreet Asslebergs
Rebel Edit & Design
Formatting by Irish Ink – Formatting & Graphics
Editing – Karen Hardlicka
Proofreading – Joanne Thompson

# ACKNOWLEDGMENTS

A big hug goes to the ladies in my team. These ladies give up their time to support and promote my books. Alison 'Awesome' Parkins, Karen Atkinson-Lingham, Marina Marinova, Ann Batty, Fran Brisland, Elaine Turner, Kerry-Ann Bell, Jodie Scott, Lou Hands, and Louise White – otherwise known as the Twisted Angels.

If you would like to receive a free copy of my novella, Evelyn, sign to my mailing list by typing the following into your browser. You'll receive a download link in the welcome email once you have verified your subscription.

https://www.subscribepage.com/v8h1g0

# Robert - Chapter One

It was in a small room in a villa in Tuscany that my life changed forever–again.

Everything I knew, or believed, had been a lie. Just over Forty years of thinking one man was my father, and that he had been killed with my mother, was disproved with a simple DNA test. I barely remembered him; I hardly remembered my mother. Just a week after discovering the letters, I'd found the man who would protect my wife, who was the love of Evelyn's life, was also my biological father. To say my head had been fucked up was an understatement.

---

"Do you want to talk?" I heard. I had been sitting on the edge of the fountain in the courtyard of the villa.

I looked up to see Brooke walking toward me. I patted the wall.

"Sit with me," I said.

She picked up my hand and threaded her fingers through mine as she did. I stared at her for a moment. Her blue eyes were ringed, faintly, with dark circles and laugh lines fanned out across her skin. She looked tired and I guessed my overactive brain working day and night had been the cause of that.

"How do you feel today?" she asked gently.

I sighed and closed my eyes; I raised my face to catch the last of the day's sun before I spoke.

"Better. One minute I have no biological family; the next, I have a father, a half brother and a half sister. It's been a little difficult to process all that," I confessed.

"No shit," she replied, with a chuckle.

I turned to look at her. I shifted my body until I was facing her and traced my fingers down her cheek.

"I've been a complete prick this past week, haven't I?"

She tried to hide the smirk. "I know of Mr. Angry, Mr. Playful, Mr. Sarcastic, and all the other misters that make up Robert Stone, but I'm a little unsure who's with us right now."

"Mr. Honest?" I offered.

"Ah, it could be. Therefore the answer would be, yes, you have been a complete prick this week. But with good reason, Robert," she said.

I laughed quietly.

"Have you spoken to him today?"

Initially, after I'd discovered Rocco was my father, we'd talked, he'd cried, but then sadness settled over me. Forty years of memories were shattered on the opening of an envelope that contained evidence and I struggled with it. I'd endured years of abuse at the hands of my aunt, yet I had a father who could have rescued me from her. It was an unrealistic thought, of course, he didn't know about me, but it bothered me. Something that niggled at the back of my brain often annoyed me. Unfortunately, I had taken that frustration out on Brooke.

"I did, we are meeting tomorrow. This affects our plans a little."

"Why?"

"I'm his oldest child, he wants to adjust his will, but I don't want him to. He has two children, how must they feel to have me walk in and take over?"

Brooked looked at me with wide eyes, she opened her mouth to speak but I shook my head and laughed.

"Okay, I get it."

"As long they don't respond in the same way Joey did, I think you're going to be just fine. But is that it?"

I looked at her. My wife knew me way better than I knew myself sometimes.

"I'm not sure I want to admit this. I'm nervous about meeting them, Brooke."

"I can imagine you would be. I bet they're nervous about meeting you, too. His daughter, she lives in London, but what about his son?"

"Marco lives in Rome but I think he spends a lot of time in Northern Italy. I didn't get to meet him last time I was there, but I don't think he's that involved with his father's business, to be honest. He works in local government, which is a little ironic…Scratch that, I'm sure an insider in local government is a perfect place for him, and us."

I stood and gently pulled my wife to her feet. I placed my arm around her shoulders and pulled her into my side.

"What a fucking few months, huh?"

"You could say that. I'm looking forward to getting back to D.C., to be honest."

"Another week, and then I'll have everything in place here," I said.

As much as Brooke enjoyed being in Italy, I was pretty sure she preferred to be back home with the girls. She never said anything but I'd watch her sitting by the pool and just staring off into space wistfully, she'd sigh occasionally with a sad look about her face. When she caught me looking, she'd smile, but it never quite met her eyes. She seemed to have lost a little of her sparkle. I'd asked her a few times if she was happy, and she would tell me she was, but I suspected she was bored.

We walked slowly toward the villa; it was a peaceful evening with just the sound of crickets and the scent of citrus in the air. Gerry was already in bed after a day of activities, Katrina and Travis had decided on a night out. There were some amazing local restaurants in the village and just outside. But then, over the past couple of years, according to the locals, tourism had started to really pick up in their 'quaint authentic' part of the country. Some welcomed it; most hated it. It was an intrusion.

"How about we have a glass of wine and talk some more?" Brooke said, as she headed to the kitchen.

I nodded to her retreating back, knowing she'd assume my answer to be 'yes.' I carried on through the living room and out to the terrace. I sat and just thought. Merging my business with my father's, which had been the plan before the revelation, was taking its time. The heads of families, who sat on the Commission, wanted a fair division of the businesses I was persuading Rocco to let go. Drugs were not my thing, money laundering was useful but not necessary; the illegal trading of arms was something I wanted to legalize, it was extremely profitable but came with a high risk. I chuckled to myself. My father had his fingers in so many fucking pies—it blew me away. Of course, there was also the matter of who would lead this new 'business.' Rocco had said he wanted to semi-retire. I'd prefer that he fully retired. I didn't do well working alongside someone, I didn't take orders. Unless it involved my wife and sex, of course.

At that thought, I felt the hardening in my pants. I smiled. No matter what happened to us, no matter what was on my mind, just the image of her was enough to have my cock ready for action.

She crossed the terrace, and I watched her concentrate on holding a bottle of red wine in one hand and two glasses in the other. The tiled floor was a little uneven in places and she kept her vision cast down. She was barefoot, wearing a halter-top dress that brushed her knees. Her nipples were erect, and I doubted that was from the slight breeze that drifted across from the valley below.

I reached out to take the bottle from her, placing it on the table, and then pulled her into my lap. I needed to touch her, to feel her body against mine. Her scent was ingrained in my senses but I wanted to refresh that. I nuzzled against her neck as she poured two glasses. She handed one to me, then settled against me.

"I worry about you," she whispered before she took a sip of her wine.

"What are you worried about, exactly?"

"Whether you've taken on too much. Whether you're putting yourself in danger, the usual," she replied with a chuckle.

"I need more people to manage all this, and we can't bring some of it into Vassago, but it will all fall into place soon."

"What about Vinny? Is he up to staying here and managing things?"

I laughed. "Vinny is just a runner, maybe security, maybe a fist for hire, but that's all. He doesn't have the business brain to run things for me."

"What's a runner?"

"I want something, he goes and fetches it."

We had *inherited* Vinny when I'd bought the villa. His grandmother owned it initially, she'd sold it to Rocco, and he and his mother had stayed on to manage the place. He was useful, he had aspirations to be more, but he didn't have the capability to. Although young, he lived in a fantasy world of old-school gangsters. That wasn't the person I wanted on my team.

"One more week, Brooke, and then we'll head home for a while."

I had no doubts our life would involve flying back and forth on a regular basis, and I knew she'd be by my side each time I did. As much as she worried for me, I did the same for her. I kissed her neck, tasting her skin, and I heard her sigh. I leaned forward and placed my glass on the table, taking hers from her hand and doing the same. She shuffled so she was facing me, her knees at either side of my thighs. I ran my hands down her throat and across her chest. The fingers of each hand then brushed gently over her nipples.

She rested her arms on my shoulders, her hands tangled into the hair at the back of my head.

I let my hands slide down to her knees and then I gently raised them back up, dragging her dress with me. A smirk slowly formed on my lips when I realized she wore no panties.

"How long are Travis and Katrina out?" I whispered.

"I don't know."

"Long enough for me to fuck you in that pool?" I stood, holding her to me as I did.

She laughed and wrapped her legs around my waist, looking over her shoulder as I walked us toward the water. I stepped off the edge, fully clothed, and submerged us both in the deep end.

I could hear her laughter underwater as she kicked her legs and used her arms to propel herself back to the surface. I grabbed her wrist and towed her until I was in a position where my feet could touch the floor, and then I pinned her to the side.

"You've ruined my dress," she said as she undid the buckle of my belt and then my pants.

"So buy another one."

I raised her dress, and once my cock was freed from the confines of my pants, I grabbed her thighs. Brooke wrapped her legs around my waist again and guided my cock inside her.

She placed her arms outstretched on the poolside behind her and raised her hips. Water sloshed over the edge as I fucked her. It wasn't easy, twice I lost my footing, my new Italian brogues not having much purchase against the pool tiles.

"Perhaps this wasn't the best idea," I whispered.

Brooke tightened her grip, and when she threw her head back, and I saw her fingers claw the tiled edge, I lowered my head and bit hard on her nipple through her dress.

Her cries as she came had me covering her mouth. Gerry was asleep, not that far away, with his bedroom door open to the balcony above us. I could feel her giggle against the flesh of my palm, and then the lick as her tongue darted out.

I pulled out of her and picked her up, placing her on the edge of the pool. I tucked myself away and climbed out beside her.

"We're getting too fucking old for this," I said, as I stood and held out my hand to her.

"Never. Now take me to bed and finish what you started," she demanded.

"Mrs. Stone, whatever you want, you shall get." I closed the gap between us. "Hard, fast, slow. You'll scream my fucking name as you come around my fingers, around my lips, and then, around my cock."

Her pupils dilated as she looked at me.

"Is that a promise, Mr. Stone?"

"You can bet it is, Brooke. Now move."

She took my hand and led me back into the living room, to the hallway, and we left a trail of dripping water as we ascended the stairs to our bedroom.

## Robert - Chapter Two

"Bro, you really ought to close your fucking windows at night," I heard, as I walked into the kitchen.

Travis was standing by the coffee machine.

"Pour me one," I said, ignoring his comment.

"Seriously, Bro, I'm sure the whole village heard your fun times," he said, as he handed me a cup.

I laughed. "My wife can't get enough of me, what can I do other than comply?" I said, with an exaggerated shrug of my shoulders.

"I guess you wore her out enough to keep her still sleeping?"

"Fucking better had. We have a meeting today," I said, as I sipped on the hot black coffee.

Travis went from brother to work mode. He downed his coffee and then straightened his tie.

"I'm ready when you are. Vinny is outside with the car."

I nodded.

"Meet you outside," I said, as I grabbed a sweet roll and broke off a piece.

I'd eaten the roll long before I reached the top step and walked into my bedroom. My wife was, indeed, still asleep. She was naked and spread-eagled across the bed, the white sheets tangled around her legs. Her hair was fanned out around her and her head was turned toward me. I walked quietly to the side of the bed and gently ran my finger down her chest and stomach. She opened her eyes at my touch.

"Hey," I said.

She smiled as she arched her body from the bed. I trailed my finger through her pubic hair and over her clitoris. I lowered my head to hers.

"I have to go. I just wanted to take a little of you with me. No time for breakfast," I said, as I plunged two fingers inside her and then withdrew them.

"That's mean," she said, opening her eyes fully.

She watched as I placed those two fingers in my mouth and sucked on them.

"Go, I'll finish myself off," she said with a sweet smile that could fell the devil.

I laughed as I grabbed my jacket from the back of a chair and gave her a wink.

I watched briefly as she ran her fingers over her clitoris. I adjusted my cock, so its hardness wasn't so obvious, and then folded my jacket over my arm.

"I won't be late. Save some for me."

"Have a *comfortable* day," I heard her call out as I left the room. I laughed as I shook my head.

Over five years that woman had been in my life and she still managed to surprise me every day.

I strode out into the courtyard and took the holster Travis held out. Once I had that securely fastened, I took the revolver Vinny handed to me and then slipped on my jacket. There had been years I hadn't wanted to conceal a gun on my body, but that had changed the minute my family had been threatened and my son had been kidnapped.

I thought of Gerry as I climbed into the back of the car. He would sleep for a little while longer and then charge around like the whirlwind he was. He and Harley would probably spend the day around the pool. Brooke and Evelyn would be planning Katrina and Travis' wedding, no doubt. I chuckled.

"We need to organize a night out," I said.

He frowned at me. "Last night of freedom for you," I said.

"Bro, no wedding ring will curb my freedom."

"Maybe not, but I guarantee a Russian New Yorker with balls bigger than yours will."

"Fuck off," he said, then turned toward the window. For a moment, I wondered if I'd taken my joke a little too far.

I let him be until we headed into the village.

"Trav, your life will be amazing, trust me," I said.

He turned toward me. "It's all happening a little too fast."

"Do you want to postpone? There's no rush if you're not ready."

"I am, I want to marry her. You know me, I don't do commitment, normally," he said with a laugh.

"Bro, you're only man I know who does commitment even when there isn't a fucking relationship to commit to. Want me to give you some names?" I could list the women he was going to marry, even before he'd been on a first date with them.

"You're just jealous. Vinny, I've had all the women, this one here…Nothing, de nada, until Brooke. Well, other than the girl in the club, oh, and Miranda! Fuck, whatever happened to her?"

"No idea."

"She was a piece of work. Anyway, I'm fine."

"Fine like your sister says," I replied, quietly.

Travis looked at me; there was no need for words. He was scared, worried about the changes to our lives, the separation that he believed would occur, and he was getting married. Travis didn't do marriage, until Katrina. He was no more capable of not marrying that woman than I was Brooke.

"They fucking got us good, didn't they?" he said.

"They sure did, Bro. And I wouldn't change one day of it, neither will you."

He nodded and then smiled.

---

The Commission was meeting in the back room of the same restaurant Rocco had taken us to a few months prior. Travis and I walked in and the seven men, already seated, rose to greet us. Before we could walk any farther, security stepped in front of us.

"I'm sorry, Mr. Stone, but…"

He didn't need to finish his sentence. I pulled my jacket open to expose the holster. He reached in and took the gun, slid out the clip and handed it back to me. He placed my empty revolver on a table, alongside others. Then he repeated the process with Travis.

Rocco walked over, they parted for him. He placed his hands on my arms and kissed both my cheeks. It pleased me to see him do the same to Travis.

"Roberto, sit next to me," he said, as he walked me back to the table.

Travis was shown to my side. Rocco sat at the head of the table, and after some shuffling, the meeting was called to order.

"Friends, you are aware of my plans and the merging of my businesses with my son's. However, Roberto wants to dispose of some of my activities here in Italy. Today, we decide what happens to those," he said. A murmur floated around the room.

"Roberto, we trust that you will treat each family fairly," I heard. I looked toward the end of the table.

"Of course, Soli. However, it will come with conditions," I replied.

"Conditions?" I heard from the side of the table.

"Alberto, of course there will be conditions. As you know, my family means more to me than anything, and this is an opportunity to protect them. You'll get part of Rocco's operation, on the condition you decide to not take what isn't yours," I said.

Alberto wasn't someone I liked. Keeping him sweet was a necessity, though. Rocco respected him, his family was very old, but he had been linked to the man who had caused me, my wife, and my son the most pain. He had supported Matteo until he had agreed; kidnapping my son wasn't the right way forward.

Alberto looked at Rocco; he spoke in his own dialect deliberately so I couldn't understand. I placed my hands on the table and leaned forward.

"Don't fucking insult me, Alberto, otherwise your family will get nothing. That will leave you weak," I said, my voice so low I wasn't sure he heard.

Rocco placed his hand on my arm.

"There is bad blood here, as you know, my friends. This is something that needs to be addressed," Rocco said.

"If anyone here doesn't agree to my conditions, then this meeting is over."

I was taking a gamble with my attitude. The Commission was an established gathering, it had been around for centuries, and although I didn't view it as part of the modern world we lived in, most of the men around that table lived for it.

I heard a chuckle and turned toward the sound.

"Roberto, welcome to the Commission. I can assure you, all these *old men* will do as you please. You were a respected man before we knew of your…origins, shall we say."

Rocco leaned to my side and whispered into my ear.

"Enrico Romano."

I knew the name; I'd never met the man. He was reclusive and ran one of the biggest drug cartels in Italy. Not even the government would take him on, so many were in his employ, and he was second only to my father in standing within the Commission. That meant he was a very influential man indeed.

"Signore, I thank you for your comments. I want to be fair. As you know, there are elements of my father's businesses that do not sit well with me, or my lifestyle in America. But I also want to ensure my family's safety going forward."

He nodded his head. "I am sure all around this table will agree with you, providing what you deem as fair is exactly that."

His English was outstanding for a man that had never left his country. I looked over to Vinny, who handed me a folder. I placed that on the table and gently slid it toward Enrico.

"Perhaps you would do me the honor to read through these, tell me whether you agree. I am open to negotiation, Enrico, of course."

I wasn't, but he didn't need to know that.

He opened the folder and picked up the first document. At the top was the family name and then a list of holdings or activities I was willing to hand over. My father had too many businesses in Italy for me to manage from the U.S.

We waited in silence as Enrico scanned each page. Eventually, he looked up and searched out each face of those sitting around that table.

"My friends, I think you will be pleased. Roberto has, indeed, been extremely fair and he has researched each family well."

He began to slide the documents to the members of the Commission they pertained to. For a moment we were back to silence, then a few members began to speak at once. One wanted more detail; another wanted to thank me. I held up my hand.

"Before you get excited, or not, take a moment to understand the condition. In simple terms, if you, or any member of your family, come after me or mine, that contract is immediately terminated. Enrico has another list, should you not comply, he will take back what is mine and give it to another."

Enrico laughed. "You are an astute businessman, Roberto, I admire that in you. I can give you my assurance, as a lifelong friend to Rocco, that won't be necessary."

My father, Rocco Sartorri, was the most powerful man around that table at that moment. But I was about to dilute his power.

"My father's enemies become my enemies, Enrico. Not many of you know me. I will only give this one piece of advice about me. An assurance, to me, is a bond. It's never to be broken. Should you be, let's say, surprised, by another family's actions, you'll stand shoulder to shoulder with me in rectifying that *surprise*."

He gently nodded his head and placed his hand over his heart. "I can give you that assurance, Roberto."

Then it was done. I had secured my place at the head of the Commission, alongside my father, and I had the second most powerful man in Italy beside me.

Alberto had settled back in his chair with his document in his hand. I had been fair, he had been given the drug route to the U.S., as much as it pained me to do so. Whether his drugs would reach their destination was another matter entirely. I smiled at him, although it wasn't necessarily a smile in friendship. He stared back at me until I had made him uncomfortable enough that he lowered his gaze and pretended to concentrate on his papers.

Of all the men around that table, he was my biggest threat, and one I intended to keep a very close eye on.

"Now we celebrate," Rocco said, and as if by magic, waiters appeared with trays of glasses and bottles of wine.

The men stood, the formality was over. I was greeted with respect by most. Cigars were passed around and wine glasses were filled. Again, it pleased me to see Travis treated the same. As much as he wasn't a decision maker in Vassago, as such, he was my brother and I would ensure he was treated as such.

After an hour of conversation, questions, most in Italian, some in English, and the promise of a second meeting to go over the fine details, some started to leave. Enrico walked over to me and held out his hands.

"You did well, Roberto," he said as he embraced me. "I don't foresee any problems."

"I'm pleased to hear that. However, problem-solving is one of my many talents," I replied with a laugh.

"So I've heard. As much as you have done your research here, I, and some of those men, have done ours. I'm impressed with your operations in the U.S., and I was impressed with how you dealt with Matteo."

"Alberto doesn't think so, I imagine," I replied. I wanted to make sure Enrico knew I was aware of Matteo and Alberto's connection.

He laughed. "That old fool will take sides with whoever is winning, he is a true Italian."

"Now we eat," Rocco interrupted us.

I was handed my revolver and I replaced the clip then slid it back into the holster. Travis and I followed Rocco and Enrico to a table on the veranda. We were immediately served wine and a jug of water was placed on the table. Rocco raised his glass.

"To my successor, my son," he said.

I enjoyed Enrico's company, although I felt bad for Travis when he switched to Italian. I often responded in English to keep him included, knowing he was already worried about this merger. I didn't want him to feel excluded in any way, whether that was the language or the new business associates.

We ate, we drank more wine, and then it was time to leave. Rocco walked with us to our car.

"Are you pleased with today?" he asked.

"Alberto will be a problem, I have no doubts about that, but it's good to have Enrico as a friend."

"I wouldn't trust any of them," he replied.

"I don't, the one I trust the least is the one I bring the closest," I said, patting his shoulder before climbing into my car.

Travis was quiet on the journey back; he kept his gaze out the side window. When the silence began to annoy me I broke it.

"So, what do you think?" I asked.

"About what?"

"Enrico and Alberto."

"I don't know them, Rob. You've met them before, haven't you? What are your thoughts?"

"I've never met either of them. As for Alberto, I only know of him and his association with Matteo."

"I can't form a judgment because I didn't understand a fucking word that was being spoken half the time."

"Does that bother you?"

"Only in the sense that, if there was a threat there, I'd never know. I can't help you if I don't understand what's being said."

"I'll make sure they speak in English next time. Although, I'm not sure whether they all can."

"I don't see a need for me to accompany you to those meetings anyway. I'm better off back in the U.S."

"You're better off by my side, like always," I replied.

Finally, he turned in his seat and looked at me.

"We are worlds apart now, Rob. That's okay; we knew this would happen. You and Rocco lead this *new* family. As I said, I'm of better use back home. This isn't my life, it's yours. This is your family, and as much as we will always be brothers, I have to step aside while we're here."

His comment brought me to an unusual loss of speech. Everything I'd ever done had been for us both. When he hadn't wanted to sit on the board at Vassago, I still made sure he got his share. When he'd voiced his concerns about the merger in Italy, I'd assured him nothing would change. I wasn't sure I could keep that promise, though. The members of the Commission had shown him respect, it wasn't their fault he couldn't speak their language and when they could, they switched to English but, and the thought pulled me up short, it was too easy to fall into a language that had begun to feel natural to me.

"One more week, and then we go home, okay?"

He sighed. "Katrina wants to get these wedding plans underway. If you don't need me here, we might head home a little earlier."

I didn't *need* him, but I wanted him to stay. Was that fair? I was conscious of Vinny who, periodically, looked in the rearview mirror.

"Okay, whatever is best," I said for the sake of Vinny's ears.

I decided I'd talk to Travis in private as soon as we arrived back to the villa. We continued the journey in silence, something that disturbed me. I could do anger, I could handle shouting, but silence wasn't Travis' thing, normally.

The car circled the drive at the villa and came to a stop. Before I could exit, Gerry and Harley rushed from the villa. Both wore board shorts and flip-flops.

"Dad, you have to come and see this," Gerry said, tugging on my arm.

"We made an obstacle course in the pool," Harley added.

The change in Travis was immediate. He smiled at Harley, ruffled his hair, and told him he'd go and change immediately. I didn't get that chance to talk to him and I wondered if Travis knew I'd wanted to. The kids were the diversion he needed.

"Buddy, how about you give me five minutes then I'll join you?" I said to Gerry. He nodded and rushed off after Harley.

Brooke was sitting beside the pool with Katrina when I walked through to the terrace.

"Hey, how was your day?" she asked as she rose from a sunbed.

"Good, I'm going to grab a coffee," I replied.

"I'll join you."

When we were far enough from the pool, and people, she asked me again.

"So, how was your day, really?"

I laughed. "It was good, got done what I needed to." She had no idea what my meeting was about and I preferred it that way.

Brooke smiled as she handed me a coffee. I shrugged off my jacket and placed it on the back of the chair.

"Can you do something about that?" she said, pointing to the holster.

I slid it from my shoulder and wrapped the excess leather around the gun. I then placed it on top of a cabinet.

"Okay?" I asked.

She nodded as she sat at the table. I sat opposite.

"How have the kids been today?" I asked.

"Gerry made an obstacle course but didn't tell Harley the 'legal' route, his words, so they argued because Gerry won every race. Of course, I intervened."

"He's very competitive," I said with a laugh.

"Sneaky, is what he is, as well."

"Can't say I don't admire that in him. It will serve him well one day."

"Mmm, not sure I agree, but they had fun."

"Children from his background always learn to 'dodge the system,' and do what they need to get their own way," I said.

"But he isn't from that background now. I'd like to think he'd play fair, be happy to lose every now and again, for Harley's sake."

Brooke's comment surprised me.

"Mmm, not sure I agree, but they had fun, right?" I said, echoing her words. "I need to get changed. Maybe we can go out later, just the two of us."

I left her in the kitchen and walked up the stairs.

"Bro, you got a minute?" I said, as Travis walked down. At the same time, Harley rushed into the living room calling for him.

Travis shrugged his shoulders. "Duty calls. Speak later," he said.

I walked into the bedroom and sat on the bed. I hadn't agreed with Travis' comments, and I didn't agree with Brooke's either. It wasn't because Gerry was my son, but I didn't agree with losing for the sake of it. Harley was older, two whole years Gerry's senior. He should be able to cope with both winning and losing. I wasn't about to teach my child to deliberately lose something for the sake of feelings.

That kind of shit could get you killed in my world.

Something had changed. There was a shift in dynamics, for sure. Was it me? I had reason to change; my world had been turned on its head. I'd discovered a family, roots, and a heritage. Like Gerry, I wasn't about to 'lose' that for the sake of feelings.

Robert - Chapter Three

"Rob, we've decided to head back home tomorrow," Travis said.

"We have a lot to prepare. Where we're going to live being one of them," Katrina added.

We were sitting at the table having breakfast. Evelyn had joined us, she had been staying with Rocco for the past few days, and although we were all happy with that, we missed her.

"Okay, I'm sure we can sort out the flights," I said, not that it was what I wanted to say, but with a room full of people I was unable to voice my real feelings.

"Already done," he said with a smile.

"I hadn't thought about where you'll live," Brooke said.

I noticed Harley looking a little uncomfortable at the turn in conversation.

"I'm sure we can sort something out, you can always build on the grounds…if you want to, of course," I added.

I watched Katrina as she quickly looked at Travis. They had already had a conversation, I was sure. They were yet to tell me their plans and I wondered why. It wasn't unreasonable for Katrina to want to live away from the rest of us, but did that suit Travis? I remembered back to the time I'd first built the house and the 'separation anxiety' he'd suffered when he moved into his own apartment. Things were different, I guessed. He was about to get married, he was already a father, but it highlighted the fact there seemed to be a gulf growing between us. Perhaps it was me that had the separation anxiety.

"We can work something out later," Travis said. He placed his arm around Harley's shoulder. "You'll have a say, buddy, don't worry."

Evelyn was standing behind the kitchen island, sipping on her coffee. I caught her looking at me over the rim of her cup. Her worry lines had deepened.

"What are your plans today, Ev?" I said, changing the subject.

"I'm spending it here with you."

"You need to spend time with Rocco," Brooke said.

"We have plenty of time to catch up, we've already had plenty of time to talk. Today, I want to spend it here."

She kept her gaze on me. Maybe she thought she *needed* to spend her day with us and I was, selfishly, thankful for that.

"Boys, one last round of your obstacle course before we do some home schooling, okay?" Katrina said as she rose from her chair.

"I'll help set up," Travis added.

The boys ran from the room and Brooke stood to clear the table.

"Brooke, leave that, we can clear the dishes later. I'd like Rob to walk with me for a little while," Evelyn said.

"You two go, you haven't spent any time alone for a while. I'm happy doing this," Brooke replied.

My astute wife had obviously picked up on my mood and was giving Evelyn and me a little private time to talk it out. I walked over to her and placed my hands each side of her face. I kissed her briefly.

"Thank you," I whispered.

"Go talk, and I'm here if you need to talk to me as well," she said with a smile.

"Did I tell you today that I loved you?"

"No, but you can later if you want," she replied. I kissed her again.

"Shall we?" I said, raising my elbow so Evelyn could take hold of my arm.

We walked in silence for a little while, crossing the courtyard and through a gate that led to the olive groves.

"What's happening, Rob?" she gently asked.

"I don't know, is the honest answer. Travis doesn't feel like he fits into my world right now. I'd planned for us to go home next week, but I guess, he rightly has a wedding to plan, and a home to organize." I then recounted the conversation we'd had in the car.

"That doesn't sound like Travis at all. You boys have been through way too much for him to not feel *part of your world*. It's his world as well and has been for as long as it's been yours. Do you think Katrina has a hand in these decisions?"

"I don't know. Possibly. I can't get involved in that, if it is the case, of course. He needs to have the freedom to do as he wishes, and I'd never want him in a position where he has to choose. So I have to back off, wait, and see what he decides."

"If you back off too much, he might think his feelings are correct."

"That's the point, to him, his feelings are correct. I tried to include him yesterday, but he doesn't understand the language. Rocco greeted him respectfully, as did some of the others, so I'm not sure where this is coming from."

We walked along the path that separated the olive trees. I ran my hand over a branch, plucking an olive off. It was hard, not ready for harvest, and I made a mental note to ask Elvira who would manage that.

"I think he's scared about the whole marriage thing, it was kind of thrown on him. He wants to marry Katrina, I'm sure, but he has a lot to process at the moment, as do you," Evelyn said.

"I'm sure that's just the case. Ev, something doesn't feel right, in here, though," I said, tapping my chest.

"Then you might need to take a little time to figure out what doesn't. You've lived on your instincts your whole life, and they have served us well many times. Focus on it, see if anything comes to you," she said.

We had doubled back and were walking toward the villa. I could see Vinny in the distance with his hand shielding his eyes. He scanned until he saw us, and then lowered his arm. He didn't indicate he needed me, so I kept my pace slow to accommodate Evelyn's.

"Who would have thought we'd be here, right at this moment, with everything that has happened these past months, huh?" she said quietly.

"You've had the most change, Ev. How are you coping?"

"I still get moments of anger, of confusion. Rocco was, is, the love of my life, Robert. He was the reason I would never marry, and there are times when I feel such an overwhelming sadness that we didn't get all those years together, but I understand why. My life was in danger for many years, I just didn't know about it. He did what he had to, to protect my family and me, but it came at such a high price. I don't know what's to happen. I'm pleased he made the decision to step back a little. I couldn't live in Rome, and I don't think he wants to live in the U.S."

"What will you do?"

We stopped walking and she turned to me. "I can't leave you and Travis, but that is my dilemma to solve. He understands and, I hope, he'll follow me. As for a visa to live in the U.S., I guess we can count on you for that?"

"You can. I'll talk to him, although I'm sure my contacts were his long before I knew them." I laughed at the thought.

"Maybe you'll do what I plan, come back and forth?" I added.

"Have you spoken to Brooke about that?"

"Yes, sort of. Why?"

"No reason, I see her sometimes and I think she might be missing home right now. She misses the girls. You fit in here because Italy has always been a part of who you are, thanks to my father, and now your own. But it's not the same for everyone else. A holiday here, that's wonderful, but long term? I'm not so sure. Even I'm hankering for a decent store and some cooler weather."

We were approaching the end of October but the heat, although not as intense as the summer months, was still draining.

"Brooke wants to be home for Christmas, for sure. Will you join us?" I said.

"Of course. I won't miss a family Christmas, Rob. Now, you need to concentrate on that feeling of yours, and we'll keep our eye on Travis. See if, between us, we can figure out what's going on, okay?"

We continued to walk to the courtyard. When I saw Vinny holding an envelope in his hand, I knew my downtime was over and it was back to business. I kissed Evelyn on the cheek and left her to walk to the villa.

"What?" I asked, maybe a little aggressively.

"This was just hand delivered for you," he said.

He held up the envelope but I didn't reach for it.

"From who?"

"I don't know, it was dropped off."

"By who?"

"A courier, I imagine."

I stared at him. "I know, but there is one in the village. Fuck knows what level of business they get," he added.

"And you've checked it out?"

"The envelope or the courier?"

"Both, you idiot. You've no idea what's in that fucking envelope. Take it to the office. Call Gary to show you what to do. I'll meet you there."

I shook my head at his incompetence and walked into the villa.

"Trav, have you got a minute?" I called out. I heard footsteps cause the ceiling above my head to creak.

"What's up, I'm just packing?"

"I need you for a moment."

He slowly walked down the stairs.

"Did you see a courier drop of an envelope?"

"No, when?"

"Some time in the last half hour. I was in the olive grove with Evelyn."

"No, but then I've been up here. What's in the envelope?"

"I don't know, Vinny was about to hand it to me."

"Had he opened it?"

"No, and I don't think anyone else knows it was delivered."

"For fuck's sake. Where is he?"

"In the office."

Travis and I walked to the front door. The 'office' was a building the other side of the courtyard. With it's concrete floor and bare brick walls, I could only guess at its previous use. Bars covered the windows and the door had once held a large padlock. We'd installed a desk and some chairs. It was a private place to talk if needed.

Gary was standing by the door and Vinny shuffled from foot to foot beside him.

"It's safe, but it's been handled so I doubt we'd get any decent prints from it if we needed to," Gary said, and then stared at Vinny.

I nodded at him. Over the past couple of years, Gary had transformed from just being Brooke's security to a very valuable member of my team. We walked into the room. The open envelope sat on the table.

"Did you look inside?" I asked Gary.

"I did. Not sure you're going to be pleased to see them."

I picked it up and shook the contents out onto the table. Three photographs slid from the unmarked envelope. Using the tip of my finger, I spread them out.

"Fuck!" Travis whispered.

One was of Brooke. She was in the town square, talking to an older woman and laughing. The second was of Katrina at the market. She was leaning over a stall and reaching for some fruit. The third was Evelyn. She was either getting in or out of a car in our courtyard.

I flipped them over and on the back of each was just a question mark in red felt pen.

Gary took the envelope and dismantled it; he laid the single piece of paper out, inspecting the inside.

"Who delivered this, Vinny?" he asked.

"Young kid on a pushbike. Said he was asked to deliver it to Mr. Stone."

"Where is this kid?" I asked.

"Gone. I didn't think…"

I held up my hand, I wasn't interested in what he 'didn't think' about.

"He was just a kid, like ten or so," he added.

I stared at him. "I don't care how old he was. I want to know who he is, though, so I suggest you get on to that right now."

Vinny hesitated. "Do you have a problem with that?" I asked.

"No, sorry. He must live locally, I'll head into the town to see what I can find out."

"You said earlier that a courier dropped this off," I said.

"That's what I assumed, but Antonio, at the gate, said some kid just cycled up and gave it to him. He gave it to me."

"Assumption gets people killed, Vinny," Travis said, as he picked up the picture of Katrina.

Vinny left the room, and I hoped when he returned, he'd have news I could work with.

"I'm definitely taking Katrina home tomorrow now," Travis said.

"We don't know what this means yet…"

Before I could finish my sentence, he interrupted, "I don't care what it means. Someone took a photograph of her, we're out of here."

Gary looked over to me. I gently shook my head.

"Okay, that's the right thing to do. I'll talk to Rocco and see if he has any ideas while we wait for Vinny." I pulled out my mobile as Travis left the room.

Gary opened his mouth to speak, he saw me raise the cell to my ear. It cut off whatever he was about to say. I hoped it wasn't to question Travis' decision; that was for me to do, no one else. Travis hadn't run at the first sign of any trouble before. I understood he had Katrina to protect, but we were safer and stronger as one unit, he knew that. As it was, we had way more allies in Italy after the meeting than we did back in the U.S.

While I waited for the call to connect, I stared at the photographs. The cameraman had been able to zoom in, blocking out the security detail that shadowed all those women. There was no way for me to tell how far away those snaps had been taken, of course, and I doubted he, or she, would have been close. The team that protected my family was at the top of their game, excluding Vinny.

"Roberto, what can I do for you?" Rocco said when he answered.

"I've had an interesting delivery today, I'd like your opinion on it."

"Is it something we can do over the phone?"

"No, I'd like you to come here, if you're able to."

"I'll be there in a half hour, sooner if I can."

Rocco had been staying in the village. He had alternated between the village and Rome, and I knew at some point, he'd have to return there. I worried for Evelyn knowing it wasn't somewhere she would want to live. I put that thought to the back of my mind and concentrated on the images in front of me.

"These weren't taken on the same day," Gary said.

"Can you date them?" I asked.

"I know Brooke's movements, and Katrina's, but not so much Evelyn's. This one, I think, was three days ago. She wanted to visit Franco," he said, pointing to the image of Brooke.

"And this?" I asked, tapping the one of Katrina.

"As far as I know, Katrina went to the market with Elvira last week, so before the image of Brooke was taken."

"Someone has been tailing them for a little while. Why hasn't that been picked up?"

"To be fair, Robert, it's still tourist season. There are plenty of people with cameras around their necks, but I doubt these were taken close up. See the background, it's very slightly blurred. I'd suspect a telescopic lens. That means, whoever took these could have been anywhere. And that angle? Probably from inside a building as well."

The image of Brooke was angled down toward her, so I accepted his statement. It also meant, obviously, it was a targeted shot and not just someone who captured the girls and thought I might like them. In the past, I'd been sent images that had been taken by the paparazzi. Fuck knows why they would think I'd want to keep images that had been taken without my permission.

"What do you need me to do?" Gary asked, bringing me out of my thoughts.

"Follow up on Vinny, and whoever accepted this at the gate."

He nodded his head and left the room. I gathered the photographs and wrapped the envelope around them. I left them in the office and headed out to find Travis. It was time for another chat.

———

I found Travis in the kitchen, alone. I closed the door behind me as I entered. He turned slowly to face me.

"Coffee?" he asked.

"Sure. What happened in there, Trav?" I asked.

"What do you mean?"

"You saw the photos and then ran. That's not you."

He sighed, turned his back to pour the coffee, and maybe buy himself a few minutes.

"Katrina is pregnant, Rob."

"That's fantastic news…isn't it?"

By the look on his face, I wasn't sure he was in agreement with me.

"We've only been serious a few months. I didn't plan for this, any of it, and it's all rolling away from me. When it was just Harley and me, I didn't feel under pressure, now I do. I have to keep them all safe, and I'm not so sure we can do that now."

"We are safer now than ever, you must know that?"

"Do I? I'm not as confident as you about that. Brooke and Gerry have the protection of Rocco's reputation. You are the top man out here. Me? I'm just your sidekick."

"That's bullshit and you know it, Trav. Those are just excuses, because I don't think you really believe that for one moment. Is it the pregnancy? The wedding?"

He shrugged his shoulders. "Maybe I'm just too fucking old for all this."

I frowned. "You're the same age as me. What is Katrina saying to you?"

"Why does it have to be Katrina? Can't you accept that I'm not happy about all this? I have my own fucking mind, Rob."

"And that mind is way off track, I want to know why."

"I'm happy about the wedding, I'm happy about the baby, I'm just…Fuck knows what I am right now."

"Bro, I need you to know, nothing changes with us, ever. You don't want any of this, then we won't have any of this. I'll tell Rocco he has to find another successor and we go home, forget about Italy."

He shook his head. "This was your destiny, and I'm pleased for you. It's just too many changes all at once. Ignore me, I don't fucking know which way is up right now. I've got Katrina making plans, talking baby names, wanting to keep it a secret until she can make the big announcement. She's pushing for me to move in with her, she has the bigger house, I don't want to."

"Then don't. As I said, build a house in the grounds; tell her how shit-scared you are of the speed it's all happening."

He nodded his head. Eventually, he smiled.

"Congratulations, by the way," I added.

He took a deep breath in and exhaled slowly. "I thought it would just be me, Katrina, and Harley. At least for a while."

"Did you ever discuss kids?"

"No, but then she's thirty-five so I guess her 'clock' is ticking."

"Is this pregnancy all that's bothering you? After what you said in the car, and earlier, I'm not sure if there's more," I said.

"I don't know. Bro, I'm just all over the place right now, like I said. So many changes and a lot to absorb, that's all, I guess."

"Let's get home and we can regroup, okay?"

"How are you handling all this?" he asked.

"I haven't stopped and thought about it just yet. Like I said to Brooke, one minute I don't know who I am, where I'm from, and the next, I have a family. Sometimes I'm angry, I could have been 'saved' as a kid, but then other times I think, if I had, I wouldn't have spent thirty years worrying about you." I added a wink so he was sure I was joking.

"Do you know what I need, Bro? I need to beat the shit out of someone, we haven't done that in a while."

"Someone? Or a session in the ring, because you know I'll kick your ass?"

"Someone might be good. Let's go find who's taking pictures of our family."

I wasn't, for one minute, fooled that the 'old' Travis was back. I also wasn't convinced that Katrina being pregnant and the rush to marry was *all* he had on his mind, but I let it go. We had a more pressing problem to worry about.

Rocco sat in the office and studied the photographs. He picked each up individually, pausing over the one of Evelyn. Without a word, he stood and walked from the room. Travis and I followed. He stood exactly where the car had been parked in the photo and looked up the hill. I shielded my eyes and followed his gaze. There was an old building, just outside the boundary of our land. Gary had already been and checked it out, of course, it was run-down and with a padlocked door.

"Follow me," he said.

We walked through a gate and along a grass path to the building. The stone wall that bounded our property was slightly lower in one place, low enough to step over easily enough. Rocco paused and I watched as his shoulders rose with a deep breath. He fished around in his pocket for a bunch of keys. We watched as he reached forward and unlocked the padlock. The door swung open with a creak.

Inside, the room housed a metal cot bed, a wooden rail, and an old metal pail. I could only imagine what the pail was for.

"They kept me here, caged like a dog. I was let out for a few hours during the day, I was fed, but for most of the time, this was my home," he said quietly.

"Who?" I asked.

"He is dead now, Roberto. I destroyed him and then I took everything he owned."

I looked over to Travis.

"Maybe it's time for you to learn what happened to me," he said.

"Is it relevant to the photos?" Travis asked.

"I think so. You see, I know where all those photographs were taken, and I don't think it's a coincidence that each one is a place I murdered in."

Rocco didn't speak again. He closed the door and locked it. He turned and walked back to the villa, past the fountain in the courtyard, and to the small wall. He stood and looked down on the village.

"So you were held near where your family lived?" I asked, not understanding how his family hadn't known he was still alive.

"Yes, the ultimate torment, Roberto. If I made contact, I'd also be made to watch their deaths. I was only here for a short time and then I was moved to Rome. When I was ready to take my revenge, I returned. By then, my mother was dead and my sister had moved away."

"Have you spoken to your sister?" Travis asked.

"She is not ready for that, so I'm told. She knows I'm alive, but for many years she mourned my death, believing she was the cause of it when I returned to Italy."

"Do you know who took the photos?" I asked.

"No, but it's perfect timing for the past to rear its ugly head."

With that he walked toward the villa. All Travis and I could do was to follow.

"Rocco, I wasn't expecting to see you," I heard. Evelyn walked across the hall.

"Bella, Roberto, Travis, and I need to talk. We have many things to discuss."

"Shall I make coffee?"

"I think we might need something a little stronger. Whiskey, perhaps?"

"Why don't you sit in the study, I'll bring some glasses through," she said.

"Give me a minute, will you?" Travis said as he darted up the stairs.

I could see Brooke in the kitchen.

"She is a good woman, is she not?" Rocco asked, following my gaze.

"The best thing that has ever happened to me, for sure," I replied. He gently nodded his head.

"Don't waste one moment of it, Roberto. I don't have the years left to make up to Evelyn, and that pains me every single day. Go tell your wife you love her, and then you, and Travis of course, need to listen to my story. I suspect we will be in for a long evening."

While Rocco headed to the study, I walked into the kitchen.

"Hey, baby," I said, as I slid my arms around Brooke's waist.

"Was that Rocco I heard?" she asked.

"It was. We have something to talk about; he's told me we're in for a long evening. It's important, so you might have to excuse us for dinner."

"I can make something and bring it in to you later, if you like. I'll keep everyone occupied, don't worry."

I leaned down to her ear. "He wants to tell me what happened to him, all those years ago."

"Wow, then you will be in for a long night. Before you get started, let me bring in some water, wine, and coffee. And if you need topping up, text me. Now, go, learn about his life," she said.

I watched her bustle around the kitchen, gathering trays. When Evelyn entered with whiskey glasses, they prepared our 'long haul' sustenance.

I followed Brooke and Evelyn as they carried the trays to the study. I positioned a small table in front of the collection of leather chairs, and once they'd left, we waited for Travis.

"Is everything okay with Travis?" Rocco asked.

"I'm not sure, to be honest. But that's a conversation for another day. If possible, as much as is possible, can we stick with English? I think his lack of understanding is one thing that makes him feel left out."

"Of course, but if I don't know the word, you'll have to translate."

I nodded as Travis came into the room.

Rocco leaned back in his chair. He studied us both.

"You two are so far apart in looks, but your mannerisms are identical. You remind me a lot of Joe, and I'm pleased that he cared you for. You are brothers, no matter who birthed you, who fathered you, because you have lived your lives together. I envy that of you, to some degree. I spent many years very lonely. I think, now is the time that you hear my story. My missing years."

Rocco: The Missing Years

Thirty years ago – Italy

# Rocco - Chapter One

My eyes opened and it took me a minute to realize where I was. I was lying on my back in the clothes I'd worn the day before, looking up at an ornate ceiling. A ceiling with plaster cherubs and painted saints, and I wondered how they felt, looking down on a sinner.

I had a plan; well, I knew the outcome to my plan. A man, a very powerful man would die by my hands. I would make that death as brutal, as painful, and as gut-wrenching as I could.

That man had ruined my life and I intended to do the same to him.

A knock on the door roused me from my thoughts, I didn't move. I had no desire to see or speak to anyone, and if they were coming for me, then let them fucking wait.

Another knock; louder that time, and more persistent, had me sighing and rolling from the bed. I didn't bother to look through the spy hole, no one of consequence knew where I was, just him and his henchmen. I opened the door, then immediately turned my back and walked away.

"Breakfast," I heard. I pointed to a small table in front of a sofa.

"And a clean shirt. Don't want to meet the Boss looking the way you are now, do you?"

I turned slowly to see the prick who had held a gun to my head. He sneered. I made a mental note, that smirk would be wiped from his face, preferably with a large kitchen knife. I ignored him and sat on the sofa. He let the shirt fall to the floor. I poured a cup of coffee, inhaling its rich aroma before I took a sip.

I lifted the silver dome that covered the plate to see deviled eggs on a toasted bun – how very European! Henchman left, slamming the bedroom door behind him.

As I sipped my coffee, I took a look around the plush room I had been imprisoned in. It had been dark when I'd been brought to a hotel, I didn't know its name or the location. Wherever I was, it was clearly expensive. Heavy brocade curtains hung from floor-to-ceiling windows on one side of the room. I stood and walked over. It wasn't windows I found myself in front of, but French doors. I opened one and stepped onto a small balcony. I instantly knew then where I was.

Below me was the piazza; its block-paved surface sloped gently down to the town hall. Arranged in a half circle around the piazza were restaurants, stores, and hotels, one of which I had found myself in—and people—lots of people. I scanned and then I saw him. Salvatore was sitting outside a coffeehouse; he looked up at me and raised his coffee cup. I did the same.

I would befriend, I would become the man he couldn't do without, I would make sure he relied so heavily on me that I became his closest ally—then I would kill him.

Sienna was awash with tourists and locals going about their business. More importantly, they were preparing for an event I'd seen only on American television. An event so colorful and majestic, despite my situation, I felt a small pang of excitement for.

Il Palio di Siena, a bareback horse race around the piazza was being prepared for.

Although early morning, the sun blazed down on the square, so I retreated into the cool room. If I had to be incarcerated, I was thankful it was in such luxury. A large bed with an ornate headboard was to one side of the room. At the other end was a bloodred, velvet covered sofa. The dark wood furniture looked old, antique. Some had claw brass feet of lions or other powerful beasts. Heavy enough to knock a man to the floor, I imagined. I shook my head of those thoughts. I'd be dead before I swung my arm.

I sat and ate, planned and tried, unsuccessfully, to push all thoughts of a previous life from my mind. I thought of Evelyn, the pain she must be suffering thinking I was dead would eat at me like a cancer. It cut me to the core and I harnessed that pain. I embraced it. I would use that pain, that *cancer,* to give me the strength to carry on.

She would know I had *died,* that I had been involved in a car accident and would be found burned at the scene. My mother would be distraught;

she'd already lost her husband and her first-born son. She'd have to arrange my funeral; she'd mourn and weep. I had no way of easing the pain the women I loved would suffer. If I did, if I tried to make contact, I'd already been warned, my sister would die; the woman I loved, Evelyn, would die. I had no doubt those threats were real, and I had no doubt those women would suffer a slow and painful death.

I rose; I needed to shower. As I walked to the bathroom, I stripped off the shirt I'd worn for two days. I unbuckled my belt, unzipped my trousers, and let them fall. The bathroom was floor-to-ceiling marble, ostentatious but again, cool and somewhat serene. A marble sink was molded into a counter, a large white bath with gold taps stood to one side. I slid the glass door of the shower open and reached in. I moved a gold lever clockwise and cool water fell from above.

Before I stepped into the shower, I stood and looked at myself in the mirror. I wanted to commit my face to memory. I wanted to remember the hazel eyes. In a year, two, three, or many more, I knew that face would be one of a very different man. That face would display the murder I intended to commit, the hatred I felt, and those eyes would be black; soulless and evil. The last thing I did before I stepped into the shower, before I stepped into a completely different life, was to remove the necklace of beads from around my neck. I kissed the silver cross that hung in the middle and then dropped it in the bin.

I'd killed before, I'd been instrumental in the death of a politician, and it was that which had brought me to where I was. But I'd done what I'd done either for revenge or for justice. I was to turn into a man who killed for pleasure, because I knew, I would enjoy every second of it.

---

"Rocco, come, come," Salvatore said.

I had been 'collected' from my bedroom and escorted to a suite. Salvatore's room spanned the width of the hotel. He gestured for me to join him at a small table out on his balcony. By small, it still had four large chairs surrounding it. The table was set for lunch. Plates of cold meats and olives, bread and oils were laid out. A waiter stood to one side. I sat in the chair that had been pulled out for me and waited for the white, stiff linen napkin to be laid over my lap before shuffling myself forward.

"Did you sleep well?" he asked.

"Surprisingly, no," I answered.

He chuckled. "You will. When we get to Rome and you see your accommodations, you'll sleep like the dead. Although, we have a stop on the way before we get home." I caught the undertone of a threat in there.

"Then I look forward to it. Being dead and free, I mean."

"Tsk tsk. You need to mind your manners, Rocco. We have a wonderful lunch, don't spoil my appetite."

I waited as the waiter poured a glass of red wine—before taking a sip—I raised it to him.

"Eat, we have much to discuss after."

I loaded my plate with meats, tore off chunks of fresh bread, and poured olive oil over them.

"Have you been to Sienna before?" Salvatore asked.

"No, it's a beautiful place."

"I thought we would take a little holiday before work. I have a horse running in the Palio. I lived here for a while, Torre was my contrada."

Contrada meant district and I knew there to be many in Sienna.

"You have a horse?"

"Yes, I loan it to my people, if it doesn't win, they eat it," he said with a laugh.

*Arrogant fuck*, I thought, and wasn't sure if he was joking or not.

"How does it work then? The Palio?"

"Each contrada puts forward a horse, they will race around the piazza tomorrow evening. It's the most important event in the whole of Italy. Did you know it's the world's oldest competitive event? Dates back to the twelfth century, although, the race originally ran through the streets."

He seemed well educated for such a prick.

He clicked his fingers and the waiter jumped forward.

"Get my friend a Torre flag, he needs to show his allegiance."

*Like fuck*, I thought.

With our meal eaten, he instructed for the plates to be cleared. The waiter left the bottle of wine and placed a pot of coffee, cups, an ashtray, and a humidor on the table. He opened the lid of the ornate wooden box to display a range of cigars.

Salvatore selected one; he ran it under his nose and inhaled deeply before sighing.

"Cuban, the finest in the world. Take one," he said.

I reached forward and selected a cigar. I took the cutter from him and snipped off the end before leaning forward so the waiter could light it. Despite my hatred for the man sitting in front me, to sit and smoke a fine cigar, with a glass of red wine, overlooking Sienna, and in one of the most luxurious hotels, was certainly something. What that something was, I was yet to determine.

We fell silent as we savored the cigars and sipped the rich red wine.

"You don't like me, I expect that. I don't need you to like me. You will respect me, though. As I told you yesterday, one job, then you will be free to leave. Where you'll go to is another matter. Everyone thinks you are dead, Rocco. I'm not a simple man; I don't like to blackmail either. I know, I know," he raised his hand as he saw the look on my face.

I was sitting in front of him because he'd blackmailed me, not because I wanted the pleasure of his company.

"You were the exception. Anyway, as you know, you killed my senator; you've caused me great distress and many problems. Before you speak, I know you were following orders, and I need to know who requested his killing. He was a prick, slime, like any American politician, the plague of the earth, but he was mine."

"I told you last night. The Commission asked Guiseppi, in return for the senator's demise; my village would be protected from, I imagine, your activities. And I didn't kill the senator."

"Ah, there you have it wrong, my friend. Not my activities, a dumbfuck of an individual who thinks he has a strong family though. He's gone; your village is safe. In fact…"

He looked at his watch.

"I imagine right now they're seeing him strung up, crucified and with his guts hanging out, just on that hill above the square." He chuckled. "Reminds me of Rio in Brazil," he added.

I smiled at his *joke*.

"I know you don't know who wanted the senator dead, but I have every faith you will find out, that you will bring me the man that caused me, and you, this much trouble."

"Why is it so important?"

"Ah, Rocco, you don't need to know. You're not high enough in my family for such sensitive information." He laughed.

*Yep, arrogant fucking prick.*

I stared out over the square, puffing on my cigar. A pang of sadness hit me; Evelyn would have loved it there. She would have sat in the square and watched the world go by with a smile on her face. I swallowed down the sadness.

*Harness it, harness it*, I thought.

Salvatore stood; he threw his napkin down on the table and stubbed out his cigar in the remnants of the wine in his glass. Very classy.

"Time for you to leave, my friend. There is a brunette waiting on my affection. I'll see you here tomorrow. We'll watch my horse then leave."

I was being dismissed. I put out the cigar in the ashtray but kept hold of it and followed him into his suite. Henchman was waiting.

"Lou, take Rocco back to his room."

So his name was Lou, I made a note. He'd be the second I'd kill.

I followed Lou to the lift, he shoved me in the back to encourage me to enter once the doors opened, what the fuck he thought I was going to do was beyond me.

I didn't say one word to him, I would not rise to his provocation, he'd get no response from me at all.

He opened the door with a card key, and it surprised me that he'd knocked earlier instead of barging in. Maybe he did have some manners after all.

"So, Lou…" I said.

"Luigi to you," he replied.

"Luigi, what am I supposed to do all afternoon?"

"Don't know, jerk off, whatever," he said with a chuckle before slamming the door behind him.

"Fucking idiot," I said.

I walked around the room. I was anxious to make my plans but knew I couldn't until I understood exactly what was expected of me. I knew I'd have to return to the U.S. and that gave me a brief smile. I'd see her; I'd make a point of seeing her, somehow.

I hadn't the chance of that cup of coffee at lunch and my mouth started to water at the thought. I looked for a telephone, I'd ring down for room service, let that fucker, Salvatore, pick up the bill. There wasn't one, which didn't surprise me when I thought about it.

I took the remainder of the cigar from my pocket and looked at it. With a smile I walked to the bedroom door.

"Luigi, would be you be kind enough to ask room service to bring up a pot of coffee and some matches? Salvatore did say just to ask you for anything I needed. I could do with some toiletries as well."

I closed the door, not waiting for the obvious answer about to explode from his lips. He had been sitting on a chair outside my room, probably bored as fuck at having to babysit, but I was banking on him not wanting to piss off his boss if he didn't do as I asked. Of course Salvatore hadn't given me permission to use him as my servant, but I doubted Luigi knew that.

I opened the French doors to allow the sounds of the square to drift into the room and removed my shirt, it was the only clean one I had. I waited.

It was a few minutes later that I heard a knock; I looked through the spy hole to see a waitress carrying a tray. I opened it, after staring at my body for a moment, she bowed her head as she walked in and placed the tray on the table. She held in her hands a small leather folder and a pen.

"He'll sign for it," I said.

She nodded and without saying another word, scuttled from the room. I took the tray to the balcony, kicked off my shoes, peeled off my socks, and sat with my feet resting on the opposite chair. I lit the cigar, poured the coffee, and started to think.

Luigi was nothing more than a soldier, the lowest rank in the Mafia hierarchy, that much was obvious and I wondered where I'd fit in. I hoped to fuck Salvatore didn't instruct Luigi to work with me, that man was an idiot but there was no way he'd allow me to go to the U.S. alone. Then a thought struck me, I would be allowed to go the U.S., wouldn't I?

There was no way I could find out who ordered the hit on the senator from Italy. Yet it would be a big deal for Salvatore to send me to the U.S., the only way he could do that and know I'd deliver was to… I didn't want to go there, I didn't want to think of them holding Evelyn or my sister until I got the job done.

I stubbed out the end of the cigar, it had soured somewhat, drank down my coffee, and returned to the bedroom. As I sat back on the sofa, I flicked through a magazine that had been left, a brochure for the hotel and things to do in Sienna. There were pictures of the Palio, close up photographs of the horses, nostrils flared and eyes wide as if racing for their lives—perhaps some were. It was one picture that fascinated me though. It was, again, a close up of a horse, a black horse. Like the others, its nostrils were flared and blood red as it appeared to be dragging air into his lungs. But it was the eyes. Unlike the others, these weren't wide with fear but courage. That horse knew it had one thing to succeed at, or die trying. His eyes were *knowing* and when I looked hard, I could see the reflection of an image. I suspected it would have been whoever had taken the picture, but against the blackness of the horse's eye, it was just a ghosted white figure. I tore the page from the magazine.

———

Hours passed. I lay on the bed, sat on the sofa, and paced the room, frustrated at my confinement. The sounds of laughter floated in from people enjoying their early evening stroll around the square. I envied them; I envied their freedom.

I returned to the balcony to torture myself some more and watched a couple stroll hand in hand, kiss, and embrace. I watched him run his hand down the side of her face as she smiled up at him. I watched them laugh. I enjoyed the experience, not the experience of watching them, but the bubbling of acid, of hate in the pit of my stomach at the thought of their freedom.

If I was to survive this ordeal, I needed to make friends. I walked to the door and looked through the spy hole. Luigi sat in his chair, head slumped to his chest, and I could hear his snores. I smiled. I pulled on my shoes, not worrying about the socks, shrugged on my shirt, and buttoned it. As quietly as I could, I opened the door. He didn't stir at the click as I closed it behind me. I walked along the corridor until I found the stairwell, sure that the ping of the lift arriving would have woken him.

As I exited the hotel, I breathed in deep. All I did was stand there and watch for five minutes before returning. That time I did take the lift; I stomped along the corridor and smirked as Luigi jolted awake.

"What the fuck..." he said, as he shot to his feet.

"Open the door," I replied.

"How..." He reached inside his jacket.

I grabbed his arm; forcing it across his chest at the same time I rammed my forearm into his throat. He fell back against the wall. I pinned him there, choking him. He tried to pull my arm away, but I was way too strong for him.

"That's how easy it could have been for me. What do you think would happen if Salvatore knew you'd fallen asleep and I'd ran?"

His eyes grew wide.

"Not so brave without the gun, are you? Shall I tell you? He'd put a bullet through your skull. I know I would if one of my soldiers were so careless. I don't care what you think about me, you don't know me. I'm about the most valuable thing Salvatore has right now, he needs me to ensure his survival."

I loosened my grip and he sagged against the wall, trying to catch his breath.

"Open the door then get me a menu for dinner."

He jumped to attention. As I walked through the bedroom door, I turned to him.

"Have no fear, *Lou*. I won't mention your indiscretion."

It had been while I was standing outside the hotel that it had dawned on me. For Salvatore to go to the lengths he had to *obtain* me, he needed me. He needed that family in New York silenced for a reason I *would* find out. That gave me a sense of power I hadn't had until that point.

A menu was slid under the door and I chuckled as I bent to collect it.

I chose a rare filet mignon, a tomato salad, and rosemary and garlic encrusted potatoes. I selected a bottle of wine, and requested a pot of coffee. I asked for two packs of cigarettes to be brought to me as well. Lou simply nodded his head, and I wondered if he had the brain cells to remember that order. I settled back on the balcony and waited for dinner.

Phase one was complete. Lou needed to know that at any time I could overpower him, he needed to be wary of me. I had no intention of running for real; I wasn't dumb, I wouldn't make it far before someone caught up with me, or worse, Evelyn. They had emptied my pockets; I didn't have a lira or a dollar to my name. I just wanted Lou to believe I could. And the fact I wouldn't inform on him, ensured he owed me.

He didn't catch my eye; the arrogance had left him when he opened the door to allow the waitress in. She placed a tray on the table and made an effort to open the wine.

"Leave that there, I'll do it." I said, after watching her struggle to get the cork from the bottle.

She nodded and left. I smiled as I slowly turned the wooden handle of the very sharp corkscrew deeper into the cork. I smiled more when I imagined that cork to be the temple of the idiot outside the door. I pulled the cork free of the bottle and raised it to my nose. I inhaled an earthy, fruity smell, removed the cork, and pocketed the corkscrew. I'd have to hide it somewhere I guessed.

I poured the wine in the oversized glass and left it to one side to breathe. My steak was cooked to perfection, browned on the outside, pink then red in the middle. Blood ran as my knife sliced through it as smoothly as if cutting butter. I inspected the knife, the sharp steak knife, but then shook my head. They'd notice if that was missing.

After I'd eaten my meal, I took the bottle, my glass, and cigarettes back to the balcony. I sat, smoked, and watched the evening's activities below. The town hall was lit up and I could still see the outline of tourists as they walked the balcony around the clock tower.

As the night drew in, I then watched the workmen prepare for the Palio. They lugged ornate railings in place to form a track; they spread sand on the ground and raked it smooth. They placed chairs in the center of the track; just those small railings would separate the spectators from ten horses galloping at breakneck speed. I saw the flags. Ten flags, one for each contrada, were raised on flagpoles and I watched Torre's flap gently in the breeze. I hadn't been given my flag at lunch; perhaps I'd receive it in the morning, not that I particularly wanted it. But it was a sight to see. I could feel the excitement starting to build.

The square got busier as the evening drew in, tourists, locals; all were excited for the following day's race. I watched some take pictures; others sat in chairs moving from one to another, presumably to see which one gave the best view. They'd have to get up very early to secure their seats, I'd thought.

There was a lot of shouting from the workmen, lots of arm waving and leaning against buildings smoking after having done an arduous five minutes of work. They were fed by the restaurateurs, and offered coffee and cold drinks. They worked late into the night, doing a job that should only have taken a few hours. In the few years I'd been in America, I'd forgotten just how 'laid back' the Italians were.

I rose from the chair after stubbing out my last cigarette of the day and headed for the bedroom. I stripped off my clothing and placed my trousers over a chair before lying on the bed. It was too warm to climb under the covers, and although the room was air-conditioned, I preferred the natural breeze that came through the still open doors.

I slept fitfully, waking in a cold sweat with a pounding heart and a stiff cock after a dream; one that both aroused and scared me.

I'd dreamt that Evelyn was lying beneath me, her naked body covered in a sheen of sweat. I was kissing every part of her flesh, her toes, up her inner thighs until I reached her pussy. My tongue licked and teased her clitoris; she writhed, moaned, and called out my name. Her hands gripped my hair and her body bucked off the bed as she came. I raised my head, my tongue trailed a path up her stomach, and then I saw her face. Her beautiful face was contorted in pain, her eyes wide with fear, her dark hair fanned out against a stark white pillowcase. Except it wasn't white on both sides of her head, it was red on one—red with her blood as it flowed from a hole in her temple.

My stomach turned as I recalled the dream and I ran to the bathroom dry-heaving. I knelt on the floor, expecting to vomit but nothing came. Sweat ran down my forehead and dripped onto the white ceramic toilet bowl I was bent over. The sound seemed magnified, it echoed around the marble room.

I stood and rested my hands on the sink, after a minute or so, I managed to calm my racing heart and splash some cold water on my face. I looked up and into the mirror. The face that looked back at me had already altered; there was a hardness to my features that hadn't been there before.

"You will not break, not yet," I whispered to myself.

---

I was showered and dressed, sitting on the balcony with a cigarette when Lou walked into the room. He called out.

"Out here," I replied.

"Breakfast," he said. His voice was a little softer than the last time he'd used those words. He placed a tray on the table.

"Thank you," I answered, as I watched him look at the packet of Marlboros next to the ashtray. Phase two was to frighten the fuck out of him and be nice at the same time.

"Help yourself," I said as I poured a coffee.

He shook a cigarette free and patted his pocket as if looking for a lighter. I handed him the matches.

"Sit, you're making me feel uncomfortable," I added.

I didn't offer him a coffee or any of the sweet rolls I'd been given.

"Have you seen this before?" he asked, indicating with this head toward the square, already starting to fill with people.

"Not for real, on TV though."

"I'm looking forward to it, although you get to see it from up there, in luxury," he said, pointing upward to Salvatore's balcony.

"I'd rather see it on TV in America, or not at all," I answered.

He didn't answer. I tore off a piece of the sweet roll and popped it in my mouth, chewing slowly as I watched the square begin to come alive again.

"I need clean clothes," I said. "I've been in these trousers for three days straight."

He nodded. "I'll see what I can do."

Lou stubbed out his cigarette and left. He hadn't asked me what size waist I was, nor had he taken my trousers for laundry. I guessed I was going to have to do my own washing.

I rinsed my socks under the tap in the bathroom, using the shower gel as detergent then hung them over the back of the chair on the balcony. They'd dry quick enough in the heat. It was as I paced the room, trying to relieve myself of the boredom, that I heard a knock on the door. It was opened before I got to it and Lou walked in with a chambermaid.

"She wants to tidy," he said.

*Yep, brains of a rocking horse,* I thought.

I waved my arm toward the bed and Lou backed through the door. A thought flashed through my mind. I unbuttoned my shirt and stripped off my pants. Her eyes grew wide and I tried not to smile at her 'not so discreet' stares. Her cheeks colored a rosy pink as she rushed around to strip the bed. I watched as she bundled it all into a laundry bag.

"Will you do something for me?" I asked in as seductive a voice as I could manage.

I walked toward her; she trembled slightly and kept her head down. I placed my fingers under her chin, gently tilting her head back up to look at me. She was so young and I swallowed down the bile that rose to the back of my throat.

"What do you need, sir?" she whispered.

"You're so pretty, why are you working here?" I asked.

"I, erm, I needed a job."

"You should be a model, or at least on the arm of a man who appreciates such beauty."

She colored some more and I took a step closer.

"My friend out there doesn't seem to want to organize some clean clothes for me. Do you think you can help me?"

I watched her pant slightly and her pupils dilate. She was staring at my chest, at the tattoos that covered my skin. Her hand twitched as if she was itching to touch them.

"I guess so," she whispered.

I slowly removed my fingers from her chin and smiled again at her. She took the trousers and shirt and initially draped them over her arm.

"My friend, he doesn't like me to be smarter than him. Do you think I'm smarter than him?"

I watched her throat constrict as she swallowed hard.

"Yes."

"Don't let him see you with my clothes."

"Oh, I...I'll put them in here." She held up the laundry bag.

"What's your name?"

"Alana."

"Well, Alana, I have a dinner appointment with a very important man, do you think you could get those back to me by lunchtime?"

"I'll try, sir," she gently said.

She peeked up from beneath her long dark eyelashes at me. I gently touched the side of her face.

"I'll see you soon then," I whispered.

She nodded before heading to the door. I would use whatever was necessary to get what I needed.

I had no doubt Salvatore would not allow me new clothes, it was all part of his 'demoralizing' or his forcing my dependency on him. If I had to tease a young girl to have clean clothes, to show him that, in fact, he couldn't strip my dignity, then so be it.

I lay down on the freshly made bed and counted the saints and the cherubs on the ceiling. It would pass some time.

***

"Your clothes," I heard, waking me from the sleep I must have fallen into.

Lou laid my freshly pressed shirt and trousers, wrapped in tissue paper, on the bed. I ran my hand over my chin feeling the scratch of stubble then swung my legs over the side. I stretched; my back ached for lying for so long.

"How many tattoos have you got?" he asked. A strange question I thought.

"Twenty, I think."

"That's a lot of ink."

"One for every man I've killed," I said and stood.

I stared at him as I passed, headed for the bathroom.

"There'll be a few more before I'm done," I added.

I stepped out of my shorts, not bothering to close the bathroom door, and into the shower. I heard the bedroom door close. Once I had cleaned myself, I turned the water to cold, the jets were like icicles that stung my skin but rejuvenated me. I wrapped a towel around my waist and walked back into the bedroom.

A brown-haired woman stood in the middle of the room. She looked at me; her eyes ran the length of my body.

"Sal thought you might like some company," she said, as she took a step toward me.

*Obviously on first name terms,* I thought.

"*Sal* thought wrong," I said.

She was standing in front of me. She raised her hand and ran her red long fingernail down my chest, following the path of a droplet of water.

"So you're his whore. How much is he paying you?" I asked.

She looked sharply up at me; removed her hand from my chest, and raised her arm. I grabbed her wrist before she could deliver her slap.

I shook my head and sighed. "Unless you want a slap back, don't even think about it."

"You'd hit a woman?"

"Only ones I have no respect for."

I shoved her arm back toward her. "He said you were feisty," she purred as she spoke.

"He knows fuck all about me. Now leave, if I wanted a whore, I'd pick one myself."

I grabbed her arm and marched her to the door; she stumbled on ridiculously high heels. I opened it quickly to see Lou jump back, one hand behind his back.

"And if you think I'm that fucking dumb, you *really* don't know me."

As I pushed her to one side, I grabbed his arm. He opened his mouth to yelp as I twisted his wrist, and he dropped the camera he was holding. I picked it up and opened the back. Using my fingers, I pulled out the film and let it unreel from its casing.

Without another word, I walked back into the room and closed the door.

"And you don't blackmail?" I shouted toward the ceiling.

I sat on the bed to dress. Why on earth would he want photos? Who the fuck would he send them to? Everyone thought I was dead, or did they?

I wondered why the imbecile that was Lou was babysitting me and not someone who had half a brain. Was it a test? If I'd been Salvatore, I would have had one decent guy, able to draw a weapon faster than the sloth outside for sure. I walked to the balcony. Outside was a hive of activity. Crowds had started to form, even though the festivities wouldn't start for another few hours. Residents of contradas were gathered together, waving their respective flags, drinking, and arguing with their neighbors. A great deal of honor rode on that race.

I dismissed Lou's invitation of lunch; I had no appetite but requested a pot of coffee. I debated on whether to take the corkscrew to dinner but expected a pat down at least. It was safely hidden under the cushion on the sofa.

I crumpled the empty pack of Marlboros after shaking loose the last cigarette and placing it on the table. I'd smoked half of it before I was collected for my date with the delightful Sal.

"Rocco, my friend, come, come," Salvatore said as we entered his suite.

The brunette was there, dressed in a short silk dressing gown and wiping her mouth. Salvatore was zipping up his fly and my stomach recoiled.

"You should have taken her up on her offer, the whore can suck better than your mamma's vacuum cleaner," he said, doubling over with laughter.

She stormed off and I cringed at the thought. Salvatore was not the most attractive man; in fact, he was what we would have said back in the village, a man who should have been drowned at birth. Short, fat, and sweaty, I guessed the only blow job he was likely to get was from a whore he'd paid.

"Classy," I whispered under my breath.

"Hmm?"

"Nothing."

He waved his hand, what or who he was dismissing baffled me. I looked around the room. The whore had gone, Lou was standing by the door with his hand on the doorknob, waiting. He didn't have to wait long; he opened it on the first knock.

A suited man, who seemed a little nervous, walked into the room. Another, a young guy, flanked him.

"Ah, my guest. Rocco meet Lorenzo, our wonderful mayor. I forget the other's name, someone in government but not important. Now come and sit."

Mr. Not Important scowled but followed on behind. Bottles of wine were set on the table, the humidor alongside them. He opened and offered it to the mayor before selecting a cigar for himself. I guessed I had been lowered to the same rank as Mr. Not Important, as we were ignored. At least we were offered a glass of wine.

Salvatore and the mayor were chatting, I tuned out. It was something to do with local funding. I guessed the mayor wanted either to raise money or line his pocket further.

"You're a friend?" Mr. Not Important said. He had leaned close and spoke under his breath.

"Nope. I'm here against my will," I said.

"Huh?"

"No, he's not a friend of mine," I explained.

"Darius," he said, and it took me a moment to realize he was offering his name.

"Rocco, pleased to meet you."

"I think we are here for the same reasons," he added.

I settled back in my chair and looked out over the view, having no real idea why I was invited. Salvatore and the mayor were deep in discussion. Their conversation was broken only by the sounds of trumpets. Our attention turned to the square. Parades of residents—some dressed in traditional costumes—walked to the track, it was a blur of color and pageantry. The noise was fever pitch as spectators shouted and clapped.

As we watched, three waiters appeared carrying trays of food. I guessed dinner was being served early. We were served crostini with chicken livers to start with, and I was appalled at the lack of manners Salvatore displayed. He talked with his mouth full, spitting his food across the table or dribbling it down the front of his shirt. I leaned back slightly away from the spray as he shouted over the balcony to someone below.

A second course of pasta was delivered, a light dish of orecchiette in a lemon and garlic sauce. It was followed with a traditional Tuscan T-bone steak, rare and served with sautéed potatoes and a lemon wedge. I squeezed the lemon over the steak and avoided watching Salvatore pick up his steak and gnaw from the bone, as if he'd never learned to use cutlery.

All the while the parade continued, the carabinieri appeared and raced their horses around the track. They were the military police and, according to Salvatore, it was usual for them to gallop around first.

With dinner eaten and wine drank, we settled back as the waiters cleared the table. Another bottle of wine was placed in the center, the humidor, and coffee. I shook a cigarette from my pack and lit it.

And then came the horses. Salvatore stood and cheered as his horse came into view, the jockey was wearing the contrada colors. It amazed me that the horses didn't freak out with the level of noise and the number people. It took forever for them to line up and then they were off. Jockeys whipped each other and their horses. Some fell on sharp corners and the crowd screamed. It appeared that there were no rules, and in ninety seconds or so, it was over.

Torre had won. Salvatore was practically wetting himself with excitement; he had jumped from his chair, spilling wine over himself and the mayor. He screamed and shouted and despite where I was, despite the situation, my heart pounded with exhilaration. I'd never seen something so thrilling. People congratulating the jockey surrounded the horse, it was a wonder no one was injured.

"Bravo, bravo," Salvatore shouted, the jockey raised his whip.

He sat back down and used the napkin to wipe the sweat from his brow.

"A toast, my horse lives, at least for another few days," he said.

I raised my glass, not to him, but to the courage his horse showed and to the freedom he'll achieve should he not make it beyond 'another few days.'

"It is time to celebrate with my people. Rocco, you will stay here," he said as he stood.

I was thankful; I had no desire to 'celebrate' with him, no desire to have *his people* think I was associated with him. Darius looked at me with a furrowed brow. I collected my cigarettes and the bottle of wine, raising it in question. I received a wave of the hand; I took that to be approval and made my way to the suite door. Lou was patiently waiting and we took the lift down to my room.

I was thankful for the time alone. I sat on the balcony and watched people party late into the night. I drank the whole bottle, hoping it would aid a dreamless sleep. At some point I passed out, fully clothed on the bed.

Rocco - Chapter Two

A loud knock woke me from a deep sleep and I struggled to open my eyes.

"Wakey, wakey, Sleeping Beauty," I heard. Lou was rapping his knuckles on the nightstand.

I groaned. "The Boss wants to leave shortly," he added.

"What time is it?"

"Time to get up."

I rolled to the edge of the bed, and it pleased me that he took a step back. I pulled my shirt over my head and headed for the bathroom. As I was taking a piss, I heard the bedroom door open.

"Over there," Lou said, and I guessed breakfast had arrived.

It irked me, not that I would show it, I wasn't able to select my own food and knew it was the control freak upstairs, again trying to demoralize. I stripped off my trousers and headed for the shower. As I passed the mirror, I took one final look. I thought the stubble around my jaw suited me; perhaps I'd keep it.

I sat with a towel wrapped around my waist, drank the coffee, and ate the pastries. When I thought Lou wasn't looking, I reached behind the cushion and pulled out the corkscrew, concealing it in my hand. I picked up both shirts, sniffing them to see if I could determine which one was the cleanest and threw on the shirt I'd worn the previous day. It had a mild smoky scent: a smell of cigarettes and sweat. It would have to do, and I quite relished the thought of sitting in a hot car stinking. They want me to smell like a pig, then they could be subjected to that.

I threw my shorts in the bin, there was no salvaging them, pulled back on the trousers, and tucked the corkscrew into the front pocket. I ran my fingers through my still wet hair and walked to the door. I was ready.

It felt good to step outside the hotel, even if that was with Lou tight by my side. I was encouraged, and by that I mean, I received a shove in the back to walk to a waiting black car, the rear door already held open by a thickset guy.

I slid across the leather seat and waited. Salvatore joined me some ten minutes later.

"Drive," he said, before resting his head back and closing his eyes.

I guessed his partying had gone on late into the night as he snored for an hour. I watched the countryside slide by the window and then straightened in my seat as my village came into view.

*Fucker,* I thought, knowing exactly what he was doing.

We continued through the village to the next and then up the hill. It was as we stopped at a set of iron gates that Salvatore woke.

"Good, home. Well, for the moment. We stay here, just a little reminder before we head off," he said. He straightened himself in the seat, smoothed down his hair, and smiled.

Once we had exited the car, I was marched across the courtyard and through a gate. We walked, or rather, I was hustled along a grass path until we came to a brick building. The door was opened and I was shoved into the dark. I heard the padlock click in place as they locked me in.

"You fucking cunt," I whispered, not loud enough for anyone to hear.

I'd kept my resolve and would not allow any one of them to see my distress. I was a stone's throw from my parents' farm. In fact, their land bordered this one. The pain I felt was immense. I was so close, yet they would never know I was. I sat on the metal cot and I cried.

Two days later, they came for me. I stank, I was hungry, but I wasn't broken. I had shut off all emotion. Lou wrinkled his nose at the stench of piss and shit, of sweat and anger.

"I think you'll need a change of clothes, I don't suppose Sal will appreciate sharing a car to Rome with you," he said.

"Too bad, unless you want to attempt to rip these clothes from my body, this is how I'm traveling."

As it was, I was bustled into a car with Lou to one side, a driver up front, and yet another henchman in the passenger seat. They were to be my companions on the drive to Rome. It sickened me as they slowed through my village, the dark windows allowed me to look out, and at one point I thought I spotted my sister. She'd never be able to see in, though. If there was ever a method of effective torture, Sal knew it. Inside I was dying, screaming, and in more pain that I could ever imagine.

The journey was endless and the heat eventually had my companions winding down the windows. I welcomed the fresh air; even I was sickened with the smell.

Four hours later, the car came to stop outside a huge villa. It had a light stone façade, a fountain in a circular driveway, and lots of people.

A woman stood on the steps to the front door, she looked a little downtrodden. As Salvatore exited his car, she walked toward him and pecked him on both cheeks.

"My wife, isn't she a beauty?" he said, to no one in particular.

*She looks like an old hag,* I thought as I stood and inhaled some deep breaths to clear the stench from my nose.

From the corner of my eye I saw another woman, a young woman. She ran to him.

"Papa, good to see you," she said, as she flung her arms around his neck.

It was unfortunate that she'd inherited the worst of both parents but she threw a smile my way.

Finally, a suited man with graying hair, an older man, greeted him. He nodded at me and whispered in Salvatore's ear. There were some nods, more whispered words, and I began to look around, bored.

I caught the daughter looking at me and she blushed.

*Keep looking, sweetheart, you may be my ticket out of here,* I thought.

I gave her a smile and a wink; she lowered her head and rushed into the house.

The suited man finally stepped forward and offered me his hand; I stared at it for the briefest moment then remembered the plan. I took it.

"Rocco, it's good to meet you, although, I wish the circumstances had been a little better. My name's Benito, you can call me Ben."

"Thank you, Ben," I replied.

"Come, let's get you settled and freshened up."

I followed him into the house and to a hallway with a sweeping staircase in front of me. If I thought the hotel was ostentatious, the house blew that away. Gold, marble, statues, and family portraits adorned every surface, the walls, and floor. A maid was on her knees in a uniform I'd only seen on an old British TV show shown in the States. All black and frilly white; scrubbing the bottom step of the ornately carved wooden staircase.

She slid to one side to let us pass and I followed Ben up the stairs, across the landing, and to a bedroom.

"Use this room to freshen up. I'm sure you will appreciate Sal isn't comfortable with you having your own place just yet," he chuckled briefly, but then saw the look on my face.

It was fairly decent sized room; a double bed sat against one wall with nightstands at either side. Opposite was a wardrobe and a door that was open into a bathroom.

"I'm staying here?" I asked.

He shook his head and seemed a little embarrassed. "No, there are accommodations outside. There are some clothes and toiletries for you on the bed. Is there anything else you want?"

"I'd like my watch and wallet back. I'm sure I had some sunglasses before my *accident* as well."

He nodded. "I'll see what I can do." I'd heard those words before. "I'll wait for you to shower then take you to your room," he said.

I took the shower and dressed in my old clothes; I refused to touch the cheap nylon shit that had been laid on the bed.

"Are you his advisor?" I asked. Ben nodded.

"Then perhaps you should *advise* him, if he wants me to do as he demands, stop treating me like a fucking animal. I will not stay caged in any room, I'm not a fucking idiot. I know the consequence of running. Do you think I'd put my family at such risk? I want my watch, my wallet, and I want clothes that fucking fit and are of *my* choice."

My patience was wearing very thin. I stomped to the door, wrenched it open, and walked back down the stairs and out the front door. Ben scuttled after me. I stood on the front drive and shook a cigarette from the pack, stuck a match, and inhaled deeply.

"This way," he said.

I followed and entered first into what could only be described as a shed, the kind of outbuilding my father had stored his tools in. There was yet another metal cot bed at one end, a bucket, and I could only guess at its use, a grimy window with wooden bars on the outside and a large new padlock sat on a dusty shelf.

"I know this is not ideal..." I heard from behind me.

I spun on my heels and stalked toward him.

"Not ideal? You have no fucking idea how *not ideal* this is."

"Rocco, calm yourself. I don't know all the circumstances, okay. I know you're here to help and I know you didn't come of your own accord. But, the quicker you get this done, the quicker you go home."

"Home? Home to where, to what? I'm dead, remember?"

I turned and walked away. I sat on the edge of the stone fountain and continued to smoke my cigarette, using the end to light another when it got too low.

I closed my eyes and saw her. Evelyn was standing in front of me; she smiled and ran her hand down the side of my face. It was that real, I felt her touch. I took a deep breath and exhaled slowly.

I was expecting to have at least been given the promised apartment, to not have to live by someone else's timetable, to choose my own clothes, and have the freedom to walk the fucking place naked if I wanted to. And there was fuck all I could about it. That was the thing that tore me apart the most.

I sat for a while thinking of ways to accelerate my plan, of ways I could get warning to Joe or to my uncle back in the village. But who did I trust? I doubted my uncle would have set me up but could Joe have? I'd thought of that man like a father; someone tipped Salvatore off that I was in the village; they had to. Or was my mind wandering along dangerous territory because of my frustration?

"Mama would like to know if you'd like lunch," I heard.

I looked up, Salvatore's daughter stood just to one side. As if on cue, my stomach grumbled and I stood.

"Thank you," I replied as I followed her. Ben followed at a discreet distance.

I had a sense of déjà vu as I walked into the kitchen. She didn't want me in her home, that much was clear. She was polite, she motioned to a chair next to Ben as she placed a bowl of pasta in the center of a pine scrubbed table, but she didn't look directly at me.

As I scooped some pasta onto my plate, Ben slid my wallet and watch across the table to me. I simply nodded my thanks.

"Felisia, tell your papa lunch is ready," she said.

So the daughter was Felisia, a pretty name for a not so pretty girl, but I was yet to know the mother's name. Perhaps I was being unkind, but I was not going to like any of those people, intentionally.

"Do you want to get clothes this afternoon?" Ben asked.

"Yes, and I want a tattoo parlor," I replied.

Felisia looked sharply at me and I heard her mother whisper something under her breath.

"Diavolo," she whispered.

I smirked. *Not yet, but soon,* I thought.

I rose from the table, having eaten my pasta, and in Italian thanked her for the meal. I wanted to be sure she knew I'd understood she'd called me the devil, that I could speak her language. I may have been out of Italy for some years but I hadn't forgotten my mother tongue.

I took myself back outside, to my *shed* and sat on the cot with yet another cigarette. I heard the click as the padlock was shut. I opened my wallet to see a wad of cash and a photograph of Evelyn. She didn't know I had it; I'd taken it from her house one day. I slid the metal strap of my watch over my wrist and clasped it shut. It was still on U.S. time, and I'd keep it that way. All the time that watch was hours off, I'd have a connection, something to remind me of what I needed to achieve.

---

"Ready?" Ben said as he opened the door. I stood. "Do I need to remind you...?"

"No," I snapped.

"Okay, wait here, we need a car."

He walked to the side of the house and beckoned with his hand. It was a minute or two later that a black car, and I wondered just how many black cars Salvatore owned, stopped in front of me.

Lou was sitting up front, alongside a driver. The thickset man I'd seen earlier was in the rear seat, and I was encouraged to sit next to him. Ben was the last to enter.

"Well, I didn't realize I was this popular," I said.

Lou chuckled; the driver scowled in the rearview mirror, and thickset ignored me. I rested back into the seat.

It was a short drive to a small side street where slightly grubby storefronts lined either side of the road. We stopped outside a tattoo parlor. It didn't look the cleanest but would do.

"Did you make an appointment?" I asked Ben.

"Oh, did I need to?"

Salvatore sure liked to surround himself with dumbfucks. Presumably that was to enhance his own level, or lack of, intelligence. I sighed and shook my head, waiting to be let out of the car.

It was as if they were shadowing the prime minister, the way I was surrounded and ushered into the store. The smell of antiseptic washed over me, it was a smell I'd come to like. A man looked up from a counter, he had been reading a newspaper. His eyes widened a little when he saw us, there was a flicker of recognition, not at me but the idiots surrounding me.

"He wants a tattoo," Lou said, with a level of bravado I'd not witnessed before.

"And he's the brains of the outfit," I said with a smile.

I received a very hesitant smile in return. "Can you fit me in now?" I asked.

"Sure, what do you want?" I was asked.

I rolled the sleeve of my shirt beyond my elbow, grabbed a pencil and a piece of paper from his counter, and wrote eight words, in my own regional dialect. He frowned at it, not fully understanding.

"Okay, any style?"

"Italic," I said, as I sat on the chair.

I rested my forearm on the arm of the chair, underside facing up. He sprayed it with antiseptic then wiped it clean.

It took no more than a half hour of watching Lou wince at the sound of the tattoo gun, and the small dribble of blood that was constantly being wiped away, and then it was done. I looked at it and smiled. After the guy plastered on some ointment, I rolled down my sleeve. I stood and walked to the counter, took out my wallet to have him wave my money away.

"On me," he said.

I nodded my thanks.

"What does it mean then?" Lou asked as we walked to the car.

I winked at him. It was something I would repeat to myself frequently. "You'll know, soon enough."

Inked down the underside of my forearm were words I wouldn't speak out loud.

*You've seen my descent, now watch me rise.*

The next stop was a clothing store, not my usual type, but it would do. The clothes were basic, nothing special. I selected some T-shirts, a couple of pairs of jeans, and underwear. I tried on some shirts and trousers, a pair of shoes, and added some sneakers and socks to the pile on the counter. The assistant rung up the total as I pulled out my wallet, again my money was declined.

Salvatore was obviously a powerful man in Rome; no one wanted me to pay. Perhaps I looked far more important than I was. Maybe by being surrounded by my jailers they thought I was being protected.

I thanked the assistant then probably shattered her illusion when I carried the bags myself to the waiting car.

I was driven back to the villa and made a mental note of the security. Two men were stationed at the gate. I noticed one patrolling the garden and another jumped to his feet to open the car door as we pulled up on the drive. Eight, including Ben, in total at that point. There would be more, many more, I was sure of that.

I set my bags down on the ground by the fountain and lit a cigarette, I watched while the guys milled around, not sure what to do with me. I smoked slowly, inhaling deep then lifting my face to the sun before exhaling. When I was done, I picked up the bags and walked into the shed.

Once I was locked in, I emptied the bags on the bed. As I turned, I noticed a suit bag hanging from a hook; I slowly pulled down the zipper and took a look inside. I raised my eyebrows in shock. Hanging up were two black suits and four white shirts. I pulled a suit jacket from the hanger and tried it on. It fit, which surprised me further. There was no way someone had guessed my size and a shiver went through me. Either a tailor had measured me while I was unconscious, unlikely, or someone had been into my home, the one in the States. It was the only explanation as to what size suit I wore that I could think of.

I hung my purchases alongside the suits on rusty hooks, put away my T-shirts and underwear in a basket beneath the bed, and lay down.

I stared at my arm; at the words only I'd understand. I was at the bottom of the pile, the lowest in the hierarchy. I'd gone from underboss to nobody, but it wouldn't be for long. I looked forward to the blood that would be shed, to the destruction I would cause, to the pain and the suffering I would inflict as I rose.

And rise I would, I was certain of that. I'd rise to the top of that family, destroying everyone in my way and take great pleasure in doing so.

Salvatore may have thought he was a great man, but he'd underestimated me. When he *obtained* me, he'd forced me not to feel, not to care—that made me a very dangerous man. I had nothing to lose.

I closed my eyes, hoping to see Evelyn in my dreams. I would keep one small part of me hidden deep, so as to not be affected by what was to come, just for her. My heart would beat just to keep me alive, but it would never feel love again. As I drifted off into sleep, the last thing I remembered was seeing her face, seeing her sitting on those church steps with her face to the sun and her eyes closed. She was smiling, she was in love, and she was perfect.

*One day, one day, one day,* were her words that ran through my mind.

---

It was dark when I woke, and noisy. Despite the villa being off the main road, I could hear the sound of traffic float through the grimy window. I could have kicked it out, I could have broken down the door had I tried, but where would I go? I'd have to run the gauntlet with the armed security outside.

The padlock rattled outside the door and it was wrenched open. Salvatore's wife stood in the doorway.

"You missed dinner," I heard. I didn't have much choice, being locked in a shed.

"I wasn't able to get out, my apologies if you cooked for me."

"Come," she said.

I followed her into the house and through to the kitchen. I sat at the chair she gestured toward. She peeled some foil from a plate of cold meats and cheese, which she then placed in front of me. She carved some bread and laid that on a second plate, which she handed to me. In the center of the table was an array of bottles, oils, and a syrupy balsamic vinegar.

"Thank you," I said, as I tore off a chunk of bread.

As she walked past, she placed her hand on my shoulder.

"We are all prisoners here," she whispered.

*Ally number two*, I thought.

I ate quickly, washed my plates before leaving them to dry on the drainer, and headed outside to smoke before being escorted to my *room*.

I was bored, so fucking bored. I lay on my bed; I paced the small room. I rearranged my clothes and paced some more. I wanted to punch the fucking wall, but there was no way I'd allow anyone to see how frustrated I was.

I had lost track of what day of the week it was; each was the same. I was allowed out of my shed to smoke, not that I didn't smoke in it, as well as to eat or to shower. I understood the mindfuck Salvatore wanted me to; I was shown the *luxury* of his house for short periods of time then caged like a dog for the rest.

It was two weeks later that I finally got to see him again. Two weeks of trying not to go out of my mind, of fighting off the urge to kick down that door and take a bullet. I had no problem with dying; I just wanted to get word to Guiseppi so he could protect Evelyn before I did.

Rocco - Chapter Three

"You have settled in, yes?" Salvatore asked, as I was ushered into his office.

I bit back the sarcasm that was dripping from my tongue.

"You have a lovely home, it's hard not to settle immediately," I replied, refusing to acknowledge the shed.

He smiled. "See, I told you that you'd enjoy being here. My wife, she's a good cook, you should watch your waistline."

She was a good cook and over the past week she'd started to speak a little more to me. Her name was Rosina, I'd finally learned after overhearing Ben talking one day. It seemed Rosina was as dissatisfied at living in that monstrosity of a house as I was in the shed. She craved the home she'd lived in back in the village.

"So now you are ready to work," he said.

I took a seat in front of his desk.

"Tell me how you managed to kidnap my senator," he added.

"It wasn't hard, he was an arrogant fuck and arrogance is a very bad attitude to have, it makes you careless," I replied.

He waved his hand, oblivious to my comment.

"A meet was arranged, he came with two Capitol Police. I had one taken out, the one who stood by his car, and the other was shot through the head while the senator watched. His coffee was laced with a drug, and when he got drowsy, he was taken to an associate. After that, I don't know what happened to *your* senator. My job was just to deliver him, not kill him."

"Your Guiseppi, does he know who ordered that?"

"Not to my knowledge, he was asked by the Commission. I'm sure you would know, that kind of information would be with them, they wouldn't pass that on."

"So this is where we have a problem then. How do you find out?"

"I'll go to America and find out."

He smiled at me, broadly, before laughing. "Oh, Rocco. You do amuse me. Go to America!" he laughed some more.

Once he was done laughing, he slammed his fist so hard down on the desk most of what was sitting on top either toppled over or jumped a few centimeters in the air.

"Do you think I am fucking stupid?" His face was puce with anger.

"You will not leave this country, you will not take a piss unless I say so," he added.

"Then you will never find out who ordered the hit on your senator," I answered quietly.

I watched Ben shake his head slightly at me; he sat to Salvatore's left.

"I have to get close to someone on the Commission, how do you think I'm going to find out from here?" I asked.

I leaned forward slightly and made an effort to soften my features.

"If I can get on the inside and you can help me with that, two things can happen. I can get the information you need and then deal with it, problem solved."

"Maybe, first I have another job for you." He leaned back in his chair with a smirk on his face.

"What job?"

"Mario will show you."

I sat looking at him, not entirely sure what he was talking about. I felt a hand grip my arm and I was encouraged to my feet. Thickset, who I guessed was Mario, walked me to the door.

---

The car had the same driver as before, and he drove for about a half hour, out of Rome and into the surrounding countryside. Eventually we arrived at an old, run-down farmhouse. Mario hadn't spoken for the whole journey. I'd asked a couple of questions, the standard, 'where are we going' type thing and received a grunt in response. Maybe he was incapable of speech.

The car came to a stop and I took a moment to let the dust settle before opening the door.

"Walk," he said. So he could speak.

I headed toward the house and pushed open the broken front door. It had come loose from one hinge and slid against the wooden floor making a squeal that had me clenching my teeth. I followed into what I guessed would have been a living room, had the house not been in such disrepair. Sitting in the middle, tied to a wooden chair and gagged, was an old man. His eyes displayed his fear and were already half-closed, due to the beating he had clearly received.

Standing alongside him was another man, a thin man with broken skin on his knuckles. I imagined he would have had to tie the old man to the chair to beat him, one puff of wind and he'd have been blown over.

"Kill him," Mario said. He indicated with his head to the old man in the chair.

"Why?" I asked. It wasn't in my nature to kill without reason.

"Because that is the order."

"Why?" I asked again.

Thin man hopped from foot to foot, he seemed excited by the prospect of watching a killing.

"He doesn't pay, he needs to learn a lesson."

"And how do you expect him to *learn* anything if he's dead?"

A knife was shoved against my chest; handle first thankfully.

"Kill him."

I guessed Mario was of limited language skills. I sighed and looked at the old man. Tears were streaming down his cheeks and he shook his head from side to side.

Thin man started to clap and I stared at him. Perhaps he was mentally disturbed, who stood and clapped at a man about to be killed? I looked over to Mario, who shrugged his shoulders and was leaning against the door.

"You want me to kill this man with that one acting like a fucking idiot?"

I was buying time. I didn't kill just for the sake of it. But I found myself in a dilemma. I was as fucked as that man tied to the chair. If I didn't do what was asked of me, my loved ones would suffer.

I knelt before the old guy and pulled the rag from his mouth. He gasped for air.

"Sshh," I said, as I attempted to calm him.

I watched him take a couple more deep breaths before he nodded. I looked into his eyes, old eyes full of knowledge. I spoke very quietly to him.

"I'm not here because I want to be. I was kidnapped and I'm being held. If I don't do what I'm told, my sister and the only woman I'll ever love will be murdered, and I have no doubt that will be slowly and brutally. I need to think."

"Kill him, kill him," Imbecile started chanting.

"I am an old man, do it quick. I'd rather die than be beholden to that pig," he said with a raspy voice.

After a minute or two, I nodded. He held my gaze as I plunged the knife into his heart. One tear leaked from one eye before they glazed over and he was dead. I held the old man's head in my hand, gently lowering it to his chest, and I silently prayed for him.

Imbecile started to dance around. I leapt to my feet and grabbed him by the hair. He screamed out incoherent words.

"Honor him," I shouted, forcing him to his knees in front of the old man.

"Honor him," I said, quieter.

Imbecile started to laugh and spat at the old man's feet. I pulled back his head and drew the knife across his throat. He wouldn't get the mercy of a quick death. I let him fall as Mario ran across the room. I turned on my heel, held out the knife, handle end first. Once he had taken it, I wiped my bloody hands on the front of his shirt, smiled, and then walked from the room.

As I reached the car, I pulled out the pack of cigarettes from my pocket. I'd need to ask Mario to stop on the way back for more. I held the lit match to the end of the cigarette, not quite reaching it as a thought ran through my mind.

*I killed an old man for no justifiable reason, yet I'm thinking of cigarettes.*

"Sal will go mad, that was his nephew," Mario said as he walked up behind me.

"That figures," I replied.

He chuckled and I offered him a cigarette.

"Do we have a cleanup team?" I asked.

"A what?"

"At some point they are going to stink, hopefully animals will find them before someone walking their dog does. What did you do with the knife?"

"We don't and I threw it."

I looked at him. "How the fuck does *Sal* run Rome?"

"Huh?"

"Go find the knife, we take it with us. That has yours, and my, fingerprints on it."

He sauntered off to some bushes alongside the dirt lane we'd driven up. I sighed as he kicked around with his shoe, having no idea where he'd thrown the knife. I joined him. I found the knife, picked it up, and handed it to him.

Salvatore really had surrounded himself with idiots, and again, I wondered how he kept control.

"Do we need to get rid of the bodies?"

"That would be a good idea but not my job, I've done what I was asked to."

I shook my head as I remembered an old cartoon.

"Come on, Clyde, let's go."

He looked at me, his brow furrowed in question.

"Anthill Mob?"

He looked blank.

"Never mind."

If I had wanted to escape Salvatore and his totally inefficient guys, it would have been real easy. But he was also dumb enough to follow through on his threat, and it wasn't a risk I was willing to take. Somehow I would get word to Guiseppi, I just had to think of a way to do that. Guiseppi hadn't only been my boss, head of the family I'd worked for, but my friend. He'd know what to do, how to keep Evelyn and my sister safe while I dealt with what I needed to.

---

"You slit his throat?" Salvatore roared.

"Yes."

"My sister will be on the phone and that's something I don't fucking need."

"Then I'll talk to her. I'll tell her how he was clapping and braying for an old man's blood, how excited he got watching that old man die." I emphasized the *old*.

"You will do nothing of the sort. Now go, get out of my sight. Mario, you had one fucking job and you couldn't even manage that!"

I walked from the room and was convinced I'd heard Mario whisper under his breath, "Prick."

Not sure whether that insult was to Salvatore or me, I smiled anyway.

Mario shadowed me back to my accommodations. I was allowed a short break for another cigarette before being locked in for the rest of the day. The only visitor I received was Felisia, who carried a plate of pasta, some bread, and a bottle of wine for me.

"I stole the wine, please don't tell Papa," she said.

"Thank you and I won't." I took the plate and bottle from her and laid it on the bed.

"I can get you out of here," she said.

"Really?" I actually wasn't that interested in her answer because I doubted very much she could.

"Papa will do anything for me."

*Ah, a spoiled bitch,* I thought.

"And I will forever be in your debt if you do," I replied.

She seemed to appreciate that answer; she smiled but it wasn't a genuine smile.

"I like the sound of that, you can be my puppy instead of Papa's."

She laughed before turning on her fat heel and walking back out. Not the naïve young girl I'd initially thought she was. I also wondered if the lack of a corkscrew, or so she thought, was her little kick in the gut as well. I laughed as I fished around inside the pillowcase and pulled out the one I'd stolen from the hotel.

Once I'd opened the bottle, I took a sip and then raised it.

"Fuck you, bitch," I said.

Hungover, stinking of alcohol and cigarettes I was collected to meet Salvatore. I swayed a little as the bright sunlight, or perhaps the booze, caused me to screw my eyelids half shut once I stepped out from the gloom of the shed.

"You need to clean up," Mario said.

"Think you can fetch me a clean towel then?" I asked.

I lit a cigarette as we reached the fountain, it had become my smoking corner, and I smiled at the small pile of cigarette butts on the ground.

"Get it your fucking self," he said. It seemed I wasn't the only one with a sore head that morning, or perhaps he'd been reprimanded for his sloppy behavior the previous day.

I pushed myself from the wall and followed him to the house. Felisia smirked when she saw me from halfway down the stairs.

"Remind me to thank Salvatore for the wine," I said to Mario, as I walked to the office.

Her face paled, she stomped down the remainder of the stairs.

Salvatore looked at me as I entered, he wrinkled his nose, and I smiled broadly at him.

I ran my hand across the stubble on my chin. "Growing a beard, I need to have some sort of disguise. People know me in New York."

"You're not going to New York," he replied.

"Then how am I to deliver your man?"

"The Commission is in New York, that doesn't mean whoever ordered the killing of my senator is as well, does it?"

I sat back in my chair; I wouldn't show my disappointment. He'd confused me at that point.

Ben sat forward. "We believe the man who wanted the senator dead isn't in America, he's in Sicily. That's where you will go."

"It would help if you told me why the senator was so important to you. I might know of any connections. I wasn't some dumbfuck back in D.C."

'Ah, Rocco. Your family, they were tiny." He held up his finger and thumb, displaying a small gap between them. "Your Guiseppi? We laughed at him."

I felt a small tic start in the corner of my eye. I would not rise; I would not bite.

"You know what," I said with a sigh. "You're right. We fought, Guiseppi and I. There was so much more money to be earned, but he didn't want it." I shrugged my shoulders. "Take the drugs, every fucking politician in that city wanted them. The whores too, but he was happy with what he had," I added.

Salvatore smiled; I was never entirely sure what the smile meant. Maybe he was pleased with the lie I'd told him, maybe he knew it was a lie and his smile was to patronize.

"Go clean yourself up. Mario, find him some luggage. Oh, before you go, Rocco, perhaps you'd like to take this."

I had stood from the chair and was about to leave when Salvatore slowly placed another photograph on his desk. It was a close up of Evelyn, a recent picture I believed. She was laughing with a boy, a black-haired boy, a boy as tall as her but clearly younger.

"She appears to have gotten over your death quite quickly," he said.

"Seems so," I said and deliberately kept my tone of voice flat.

"Fuck up and she dies, slowly, painfully. I wonder what she'd be like to fuck. Did you fuck her? Maybe I'll fuck her before I kill her," he said.

I clenched my teeth together and didn't reply.

"I bet she's a good Catholic, she would have been saving herself. Imagine that tight pussy, Ben. She'd bleed, I bet, and that makes it all the more erotic, don't you agree?" he added.

Ben had the grace not to answer. I walked from the office and Salvatore's laughter followed me.

If I could have, I would have cut off his dick and shoved it down his throat, watching him choke on his own cock. In fact, that thought made me smile, maybe that's exactly what I'd do, when the time was right.

I walked to the shed to collect some clean clothes then headed to the house for a shower. I brushed roughly past Felisia, who seemed to spend most of her time halfway up, or down, the stairs. Perhaps she needed a rest, twenty steps was a lot of exercise for the pig.

She opened her mouth to speak, perhaps to cuss or berate but closed it quickly. I imagined the look on my face had her change her mind. I was in the mood for murder. I needed to know how that fucking prick was getting close enough to Evelyn to take her photograph. Why was she not being protected? I felt so useless and angry. I was angry with Guiseppi for allowing her the freedom that may ultimately result in her death; angry with the young boy for making her laugh when it should have been me. I was angrier with myself; I should never have left her.

As I stood in the shower I remembered the last weekend I'd spent with Evelyn. She'd lied to her father, told him she was staying with a friend, and we'd spent a whole weekend as a real couple. There was none of the hiding and secret dates we'd been forced to share for the previous year; just a weekend of being together.

I remembered the call I'd received from my uncle: my sister had gone missing. I cursed myself further for not waiting for news, for jumping on a plane and rushing back to Italy, just to find her sitting by a roadside with a broken-down truck.

I refused to cry, I refused to feel any emotion other than rage. Anger was good; anger fueled the *cancer* that was eating away inside me. One day, that anger, that *cancer,* would come exploding out and I looked forward to it.

---

We checked in at the airport and I followed Mario to the departure gate. Ben and Alex, a guy I'd not had the pleasure of meeting until we'd left for the airport, sat in the row in front of us.

The flight was cramped, mainly Italians heading off either home or for their holiday to the coast. However, across the aisle from me sat a blonde. She was engrossed in a magazine and I wanted to catch her attention. I wanted to know her nationality.

During the one-hour flight, the stewardess walked the aisle offering refreshments, I waited until she reached the blonde and hid the smile as I heard her ask for water with an American accent. I needed to think. Could the blonde help me get a message back home? I watched as she folded her magazine and accepted the water. Once the stewardess had moved on, she glanced over at me and I smiled. She gave me a hesitant smile in return.

"What the fuck you doing?" I heard. Mario sat beside me.

"Can't I admire a pretty woman?" I whispered.

"Just keep your mouth shut," he replied.

"I only want to fuck her, not have a conversation," I replied.

He looked sharply at me. "Got needs, my friend," I added.

I settled back for the remainder of the journey, wondering how I could make contact with her and whether I could write a note and slip it to her. But then, would she take it seriously? Would she want to help?

The plane landed in Palermo, and as we came to a halt, I unbuckled my belt and rose. I reached to the overhead lockers to retrieve the small carry-on I'd brought and placed it on my seat. I turned and reached for the one opposite.

"Is this your bag?" I asked.

The blonde looked up at me, she smiled.

"Thank you and yes."

I pulled down a backpack and handed it to her. I took up the aisle, making sure to stand and stretch, anything to stop Mario climbing from his seat by the window. I stepped to one side to allow the blonde to stand as the aircraft doors were opened.

"First time in Sicily?" I asked.

"It is, I'm traveling around Italy. You?"

"Yes, here on business. Perhaps I'll bump into you somewhere, maybe for dinner?"

"Sure, I'm spending a few days here before moving on."

I felt a jolt to my back as Mario managed to stand. The jolt wasn't accidental. The blonde started to walk toward the door and I grabbed my bag from the seat.

"What the fuck do you think you're doing?" Mario growled.

"Talking to a pretty woman, don't for one minute think you can tell me who I can and can't talk to," I replied.

"Enough, both of you, now move," I heard. Ben had spoken.

"The *boss* has spoken," I said quietly to Mario. I watched him scowl at Ben's retreating back.

As we walked through the airport, I caught sight of her a couple of times. She had stopped to collect a map of the island, from a rack beside the door. Palermo wasn't that big and I prayed I'd bump into her again. She would stick to the tourist areas; the cheaper tourist areas, so finding her wouldn't be difficult. Losing the fucking entourage would be the hardest part.

"Don't even fucking think about it," Ben said, as he followed my gaze.

"Fucking is all I can think about and you have no control over that," I replied.

He smiled and gave a small laugh.

We made our way out and into harsh sunlight; I raised my palm to shield my eyes. A suited man, with his shirt open halfway down his chest, walked over to greet us. He embraced Ben then ignored the rest of us.

"Benito, my friend. It's good to see you again," he said.

"And you, Aldo. Salvatore sends his regards to you and your family and his apologies for not attending himself."

"Another time, I am due for a trip to Rome. Now, shall we get going?"

He waved to a car, which crept slowly to where we stood. A second followed. I made my way to the second.

"Rocco, you're to join us," I heard, spoken in broken English.

I turned and frowned. How did he know my name? Silently I walked toward him. Aldo's driver opened the rear door and I was encouraged to climb in. I slid across the soft leather seats to take my place behind the front passenger seat. Aldo climbed in after me and Ben sat up front. I was confused; I wasn't high enough in the food chain to be sitting where I was.

"Rocco, I've heard good things about you," Aldo said.

"From whom?" I asked.

"Sal of course."

"He doesn't know me."

Aldo chuckled and I was unsure if he knew the circumstances in which I'd found myself. I also saw Ben half-turn in his seat.

"He believes that you will be, how do you say it? *Compliant?*"

"I have a job to do, and then I will be returning home, nothing more."

"Is that what he told you?"

I turned to face the window. The *job* I had wasn't just the delivery of the man who ordered the senator's killing, it was to also give a little payback. Only then would I be done and return home.

"We should eat first, then discuss your problem," Aldo said as we pulled alongside a restaurant.

I wasn't sure what 'my' problem was. The dead senator was Salvatore's problem, not mine.

I guessed Aldo was important by the way the restaurant manager ushered customers from a table outside and under a canopy. He spoke rapidly in his dialect to Aldo; it appeared he was apologizing profusely. The customers that had been moved grumbled until a bottle of wine was placed on their new table. As we sat, I shook a cigarette loose from the pack I'd pulled from my top pocket.

I patted my pocket, looking for matches, then smiled when Aldo clicked his fingers toward Mario who jumped forward with a lighter. I inhaled and as I rested back in my chair, exhaled slowly.

The restaurant was in the harbor and a welcome breeze blew in from the sea as the sun set. I looked out over the ocean. I'd lied when I'd told the blonde I'd never been to Sicily. I sat and remembered a time when I was young, and I'd visited with my family, the one holiday we'd had together. We stayed with some distant cousin of my mother's and spent each day on the beach. I fought back the sadness that threatened to engulf me.

A carafe of red wine was placed on the table with three tumblers, Aldo poured and offered one to me, one to Ben, and one he picked up himself. Mario and Alex were left to fend for themselves.

"So, the senator, that is why we are all here, isn't it?" Aldo said.

"It appears so," I replied.

"Sal doesn't believe the order came from any family in America but from here," Ben said.

Aldo rubbed his chin, it was supposed to be in a thoughtful way, but the gleam in his eye told me he was just playing games. I liked him because I didn't think he liked Sal very much.

"And why is the senator so important, Ben?" he asked, before resting back in his chair.

Ben looked uncomfortable, more so after watching me mimic Aldo's behavior. I was anxious to know as well.

Ben looked at me. "The senator had information on some of Salvatore's activities in America. Specifically, the importing of our heroin. He obtained that information because his nephew, a high-ranking police officer, intercepted one of our shipments. To *control* his nephew, the senator was paid a percentage of what we earned."

"The senator was the one to push the Rico Laws through Congress, why?" I asked.

"To take out another family. That would clear the way for Sal to expand his operation and for the senator to earn a damn sight more than Congress pay."

"How does that lead you here?" Aldo asked.

"The heroin is kept here, the family that the senator wanted taken out are in New York and also here."

There was a silence and from the look on Aldo's face, realization had struck. I was none the wiser.

"You're taking on *that* family?" Aldo's face reddened, tears formed in his eyes, and then he threw back his head and laughed, seriously laughed.

Tears ran down his cheeks and he slapped the table, I grabbed my glass before it toppled over.

"Someone want to fill me in here?" I asked.

After what seemed like minutes, Aldo managed to get himself under control.

"Your Sal wants to take on the Gioletti family, that should prove to be very interesting. They are one of four that control the heroin. And you think this family took out your senator?"

"We do," Ben replied.

"Then why are you not in New York?"

"Because Sal wants to ensure your support in maintaining his supply. We're not here to take out anyone, not yet. We're here to put plans in place."

"And why, since you know who took out the senator, am I being asked to find that information?" I asked. Ben sighed before shrugging his shoulders.

Aldo chuckled some more, all the while shaking his head.

"First we eat," he said, as he waved for a waiter.

There was something in the way Aldo's eyes shifted, very subtly and occasionally to the table behind me, which had me on alert. I thought on what he had said as the waiter placed menus on the table. There were four families that controlled the heroin in Sicily, and I was betting his was one of them. Why else would Sal need his cooperation?

The night was drawing in, the waiter lit a candle he placed on the table, and I notice the slight shake to his hand as he did.

"Want to order for me? I need to take a piss," I said as I stood.

Mario stood at the same time; I guessed I wasn't allowed to take a piss on my own. I wasn't concerned, taking a piss was not why I wanted to leave the table. With Mario following, I walked into the mostly empty restaurant. It had been buzzing when we'd arrived, no more than a half hour prior.

"Notice anything?" I asked as we stepped into the toilet.

"No, what?" Mario replied.

"The restaurant was full when we arrived, now it's empty. There are half eaten dishes on the tables. What does that tell you?"

He shrugged his shoulders.

"People have been asked to leave. The table behind us? Aldo keeps looking, very subtly, at its occupants."

"So what does that mean?"

"It means, Clyde, something is about to go down. You carrying?"

"What's with the fucking Clyde? And yes, of course I am."

He pulled his jacket to one side to show me the revolver he had holstered.

"So what do we do?" he asked.

"You just keep that gun in your hand and your eye on the guy behind me. If you see anything suspicious, shoot the fucker."

"You want me to shoot someone in the middle of the street? Why would I want to save your ass?"

"The street is deserted, and think of it as doing Ben a favor, if they miss, they'll hit him and then go for you and Alex."

"What about his drivers?"

The two cars we had traveled in had parked up farther along the harbor. Both drivers sat waiting patiently in their respective vehicles.

"If they leave the car, you or Alex takes them out. You can shoot more than once, I take it?"

We walked back through the restaurant and I paused, nudging Mario as I did.

"No staff, see," I whispered. The restaurant was empty.

Mario pulled the gun from its holster and tucked it in the waistband of his trousers. As we walked back to the table, I made a mental note of exactly how and where the two guys on the table behind were sitting. I'd have one chance if my instinct proved correct.

"Ah, Rocco, I've ordered you some local dishes, I'm sure you'll approve," Aldo said as I took my seat.

It was simultaneous. Aldo 'dropped' his napkin and leaned down under the table to retrieve it, at the same time I heard the click of a hammer being cocked. I jumped from my seat, pushing Ben to the side and spun on my heel. As the gun was raised, I lifted the table behind me and threw it over the two guys sitting there before running around it. Mario, much to my surprise was on his feet, gun raised, and by my side in seconds.

Two guys lay on the floor, one still held a gun. As he raised it, I kicked him hard in the elbow. The gun flew through the air, clattering on the cobblestone street some feet away. Mario put a bullet between his eyes.

"What the fuck…" I heard as Ben clambered to his feet.

"Set up," I said, as I punched the other guy in the face before kicking him hard to his ribs, snatching his gun from the floor. He'd obviously dropped it when the table hit him.

The sound of a gunshot rang through the air; I ducked, unsure who was firing at whom. As I spun around, gun raised and arm locked straight, I saw Alex leaning through the window of one of the cars. The other had driven away.

Aldo lay on the floor looking up at me; he had one hand raised in defense.

"On your feet," I shouted.

He took his time, so I grabbed his arm and dragged him to his feet as I ran for the car.

Ben, being Salvatore's advisor, rarely saw 'action' so he seemed to be frozen to the spot.

"Move, Ben," I called over my shoulder.

Mario grabbed his arm and dragged him along. In the distance, I could hear the wail of a police car. Alex had climbed into the driver's seat, having deposited the original driver on the ground.

"Open the boot," I said, banging my fist on it.

When it opened, I shoved Aldo in and slammed it shut. Mario threw Ben across the back seat and joined him; I climbed in the front.

"Drive," I said.

"Where to?"

"Anywhere, just fucking drive!" I shouted, as I looked back through the rear window.

The restaurant owner was running up the street away from the car and waving his arms, attracting attention. I could see the blue and red lights of a police car illuminate the unlit road that ran alongside the restaurant. Alex started the engine and put his foot hard down on the accelerator.

I turned back in my seat. "Good thinking, Alex," I said. He nodded.

He navigated the small roads that weaved between buildings as if he'd lived in Palermo all his life. Eventually, we found ourselves in open countryside and heading inland.

"You fucking shot Aldo's men? You any idea of the shit that will cause?" Ben said, his voice rose in fright.

"If he hadn't, they would have shot you, so stop complaining," I said.

"How the fuck could you know that?"

"The restaurant emptied, diners were asked to leave before they'd finished their meals. Aldo spent most of his time looking over my shoulder to the only two people left, two guys. And the click of a fucking hammer being cocked, you know that thing on top of a gun, pretty much confirmed we were about to be fucking shot," I said, the sarcasm dripped from my tongue.

Ben slumped back in his seat. "Where to?" Alex asked me.

"There, kill the lights."

I pointed to a dirt lane that snaked its way through the middle of a recently plowed field. I could make out the outline of a farm building ahead of us. Alex drove around the side and shut off the engine.

"Now what?" Mario asked.

"Now we find out what that was all about," I said, as we heard thumping from the inside of the boot.

We left the car and walked to the rear. I took the gun from my waistband and checked the barrel. Six bullets.

"Give me the gun," I heard. Ben was standing behind me with his hand outstretched.

"Not a chance, now, if you're squeamish, I suggest you get back in the car," I said.

"I said, give me the gun."

I slowly turned around and took a step toward him.

"You want this gun? Come and fucking get it. I just saved your fucking arse. If you think I'm about to kill you with it, let me tell you this. I could have killed you many times over, and I don't need a fucking gun to do it. I could have slashed his throat when I killed the idiot, but I didn't." I looked over to Mario.

"I could have choked Lou in Sienna when he fell asleep and I walked out of that hotel, but I didn't. Don't think for one moment I need a gun," I added.

"Then why haven't you?" he asked, and I noticed the slight tremor to his voice.

"When you were party to my *kidnapping*, when you were party to threatening the only thing I have to live for, you made the biggest mistake. You took away the only reason my fucking heart beats. I don't care, Ben. I don't fucking care if I die today, tomorrow, or next week, and you know what? That makes me a dangerous man. But before that happens, there is something I must do…" I left the sentence hanging.

Silence followed.

"Now, let's get to work," I said.

Alex opened the boot of the car and Aldo looked up at me. His brow was furrowed in question; he would have heard our exchange.

"Out," I said, as I grabbed the front of his shirt and hauled him up.

He fell to his knees on the dusty ground at my feet. I grabbed a fistful of hair and dragged him to the doors of the wooden barn. Aldo grabbed my hands and twisted, trying to break free. I kicked the barn door until the old rusty lock gave way and threw him in.

The barn was empty, save for a few old musty-smelling bales of straw stacked alongside one wall. The faint odor of animals wafted from the ground and we walked around disturbing the dirt.

"Get that," I told Alex. In the corner was an old wooden chair.

Alex carried the chair to the middle of the room; I grabbed Aldo by the front of his shirt and lifted him from the floor.

"Sit," I said.

Moonlight filtered through the broken windows, it gave enough light for me to do what was necessary.

"Who are you working for?" I asked.

Ben, Alex, and Mario stood to one side. Aldo looked toward Ben.

"*I* asked you the question!" My voice echoed around the room.

"I don't know what you mean?" he said.

"I have six bullets in this gun. I need one so that leaves me five. One for each kneecap and one for each elbow."

I turned to Ben.

"Do you know how fucking painful it is to be shot through the elbow? I saw it once, totally shattered the bones. The lower part of this guy's arm was hanging like a piece of thread."

Aldo whimpered. "By that point, Aldo, you'll be begging me to kill you, and thankfully I'll have one spare bullet. Where would you want that?"

I walked around him, tapping the gun on his temple. "Here?" I said.

"Or maybe here?" I placed the gun to his forehead.

I stood in front of him not speaking, just looking. His eyes were filled with unshed tears; he was trying to keep it together, to not break down in front of me. I crouched down on my heels, far enough away to not be touched should he decide to kick out.

"Who are you working for?" I asked, my voice gentler than before.

He stared at me, not answering. I placed the gun on his left kneecap and pulled back the hammer, priming the gun ready to fire.

"The Gioletti family," he whispered.

"Why do they want us dead?"

"They don't want *you* dead, they want to let Sal know he doesn't dictate, that he needs to drop his quest to find out who ordered his senator's death."

"So they definitely ordered the senator's death?"

"I don't know. I follow orders, Rocco, just like you."

"And that order came to you directly?"

"No, via the Commission."

"According to Sal, the Commission has no place in Italy, is that incorrect?" I lied because at that point I wasn't sure of the outcome for Aldo. If he lived, I wanted word sent back that Sal wasn't respectful to the Commission.

"There are many Commissions, some share heads of families. They overlap."

"How did you know we were coming here?"

"Huh?"

"It's an easy enough question, who arranged for you to meet us at the airport?"

"Sal, of course."

"Then who told the Giolettis we were meeting? You've just told me they ordered you to take one of us out as a warning."

"I…I didn't…I."

"Aldo, let's recap. The Gioletti family wanted to send Sal a message that he's to drop his quest to discover who ordered the killing of the senator, yes?" I spoke slowly. "So, the Giolettis ordered his killing, and they don't want Sal to know, yes? That means, the two goons that were supposed to shoot Ben, whoever, or me, were there with you, yes? You knew, Aldo."

"I didn't, they were there just to protect me from you. I had no fucking idea what was going on. I swear." Aldo looked between Ben and me.

"You lie," I shouted, and I heard the quick shuffle of feet as my loudness spooked Ben.

"Someone betrayed us all, Aldo. It was either you, someone in your family, a traitor maybe, or someone in Sal's," I said, gently.

"I sure as fuck didn't, I was given an order. Okay, one of you was to die, only one of you."

"And what happens when they find out you couldn't execute that order? I mean, you didn't think it through very well. You had two guys sit behind Ben and me; both of us were unarmed. Alex and Mario, who are armed, sat behind you. Your guys would need to be fucking good shots to have taken them out first, because that's who they should have been shooting at."

Aldo didn't answer. I stood and walked about, thinking. Someone had informed the Giolettis we were meeting. There was not much that was making sense, other than the fact we had been set up.

"What are you...?" Aldo said as I paced.

"Quiet, I'm thinking," I replied.

The only noise, other than my feet dragging through the dirt floor, was the scampering of animals, rats I imagined, that had made their home among the rotten straw.

I walked back to Aldo, and without speaking, placed the barrel of the gun on the top of his knee and pulled the trigger. His screams, the gunshot, and the gasps from Ben echoed around the barn.

"Tell me exactly what Sal does here?"

Aldo was sobbing, he had his hands wrapped around his knee, blood dripped through his fingers and splashed onto the floor.

I pulled back the hammer again.

"We provide the heroin, then he ships it to New York," he said between sobs.

"So you are one of the four?" He had said, 'we.'

Aldo was panting, trying to absorb the pain. His face was screwed up but he nodded his head.

"Rocco, where the fuck are you going with this?" Ben asked.

"Someone set us up, someone wants all of us dead, and I don't think for one minute it has anything to do with a fucking senator."

"So what the fuck does it have to do with?" he asked.

"The heroin, obviously. Someone wants Sal's route, maybe his contacts in the U.S., maybe, one of the *four*. We just have to figure out who."

I knelt in front of Aldo and placed the muzzle of the gun into the wound in his kneecap. I pressed down, turning the gun as I did. He screamed out, the sound only just covering the squelch of flesh being twisted around the barrel of the gun.

"There is a way out of this, you know?" I said.

Sweat rolled from his forehead mixing with his tears. He bit his lip so hard, to suppress more screams, a trickle of blood ran down his chin. I pulled the gun away from his leg.

"Who gave you the order?"

I wanted to know the name of the man who had ordered the killing. For Aldo to tell me meant he had to become a traitor and sign his own death warrant. It was a testament to his loyalty, and I respected the man, when he clamped his mouth shut. I shot him through the other kneecap, knowing it to be a fruitless endeavor.

"Answer me one thing, this has nothing to do with the senator does it?"

He shook his head. "They took out the senator because he was working with Sal. But they want control of Sal's operations because they don't trust him and, Rocco, they will get it," he replied through clenched teeth.

I nodded in reply. "So, what to do with you."

"Make it quick," was all Aldo replied.

I shot him through the forehead, and sealed my fate.

"Now what?" Ben asked.

"We head back to Rome," I replied.

We were in the car, Alex was driving, and we headed toward the airport under the cover of darkness.

"We should have found out more," Mario said from the back seat.

"Do you think he would ever have told? He was a dead man, he knew that so there was nothing to gain by talking."

I rested back in the passenger seat and closed my eyes. I'd killed a high-ranking official of a prominent Sicilian family. I would be a marked man. The only way I could secure my safety was to become a high-ranking official myself. I also knew I would not be returning to Evelyn any time soon. All the time there was a price on my head, anyone around me would be in danger.

As we came off the road that bordered fields, using my shirt, I wiped the gun clean of fingerprints and tossed it from the window. We'd driven most of the way in silence, but there was a shift in the atmosphere. Ben— even Mario to a degree—relaxed around me, they weren't on 'alert' that I'd run. I didn't care about saving them; I didn't give a fuck about them in the least. I only cared that what I had done may have accelerated my plan. I smiled as we pulled to a stop a short distance from the airport entrance.

"Let me see if I can get us new flights," Ben said as he opened the car door. "Wait here."

I shook a cigarette loose from the pack and lit it before offering them around. Alex took one; Mario shook his head. With the windows down, we smoked and waited.

"How did you get here?" Alex asked.

"On the same flight as you," I replied, knowing full well what he meant.

He smirked. "Your friend, your boss, Sal, kidnapped me, basically," I said.

"Why haven't you attempted to run?" Mario asked from the rear seat.

"Everyone thinks I'm dead, and I'll stay that way for a little while. But here's the thing, my resurrection is going to be fucking epic and you will have a choice to make."

"And that would be?"

"You'll be with me—or dead."

We fell silent and I continued to smoke my cigarette. As I watched Ben stride from the airport, Alex spoke.

"I'm with you," he whispered.

"And me," Mario added.

I nodded. "Breathe one word about this conversation and it will be your last."

Ben had secured us flights home, although, we would not be sitting near each other, which seemed to make him uneasy. He was three rows in front of me as I sat and buckled my belt. I caught him on many occasions looking over his shoulder. I laughed, wondering where the fuck he thought I could run. I laughed more when we were thousands of feet in the air and he still checked. What I did do, though, was scan the aircraft. I remembered the blonde on the journey out, I'd missed an opportunity to get word out that I was alive. But then I thought about it. I needed to stay dead, I'd live my life on the run, and everyone I loved would pay a price if I didn't.

I put all thoughts of contacting home, of Evelyn, and my family from my head that day. I focused on one thing only. I looked at the tattoo on my arm, visible through the thin white cotton of my shirtsleeve and knew.

Hell would open up the day I commanded it, and those that had wronged me would feel the wrath of the devil himself.

---

There was much shouting, screaming obscenities, and slamming of fists on desks coming from Sal's office. I sat outside while Ben debriefed.

I was bent at the waist, my forearms resting on my thighs, when I saw a pair of bare feet stop in front of me. My eyes trailed a path from the red painted toenails to the slender gold chain around one ankle and up the legs of Felisia. She wore shorts, tight denim shorts that I'm sure her mother would disapprove of. Her midriff was exposed beneath the shirt that was tied in a knot under her ample breasts. She smiled and swiped her tongue over her cherry red lip.

"Rocco, I've missed you," she said.

"I've only been gone since yesterday, I doubt it."

"Why are you never nice to me? I could make your life easier if you were nice to me."

I stood, towering over her. "You look like a whore, now go, wipe that shit from your face and put some clothes on."

She gasped, her mouth opened and closed and she raised her hand to slap my face. I grabbed her wrist and roughly pulled her close. I placed my free hand under her chin, raising her face and squeezing until I saw tears form in her eyes. Letting go of her wrist, I used my fingers to wipe the lipstick from her mouth. I cleaned my fingers on the front of her shirt, brushing over her erect nipple.

"When I fuck that mouth, when I claim you, you will not wear that shit, understand?"

Her eyes widened and she gently nodded. I released her from my grip and pushed her away. She stumbled slightly before running off.

I sat back down and placed my head in my hands. I prayed Evelyn would forgive me for what I knew I had to do. I was to betray her.

"Rocco!" Sal shouted from his office. I stood and entered.

Mario and Alex sat facing him, Ben, as usual, was to his side. The place was trashed. Papers were strewn over the floor. Sal stood with his hands placed on his desk. His face was puce with anger and sweat rolled from his forehead.

"Sit the fuck down and you tell me what fucking happened," he shouted.

I looked around the room for a spare chair, taking my time to walk to the corner and retrieve one.

"We were collected from the airport by *your* friend and taken to a restaurant…"

"I know all that. What did he say, in the barn?"

"Nothing."

"You shot the fucker before he told you anything."

"I did him a kindness. He was a dead man, regardless."

There was a short silence, I watched Sal as his face reddened further and wondered if he was about to have a heart attack.

"You did him a kindness?"

He slammed his hands down on the desk with such force I heard a crack. I wasn't sure if it was the desk or a bone. I held back the smile that was making my lips twitch.

"I saved their lives…" I indicated with my hand toward the other guys in the room. "And found out that your *empire* is about to be under attack from the Gioletti family. They want your heroin routes. More importantly, *Sal,* someone in your organization set us up. They told the Giolettis we were in Sicily. Who could that have been?"

Sal shook his head and took a deep breath. He finally sat. "Now they will come after you," he said.

"No, they'll come after us."

"You started a fucking war," he shouted.

"No, we defended ourselves and showed whoever set us up, it wouldn't be that easy. Now, tell me what's happening to your shipments?"

"Nothing is happening to my fucking shipments."

"So you don't lose one or two?"

His silence told me all I needed to know.

"If you want my fucking help, Sal, you need to tell me something."

I watched him lean back in his chair.

"I think he has proven his worth, don't you?" Ben said to him.

Sal looked at me. "What do you recommend then?"

"First, you tell me the process."

"Alex, get us some coffee," Sal said before he settled back in his chair.

"The heroin is taken by boat, initially, then road. All the boats make it, not all the trucks. It arrives in New York and it's then distributed through pizza parlors," Sal chuckled at the thought.

"Who controls all this?"

"One guy, a Sicilian and head of the Bolognetta family. We get a payment for the trucks and a percentage of what's sold is given to American families to keep them happy."

"How did you get involved? Why you and not just the four families in Sicily?"

"Because I was one of the four families in Sicily until an opportunity arose for me to relocate here."

I wasn't about to ask what that opportunity was; I'd find that out for myself.

"Is there any pattern to the missing trucks? Same driver, license plate?"

"We rotate the drivers, most think they are carrying coffee or food," Ben said.

"But is it the same truck?"

"No, although there is one more than the others."

"Then as I said, someone in your family is working for the Gioletti. We drive the trucks."

Salvatore fell silent.

"We drive the trucks knowing one will be handed over. You need a new traitor, Sal, but a traitor working for you."

"And you have your feet on American soil," he said.

I leaned forward in my chair. The atmosphere in the room had changed; some of the hostility had abated.

"Let me tell you one thing. You've kept me prisoner here and I've allowed that."

His eyes widened and his mouth opened as if to speak. I held up my hand.

"Do you think I couldn't have gotten away? Do you honestly think that many times over the past months I haven't had the opportunity to put a bullet in your skull, in theirs, and leave? But I haven't, have I?"

I heard the shuffle of feet and a sigh from Ben. I kept my gaze trained on Sal.

"Why?" Sal asked.

"Because I have a plan. I will return to America, once I know who, in my family, collaborated with you. Someone told you where I was, who I was.

And if it takes me years, I will find out and I will kill him. In the meantime, you need me and I need you."

I sat back in my chair and let the silence deepen, allowing Sal to absorb my words. He looked uncomfortable. For such a powerful man, and I was yet to determine just how powerful, my words had struck a chord.

"I don't fear you, Salvatore. I don't fear anyone but God. And I fucked up my position with Him a long time ago," I said with a chuckle. "But whoever it is in America is my enemy and the biggest threat to Evelyn. If it means I lose her forever, that's the way it has to be. But make no mistake, if even a hair on her head is harmed, you will witness endless pain."

"Are you threatening me?" he said.

"No, merely stating a fact. Unless you kill me, of course, and I'd recommend you do that. The day you caged me, the day you began to treat me like an animal was the day you made a big mistake. Right now, I'm not your enemy. The Gioletti family is. That's a family with the potential to wipe you out and I set that in motion. I didn't kill Aldo for information, we both know he was never going to talk. Think about it, Sal. You have a war coming and you need the best, that's me."

I stood, buttoned up my suit jacket, and made to leave the room.

"Oh, I want an apartment, and by dinnertime," I added.

"Where the fuck do you think you are going?" he said, his voice beginning to rise.

Had I pushed him too fast? Shown my hand a little too early?

"For a smoke. Then we plan."

I left the office and the house. I took up my usual position, resting against the fountain in the courtyard and shook a cigarette from the packet. I inhaled deeply. I wasn't as confident as I'd sounded. I worried I'd shown my hand a little early. The outcome of what I'd said would go one of two ways. I'd be on that next rung of the ladder or I'd be dead. Time would tell.

I thought of Evelyn, of the things I had to do to be able to return to her. And although no one would ever know, my heart turned to ice that day. I'd set the wheels in motion. I wanted those four families to come after Sal; I wanted to flush out whoever had betrayed me, yet I prayed it hadn't been Joe.

"*Do* we have a plan?" I heard in a whispered tone.

Alex took a seat beside me, he handed me a coffee.

"Yes. And I will ask that you trust me, follow me without asking questions."

"Or die?" he said with a chuckle.

I turned to him and shrugged my shoulders. "It's always our choice, Alex, whether we live or die. I will tell you this, I don't operate the same way as him. I don't need to rule by fear. I saved your life, you owe me, but it's your choice. You repay that by standing alongside me, Alex. Not below me, alongside."

We stared at each other for a short while before he slowly nodded.

"What did he say after I left?" I asked.

"To find you, watch you, and he told Ben to get the keys to an apartment."

I chuckled. "Then I guess I need to go and pack."

I flicked my cigarette to the ground and walked to my 'shed.' The padlock was hanging on the bolt and I took it off. I raised my arm to throw it but then stilled. I opened my palm and looked at that padlock. It had aged, weathered over the past months it had been party to my incarceration. I chuckled as I pocketed it. It would serve as a reminder. A memento that no man has the ability to lock me away. Maybe my body could be, but never my mind, and never my soul.

I moved into an apartment just a short walk from the house. The apartment wasn't the plush penthouse as promised, but a house that had been converted. At least I had the upstairs. It contained two bedrooms, a living room with kitchen at one end, and a basic bathroom. I'd given a list of requirements to Sal for modernization, but it would do as a temporary base. I also expected to start earning.

The apartment was sparsely furnished, with just a sofa and one bed. Rosina, I suspected, had donated the linens. At least there was a coffee pot. I didn't need much else; I'd lived my whole life sparsely.

For a week we planned.

"Tell me about the Bolognetta family," I asked.

While Sal was out on business, Alex, Ben, and I were sitting in his office, and before Ben could answer, there was a knock on the door. It slowly opened and a very demure Felisia walked in carrying a tray. She kept her head bowed, only glancing at me from the corner of her eye. She wore a blouse with the buttons done up to the neck and smart trousers. She had little makeup on her face.

"I have coffee for you," she said. Her voice was low.

"Good, place it there," I said, pointing to small table across the room.

I then ignored her. She hesitated, not sure whether to stay and pour the coffee. If she was waiting for a response from me she wasn't getting one.

"Erm, I'll leave that right there," she said before rushing to the door.

Once she had left, we continued our conversation. Ben explained the heroin was sold in the U.S. and the money laundered through the pizza parlors before being sent back to the suppliers. Each of the four families shared the profit. Sal's involvement was not in production but in the shipping. It appeared the four families were not happy with the fact that part of the shipment seemed to never reach it's destination.

I began to suspect the *disappearance* of the trucks might have been orchestrated by Sal himself. And to do that, he'd need a high-ranking official. I kept that suspicion to myself. Perhaps I wasn't the only one who suspected the same.

"How much is a missing truck worth?" I asked.

"Millions of dollars," Ben answered. "We're talking many billions of business here. Each month five trucks reach New York. Well, I say five, for a while now it's been four. One truck is found missing its cargo."

"And the driver?"

"Sometimes dead, sometimes missing."

"Who employs the drivers?"

"Sal, obviously, but Massimo Gioletti is one of the most powerful men in the U.S. Although he allows the Bolognetta family to assist with the transportation of the heroin, he takes control of it as soon as it hits the pizza parlors. He's as upset about the missing truck as the four families are."

"And presumably Sal has spoken with Massimo?"

"Yes, many times. We're confident Massimo is not directly involved, I can't see a reason for that, it's lost revenue. I wonder if they think Sal is incompetent and that's why they want to control the route."

I caught a glance from Alex and suspected his line of thinking was aligning with mine. I kept my face neutral.

"I don't think using you as a driver is going to be approved. Sal won't run the risk of you in the U.S."

"Why?"

"Because…" Ben paused and took a deep breath.

"Because when he did what he did, he alienated most of the Commission. He doesn't have the backing he once had and he knows that. If you return, he's lost you, and that puts him in a dangerous position. For now, you're his insurance policy from them. They show their displeasure in any way, he kills you and then…" He left his sentence hanging for effect, I thought.

"So they know I'm alive?"

"I imagine so. And if they do, then they'll also know of his threats to your family. And if they don't, I suspect they will after the events in Sicily."

That news put a completely different spin on my plan. If they knew I was alive, did Joe? Did Evelyn? My heart started to beat a little faster.

"I've said too much already but I like you, Rocco. I didn't agree with any of this, and Sal is in a weak position now."

I slowly nodded my head. What Ben was telling me was that if my plan involved overthrowing Sal, sooner would be better than later. However, Sal still had his 'friends,' he had people reliant on him for transporting their heroin. I needed to make alliances with those same friends. That wasn't going to be easy considering I'd killed one.

"Were the threats to Evelyn real?" I asked.

"Very. He has someone in Washington who watches her and Joe. I can't tell you who that is. I will, when the time is right. This person is very close, Rocco, so you need to tread carefully."

"Why, 'when the time is right'?"

"Because that's my insurance policy. Are you going to kill me knowing that I have something of great importance?"

The room fell silent. I gave him one nod of my head and a smile. "All the time Evelyn is safe, so are you."

It was that day I realized I wasn't heading back to the U.S. any time soon. It was that day that I gave up my dream and any hope of a life with Evelyn. One day, in the future, I had no doubts I'd see her again, but for now she was lost to me. I had a lot of work to do; I had to overthrow Sal. I had to make alliances with men I wouldn't spit on, and before I could do any of that, I had to get closer to the man who had fucked up my existence in more ways than he would ever know.

---

It was late one night when I heard a knock on my apartment door. Mario lived downstairs and the property was pretty secure. No one could get to my door unless they had a key to the main property. I rose and crept to the door. I stood and listened for a while. I could hear the shuffling of feet and then a delicate clearing of throat. I opened the door to see Felisia.

"Yes?"

"I, err, Mamma thought you might like some meals. She worried you hadn't joined us for dinner."

I'd been eating at the house, using the apartment to bathe and sleep in only for the past few days. But that evening I'd opted to spend my time alone.

I pulled the door open wide and stood to one side. Felisia was hesitant at first but eventually walked to the kitchenette and placed her bag on the countertop. She began to unload plastic containers of food.

I heard the hitch of her breath as I walked and stood behind her. I saw the tremble to her hands as she placed the containers in the fridge. As she turned to face me, she lifted her chin in defiance; she wouldn't want me to see her nerves.

"If you were nicer to me, Rocco, I could have made sure you had a decent place to live." She looked around my apartment with disdain.

"This suits me just fine, Felisia. I don't plan on staying here long enough to worry about it."

"Oh, are you going somewhere?"

I chuckled and took a step closer to her. She took a step back.

"Why would I be nice to you?" I asked, ignoring her question.

"I can make your life a little easier. Papa will do anything for me."

"And you think being your puppet would be better than his? You really don't know me very well at all, do you?"

"I'd like to," she said, her voice was husky.

"Do you know what it's like to want, Felisia?" I drew out her name and watched her pupils dilate.

"I've never wanted for anything," she said breathlessly, as I took yet another step toward her.

"You want me to fuck you, don't you? You want to feel my hard cock inside you. Are you a virgin?"

I took another step forward; she took another step backward until she hit the countertop. I placed my hands either side of her, trapping her. My face was inches from hers. I could feel her breath on my skin as she fought to control it.

"Let me tell you what a man like me can do to you. I can have your body burning like it's on fire. Your heart will beat so fast—you'll struggle to breathe. You'll scream out my name when my fingers touch you, when my tongue teases you. And when I decide to fuck you, you'll claw at my back. You'll feel pain, Felisia, and then a desire so great it will bring you to tears. Is that what you want?"

She nodded her head, her lips were parted, and her breathing erratic.

"I'll fuck your pussy, I'll fuck your mouth, and I'll fuck your mind."

She moaned, and her whole body trembled. I looked at her and swallowed down the bile that rose to my throat. I hated the woman standing in front of me; she represented my pain and my loss.

"I want that, Rocco. I want you to fuck me."

"Now you know what it feels like to want."

She opened her eyes and I saw the anger. She raised her hand as if to strike me, but I was too close. I grabbed her wrist and forced her arm back, holding her hand to the countertop. I grabbed her chin with my fingers and lowered my head to hers. Her lips parted. My mouth was millimeters from hers. Her tongue darted from her mouth, licking over my lower lip. I felt nothing for her; she was simply an instrument, a tool I would use.

My mouth crashed on hers, I devoured her and took no pleasure from it. I bit at her lip, her tongue. She placed her free hand over my cock and gently squeezed. The hardness was painful. She pulled her head back slightly.

"You want me, I can feel it," she whispered.

"No, Felisia. I want to fuck, it doesn't matter who."

I watched her chest heaving and her cheeks flush. Whether that was desire or anger I wasn't sure.

"You bastard," she said.

I reached down and grabbed her skirt, lifting it to her hips. She placed her hand on my chest and tried to push me away. I slid my fingers between her thighs. Her wetness had soaked through her panties. I ran my fingers over her, just the once, but it was enough to entice a moan from her lips. Her hand fisted in my shirt and her head fell back. And then I took a step away. I placed my hand around the back of her head and gave her a smile. She smiled back.

I propelled her toward the apartment door, opened it, and then pushed her out. She stumbled as she turned to face me. I laughed at the look of shock on her face and closed the door before the spew of profanities erupted from her mouth.

She banged her fists on the door, shouting obscenities before finally leaving. I heard her stomp along the corridor to the stairs and the slam of the building's door. I watched through the window as she pulled her cardigan tightly around her and ran back to her own house.

I walked into my bedroom and lay on the bed. Taped to the headboard was the only photograph I had of Evelyn. I reached up and placed my fingers on her face.

"I'm sorry. I'm so fucking sorry," I whispered.

---

I woke still dressed in the previous day's clothes. My head thumped as I swung my legs over the side of the bed. I looked at the photograph and swallowed down the lump that had jumped into my throat. She'd understand, I was sure of that. If she knew my situation, she'd give me permission to do whatever was necessary, but that didn't make the guilt lessen or the pain in my heart subside.

I stripped off my clothes and stepped into the shower. I was done before the water managed to change from lukewarm to hot. I wrapped a towel around my waist and sat back on the bed. My cock throbbed painfully as I stared at the face of the only woman I'd ever love. I let my towel fall open and wrapped my hand around it.

I closed my eyes and pictured the last weekend I spent with Evelyn. I heard her moans in my head, and saw her body in my mind. As I stroked I imagined it was her hand. Tears pricked at my eyes as I came.

Once dressed, I made my way to Sal's house. I dragged on my cigarette as I walked, wishing I'd taken the time to drink a cup of coffee.

"Rocco," I heard as I made my way up the drive.

Mario upped his pace to catch up with me. "I have news," he said.

We stopped by the fountain. "Not here, later, okay?" I said.

He nodded and together we made our way into Sal's office. He was sitting at his desk and on the telephone. I noticed a fresh pot of coffee had been left on the side table. I picked it up, waved it at him. He nodded and I poured four cups. I had no doubt Ben would be joining us soon. Mario and I sat and waited for him to finish his call.

"It seems a meeting has been called," he said, as he sipped from his cup.

"Are you invited?"

"Yes, it's to be held here, in Rome."

"Are you going to put forward my proposal for us to drive the trucks?"

I knew what the answer was going to be, but I wanted to push it. Whether I got to the U.S. or whether I got to one of the Commission, it didn't matter. All I needed was for a message to be sent.

"That has already been dismissed, the Commission will figure out who is hijacking my trucks," he said. As his eyes shifted to the left I knew he was lying.

"In the meantime, I have some outstanding payments I'd like collected. Go with Mario," he added.

Mario and I stood and left the office, as we did Felisia walked down the hallway.

"Wait outside for me," I whispered to Mario.

I stood and watched her falter. She tried to hold my stare, but as she got closer it was clear that had become difficult. She tried to square her shoulders and lift her chin but kept her eyes downcast.

"No words of endearment this morning, Felisia?" I said as she drew close.

"I have nothing to say to you."

"Other than scream out my name when I make you come, that's fine by me," I whispered as she passed.

I heard the soft gasp that left her lips before I turned and joined Mario outside the house.

"We need to unravel this," Mario said and he and I walked to the fountain. "What do we really know?" he asked.

"Aldo has his own family, yet he said he worked with the Giolettis. That's two of the four families that have collaborated. It's suspected the Giolettis were the ones who wanted the senator dead. Tell me about them and your thoughts."

"The Giolettis are the largest family in New York. They allow the Bolognetta to manage the distribution of the heroin, I guess, so they are distanced from it. I think Sal has his own truck hijacked because the other families are taking a larger cut of profits. He also needs a federal agent or high-ranking police officer on his side to ensure *his* hijacked truck then makes it to some kind of safety," Mario said.

"I need to get in on that meeting with the Commission. Before that, I need to meet with the other families in Sicily."

"That's never going to happen."

"We need to think of a way." I started to walk back to the house. Ben was the key to getting me back to Sicily.

---

"Rocco, there is no way Sal will allow any of us back to Sicily until this has calmed down," Ben said.

"Then we find a way to change his mind. If I can get back there, call a meeting with the families and form a plan."

"I told Sal that someone on the inside was feeding information about the truck route, but we know that isn't true. Sal is arranging for one of his trucks to go missing every time. The Giolettis know that. We prove it, we can hand them Sal and we are halfway down the home stretch."

Ben stared at me for a moment. "They won't believe you, Rocco. Whatever you thought of Joe and his family, he is small fry compared to what goes on here."

"I don't doubt that, and never disrespect Joe, he is more respected in America than Sal, so we use that to our advantage. Find a way to convince Sal to let us go back to Sicily."

"Do you really believe he's hiding one of his own trucks?"

"I do, it's the only thing that makes any sense. Four families in Sicily produce the heroin. They trust the distribution to him, but he won't get the same payment as they would, right?" I said, Ben nodded.

"Sal has gotten greedy, he wants more. He needed the senator to ensure one truck got lost, the Giolettis needed the senator to ensure all the trucks made it to their destination, right?" Ben nodded again.

"The four families in Sicily need the Giolettis way more than they need Sal. So we give them a choice. They can side with the Giolettis and cut out Sal, find another distributor, or they can work with me, and I'll make sure all those trucks reach their destination."

"Work with you?"

"I'll take out Sal, I'll run this fucking sham of a family."

No one spoke. I heard the rattle of a cup in a saucer as Ben lifted it to sip on his coffee.

"Have no doubt, Ben. Sal will die at my hands. Like I've said before, you can stand beside me after that, or you can go down with him. You hold information, but the thing is, that information isn't as powerful as you think. I can never return to America. Evelyn is lost to me, so tell me or not, my plan is going ahead."

"How on earth do you think you're going to take out Sal?" he asked.

"I won't tell you that, not until it's time. Do you remember my words at that barn? I have nothing to lose, Ben. The only freedom my heart will ever feel is when I'm dead. That might be now if you tell Sal of my plan, I'm hoping it will be old age."

"I need time to think. I have been loyal to Sal for many years, but I agree with you, he is responsible for the missing trucks, and I don't like the way this is headed. He's put us all in danger."

"You have one day, Ben. We need to strike soon, I don't have the luxury of time."

As it was, it was just a few hours later when Ben aligned with Mario, Alex, and I. It was then time to take on the biggest fight of my life. I wasn't confident I'd survive, I was hoping to, of course. Whatever the outcome, Sal would go down and I'd be the one to instigate that.

---

"Sal, I have an idea for you," Ben said.

For the past couple of days the house had been on lockdown. Sal had spent most of his time on the phone trying to convince the other families I was a rogue, and the shooting of Aldo had been done without his orders.

"What?" he said, not looking up from some papers on his desk.

"Let Rocco go back to Sicily…"

"What? Are you fucking kidding me?"

"Hear me out. Send him back. Let him face the families. They'll want to hear why he did what he did. We use Rocco to feed back information that Aldo was working for the Gioletti family, who wants to take over the route and keep the majority of the share for themselves. It's not a lie; we are losing a truck a month at the moment, that's millions of dollars, Sal. Dollars that should be coming back to us, to them."

"I can tell them that," he said.

"But if you do, you are seen as protecting me and they might want to know why," I added. Until then, I'd sat quietly in the corner.

Sal waved his arm. "Organize it," he said to Ben. "And you, one fuck up, one slight deviation from the plan, and Mario will put a bullet through your fucking skull. Not only that, I will personally see to it that Evelyn meets you in hell as well."

I bowed my head in mock deference. "You have my word, Sal. I will convince the families the Giolettis want control, which is why they wanted to stop your search for who ordered the senator's death. They have taken you on, Sal, not the families in Sicily. Those families are your allies—it's time to call that in—get together and you are a stronger force than the Giolettis. I mean, there's nothing stopping you organizing the final stage of that heroin, is there? You have contacts in the U.S., yes?"

His greedy little eyes started to glisten as he thought. "Yes, yes, I have contacts, in fact…" He never finished his sentence but waved me away instead.

Once my back was turned, I smiled. The wheels had been set in motion. Now I had to pray I could convince the four families in Sicily to align with me.

---

It was a few days later that I encountered Felisia again. During that time she'd kept out of my way, but as I sat in her mother's kitchen, she had no choice but to wait on me. I saw the not so subtle glances, the licking of lips, and the closeness each time she placed a plate in front of me. So had Sal. He stared hard at me, scolding his daughter enough to have her scuttling away.

"It is set," he said, spitting his mouthful of food across the table as he spoke. "You will go with Ben and meet with the Romano family. Enrico is a very good friend of mine, but he is troubled by recent events."

I watched Rosina wince, and I assumed that was at the food that landed close to her plate.

"Good, I look forward to it," I said. I sat opposite Sal; close enough to have his chewed and discarded food land on the side of my plate. I pushed it away.

Rosina stood; she took her plate, then leaned over and picked up mine, to the kitchen counter. She returned with fresh ones. Sal was oblivious as to why.

"You will be there no more than one day, that's assuming you return, of course," he said, laughing. "I cannot guarantee your safety, Rocco."

"I don't expect you to. But I intend to come back, Sal, make no mistake about that."

When dinner was finished, I thanked Rosina and left the house. I stood beside the fountain and lit a cigarette. Behind me, off to one side, I heard a sob. I couldn't see anyone so followed the sound. Behind a row of bushes, Felisia sat on a bench in a grassy area. She startled when she saw me and angrily brushed her tears away. She straightened her back and planted her usual scowl on her face. I sat beside her, shaking another cigarette from the pack. I offered that to her, she shook her head.

"Why are you crying?" I asked.

"I'm not. I was getting some air."

"Okay, sure sounded like sobs to me. But then, what do I know?"

She mumbled under her breath.

"When you curse, it makes you ugly, Felisia."

"What the fuck do you care?" she replied, baiting me.

She snatched the cigarette pack from my hand and with shaking hands pulled one free. By the way she held it, I wasn't sure she was a seasoned smoker. I struck a match and held it, as she placed the cigarette between her lips. She inhaled, and then coughed violently. I reached forward to take the cigarette from her fingers but she pulled away.

"What was America like?" she asked, quietly.

"Wonderful. Busy," I said.

I didn't want to talk about America to her.

"I want to go one day. I want to go anywhere, even our village is better than here."

"Why?"

"I haven't been allowed to walk through those gates since we came here."

"You came to me."

"I snuck out, and I paid a price for that when I was caught sneaking back in."

"You should have your freedom, you are too young to be locked up here, in this monstrosity."

"Mamma is desperate to go home. I listen to her cry, night after night, and I hate him more each time." Her voice had lowered to a whisper.

I turned on my seat. "One day, you can take your mamma home."

She huffed and took a second drag on the cigarette. I watched her cheeks redden, her eyes water. I reached out and pulled the cigarette from her lips and ground it out on the ground.

"Smoking makes you ugly as well," I said, taking a drag of my own.

"Yet you smoke?"

"I'm black on the inside, Felisia, haven't you figured that out yet?"

I stood and started to walk away.

"Not to me," she whispered. I doubted she intended for me to hear her words, but I had.

I stopped and turned. "Do you want to see my blackness, feel it? Have it absorb your soul?"

I took the few steps back to her. She nodded. I reached down and pulled her to a standing position. Her body began to shake and her eyes filled with tears. I had no love for the woman in front of me, I'd never love another, but in that moment, I was lonely. Of course, it helped that she was part of my plan. I swallowed down the guilt and I kissed her hard. I placed my hand on her back and held her to me, not because I wanted to feel her body against mine, but simply because her legs shook and I needed to hold her up. She gripped the hair at the back of my head and moaned her desire.

When I pulled away, she struggled to gain her breath.

"Tonight, I will come for you," I said, and then I walked away.

Was I being fair? Absolutely not. I was going to fuck her in her bedroom, in her father's house. Not because I wanted to, but it was probably one of the greatest insults I could give to Sal. I'd take his daughter's virginity, right under his nose, so to speak.

I headed back to my apartment for a shower and change of clothes. It was as I sat on the bed with Evelyn's photograph pinned to the headboard that I wondered if I was making the biggest mistake. I'd convinced myself that Evelyn would understand the need to do whatever I had to, and I brought that thought, in her voice, to the front of my mind. Using Felisia, initially, had been one thing, but fucking her simply to spite her father was low, even for me.

I pulled on a pair of jeans and a dark short-sleeved shirt. I slipped on my loafers and grabbed my keys. I had to brush all thoughts of morality to one side. I'd make my peace with my guilt at some point, when I was free to do so. In the meantime, I had no choice but to use all means available to me, and Felisia was available to me.

---

The house was quiet, although security still patrolled the grounds, I was waved through. I checked my watch and noted the time. At nearly midnight, I was banking on Sal and Rosina being in bed. Alex let me in the front door, he had no idea why I was there, but like the good soldier he was, he didn't question me. He raised his eyebrows in surprise, of course. I just gave him a wink and carried on. I silently climbed the stairs and walked the corridor to the bedroom I knew belonged to Felisia. My heart beat a rapid rhythm. Not in excitement at what I was about to do, in excitement at the thought Sal would fucking freak out.

I paused outside her door. For a fleeting second, the thought that what I was doing was so very wrong, came to mind. I pushed it back down. I placed my hand on the doorknob and turned. The room was mostly in darkness. A bedside lamp gave a very subtle glow and sitting on the edge of the bed was Felisia.

"I didn't think you'd come," she whispered.

"How would that have made you feel?" I asked, stalking toward her.

"Awful, I guess."

"How nervous are you?"

"Not very," she replied.

"Then I guess the room is pretty chilly because you're shivering. Rule number one, don't lie to me, ever."

She nodded her head slowly. As she stood I could see that she wore a silk robe. I reached forward and untied the belt, letting it fall open. She sucked in a deep breath, as I hooked one finger in the front of her bra. I pulled her gently toward me.

"Turn around," I said.

I slid the robe from her shoulders and unclipped her bra. I slid the straps over her shoulders and let it fall to the floor. I ran my hands down her sides, catching her panties as I did. I lowered them, until they, too, fell to the floor. Her breathing was rapid and I could see her flesh pimple. Her legs shook slightly. I placed my hands on her shoulders and turned her back to face me.

"This may hurt," I said quietly.

"I hope so."

I unbuttoned my shirt and slid it from my body; I then undid my jeans, kicked off my loafers, and stepped out of them. She reached forward to place her hands on my chest. I took hold of her wrists; I didn't want her hands on me. I gently walked her backward until she sat on the bed.

"Lay down," I said.

When she did, I climbed on the bed beside her. I ran my fingers over her stomach, feeling her quiver at my touch. She parted her legs slightly and I heard her gasp, I felt her hands fist as I inserted a finger inside her. She was so tight, so hot, and so wet. My cock hardened and my mind fought the primal instinct that flowed through my body. I didn't *want* her. My cock hardening was simply a bodily reaction, not an emotional one.

When I thought she was wet enough, I slid across her, forcing her legs farther apart with mine. I held myself above her and gently eased inside her.

She wrapped her hands around my biceps, opened her mouth, and moaned. I had no choice but to kiss her, simply to silence her. I didn't want to be caught in the act, not just then. It was a perfunctory fuck, basic, and with little thought to her pleasure. I banked on her not knowing if it was good or bad, really. As I was about to come, I pulled out and spurted over her stomach. She had a look of surprise on her face.

I rolled to one side and reached to her nightstand. I pulled a tissue from the box and cleaned my cum from her stomach.

"It didn't hurt at all," she said.

"Good. Next time it will, because I'll fuck you properly. That was just a little introduction."

I slid from the bed and dressed.

"Are you leaving already?"

I guessed I hadn't been in her room no more than a half hour.

"Yes, you don't want your papa to find me here, do you?"

"No, he can't know, Rocco."

"He'll only know if you tell him."

Once I was dressed, I left her room without another word. I smiled, bitterly, as I descended the stairs and left the house.

"What were you doing?" Alex asked as I met him patrolling the front.

"Fucking his daughter." I shook a cigarette lose and lit it.

"Rocco, for fuck's sake. Why risk what we have going on?"

I patted Alex on the chest. "Because it's just my little secret *fuck you* to him."

"She's like a vampire, Rocco, I don't know if you understand what you're getting involved in. She's a spoiled bitch, overindulged, she won't keep quiet about that," he said, panic lacing his voice.

"I'm banking on that. See you tomorrow."

I left him standing there, hopefully wondering what the fuck I was doing.

When I reached my apartment, I showered again. I scrubbed my skin until it was red, and kept the water as hot as it would go until I thought I'd washed all trace of her from me. Until I thought I'd cleansed myself of my sin.

I couldn't look at Evelyn's picture as I climbed into bed, I felt nauseous. Before I closed my eyes, I whispered to her, though.

"Forgive me, Bella, please, forgive me."

The following day we were sent to Sicily. As we settled into our seats on the plane, I asked Ben why Sal never accompanied us.

"He had to leave Sicily, under a bit of a cloud. Rosina was the fiancée of the man we're about to meet. Fuck knows why she decided on an affair with Sal."

"Interesting. Are you sure it was an affair?" I asked. Like Ben, I couldn't imagine anyone wanting to voluntary sleep with Sal. He was a pig.

Ben shrugged his shoulders. "Who knows, but Enrico never recovered from it and although Sal will tell you they are best friends, I doubt that to be true."

"Then we have our first ally with him," I said.

I settled back into my seat and watched Italy fall below me. The flight was short, uncomfortable, and I was pleased to disembark and stretch my legs. A man, who introduced himself as Freddie, met us outside the airport. He showed us to his car and, in silence, we drove through Palermo.

I was surprised to be taken to a compound instead of a house, and my senses went on high alert. When the car came to a halt, armed men surrounded it. I raised my hands slightly as I climbed from the car. We were patted down, we expected that.

A man walked toward us. His arms were outstretched.

"Rocco, Ben, it's good to see you. Please accept my apologies for the location, but it's a busy day. We meet here. Come, come," he said, as he patted me on the back.

Ben leaned toward me. "Enrico," he said.

I was expecting someone a lot older. "Son of Enrico Sr. I wish these families would come up with an original name for their firstborn sons."

I chuckled as we headed toward an old barn. Boxes were stacked four high and I didn't have to look to see what they contained. I guessed they were busy readying themselves for a shipment. We were shown into an office, where an older guy sat smoking a cigar. He rose, a little unsteady on his legs, gripping the arm of his chair as he did. He extended one hand to me.

"Rocco, sit, you have an explanation to give I believe," he said, his voice raspy, and I waited until his coughing fit ended before I spoke.

"Signore, I can't apologize for what I did to Aldo, but I will tell you that you are better off without him. Let me explain."

"Coffee first," he said.

At first I only saw the back of her. A young woman walked in carrying a tray. She kept her head bowed but her height, the color of her hair, had my breath catch in my throat. When she turned, her dark brown eyes and soft features did two things to me. I was disappointed and I was intrigued. She looked so much like Evelyn I wondered if they could be related.

She gave me a small smile before she left the room.

"My daughter, keep your eyes facing this way," Enrico Sr. said with a chuckle.

"She is very beautiful. She reminded me of someone," I said.

"Yes, they are very alike, unrelated of course."

I stared at Enrico Sr., he knew exactly who I was thinking of, and I wondered if using his daughter was a deliberate ploy to remind me of what I'd lost.

"So, you have an explanation," he added.

"One of us was meant to be killed that night. Or maybe all of us, who knows? Aldo was working with the Giolettis, and maybe others, who want to take over the routes from Sal. However, Sal doesn't know that yet. Our murder was meant as a message to Sal, to encourage him to back off searching for whoever ordered the senator's death."

"Aldo told you that?"

"Yes. It's amazing what a man will divulge when he knows he's about to die," I said.

"Why was Aldo working with the Giolettis? A family, I should add, that we all work with."

"One truck never makes it through, does it? The senator was playing two sides, Enrico."

"I don't care about the senator, he's better off dead. So why was Aldo working with the Giolettis?" Enrico asked, again.

"To discover what happens to the missing heroin," I said.

Enrico had a smirk on his face, somehow I didn't think this was news for him.

"So where does this leave us?" he asked.

"It leaves *you* with Sal. He is organizing the missing truck himself," I replied.

For a moment, Enrico sat and stared at me. Eventually, he leaned forward and reached for his coffee cup.

"Tell me, Rocco. Why should I believe you?"

"You have no reason to. But I'm there, in his house. Against my will, I should add, and I don't take too kindly to that. Don't, for one minute, think I won't do something about that when the time is right."

"In the meantime, while you're deciding when the time is right, our drugs go missing," he said.

"My timing is entirely dependent on you, Enrico, and the other families here."

He laughed. "You have, what is it you Americans say…Spunk?"

"I'm not American, as you know. But yeah, I have that, and more."

"So, let me recap. The Giolettis killed the senator. Maybe they are aware of Sal's activities, maybe not. We don't care about how the drugs get there, just that they do. It's a very lucrative market, I'm sure you're aware," he said.

"I understand that but the route is in place, it's secure, it's been running for a long time. If you cut out Sal, you have to start all that again. However, I will secure those routes for you, and I will make sure every truck reaches its destination."

"You're serious, aren't you?" he said, settling back in his chair.

"Deadly serious. I can't go back to America, Enrico. Sal has made sure of that. There is someone inside my family working for Sal. If I step on U.S. soil, someone will be killed and I won't take that risk. Ben knows who that person is, but that information is his insurance policy. It ensures I won't kill him, just yet."

Enrico laughed. "Ben is an intelligent man, and the fact you have told me all this in front of him suggests he is in agreement with you." He turned to look at Ben.

"Enrico, I have been loyal to Sal for many years. Like Rocco, I believe he is diverting the trucks for his own financial gain, and knowing how close the families here are, that doesn't sit well with me. I know you could deal with that, but do you want to? Rocco is in the perfect position to deal with Sal but, of course, he'll want something in return," Ben said.

"And that is?"

"Sal's operations, the safety of my family both here and in the U.S., and a seat on the Commission," I said.

"And if we don't agree to that?"

"Then I will take the operations anyway, I will take out any threat to my family, and I will force the Commission to accept me."

Enrico looked at me, amusement at my words had his lips twitch as if he was trying hard not to smile. It was clear he didn't take me seriously and I understood that. He didn't know me. He, and his associates in Italy, dismissed Joe and his activities in the U.S., and that was only because Joe was far more advanced with his thinking than this lot. He didn't want to deal in hard drugs because he understood the level of attention that meant he'd get from the authorities. All the time he was under the radar, he was able to do way more than anyone here could.

"Enrico, I know you don't know Rocco, but in the time he has been with us, whether that is voluntarily or not, he has shown us what he's capable of. I would listen. Something is very wrong with what Sal is doing, and you know me, you've known me for a while. I wouldn't be here if I didn't trust Rocco."

He thought for a moment. "Rocco, go smoke, or get some fresh air. Let me talk with Ben alone," he said.

I left the room and was pleased to. I wanted a cigarette, but I also wanted to see exactly what the compound housed.

I lit my cigarette and walked slowly around. There were three barns in total, and as I passed them, I glanced in the windows. One was the lab, the other was some kind of bunkhouse. I guessed whoever made the heroin lived on site.

"Can I have one of those?" I heard. I turned to see the woman, Enrico's daughter.

Once again, my breath caught in my throat and my heart missed a beat. I shook a cigarette lose and as she placed it to her lips, I struck a match. I watched as she expertly inhaled, raising her face to the sun to exhale.

"You are the talk of Sicily right now," she said.

"I imagine I am. What is your name?"

"Chiara," she replied, taking another drag of her cigarette.

"What do they say about me?" I asked.

"That you are one to watch. They don't fear you, of course, you are unknown, but when you killed Aldo, you ruffled some feathers."

"I guess I didn't particularly want to be killed myself that day."

She didn't respond but stood silently beside me while she smoked.

"What do you do here?" I asked.

"Nothing. I called in to see Papa. I'm going home soon."

I wasn't entirely sure I believed her but she intrigued me further, although what it was about her, I didn't know. She resembled Evelyn in looks but was the total opposite in manner. Whereas Evelyn was quiet and unsure, Chiara was confident and outspoken. I couldn't take my eyes away from her. I wanted to step closer to her, to see if she would smell the same as Evelyn, and then I wanted to slap my own cheek for that thought. Why would she smell the same?

"I need to get back," I said, immediately walking away from her.

"I hope to see you again, Rocco," she called after me, in a sultry voice.

I shook my head and closed my eyes momentarily to rid her image from my mind. I walked back into the barn, not caring whether they had finished their discussion about me.

"Rocco, we were about to call for you," Enrico said.

"Then I saved you the trouble. Enrico, I have explained why I shot Aldo; I hope that you understand my reasons, and I would like to think you have believed what I've told you. It's up to you now. I need to get back to Rome. I have things to do. You have to make a decision, I guess."

"Why the rush?" he said.

"Like I said, things to do."

"I believe you. In fact, I suspected a long time ago Sal was the one to *lose* his truck. You go do your *things* and we will talk again."

"And the other families?" I asked.

"They will do as I advise. As for the Commission, Rocco, I sit at the head, so don't for one minute think you will take what you want where that is concerned. When you are worthy of it, I will invite you to join us. Not until then, are we clear?"

I nodded as I rose. Enrico stood and we embraced, he then waved his hand to dismiss us. Enrico Jr. walked us back to our car. He chuckled as Mario opened the door.

"You have some balls, Rocco. My father will admire that in you. Keep us informed. Perhaps you know, I despise Sal, my father more so. You will find an ally in our family," he said.

"I know the history, and if it's any consolation, Rosina is very unhappy."

"I don't know the facts, obviously, this was before my time, before my mother. I do know my father has never forgiven Sal for stealing her, and from the little I do know, Rosina wasn't one to have an affair. There is more to that story than any of us know."

"Why didn't your father try to win her back?"

"I honestly don't know. She isn't someone he likes to talk about that often," he said. He nodded and then walked away.

I climbed into the car with Ben, Mario took the passenger seat. We were driven back to the airport for our return flight to Rome.

"What do we do now?" Ben asked, as we settled in our seats.

"We start a war. The three of us can't take out Sal on our own, and I don't necessarily trust any of his guys."

"How the fuck are you going to do that? More importantly, how do we survive that?" Mario asked.

"I need to speak to Massimo Gioletti."

"Impossible!" Ben replied.

"Nothing is impossible, Ben. It's time to think outside the box. What would bring Massimo to Rome?"

"The last time he visited was for a wedding."

"Then someone needs to get married."

Sal was told the families in Sicily were happy with my explanation, and that I had convinced them the Giolettis were responsible for the missing trucks. I had to work fast; I couldn't risk Sal speaking to anyone. He had agreed that, for the moment, we needed to keep the information to ourselves until we could formulate a plan. Of course, we knew he was tied. He couldn't afford to take on the Giolettis and cause any rift in his distribution chain.

Ben, Mario, Alex, and I met regularly. We sat in my apartment, or Mario's since his was a little larger, and discussed our next move. I was convinced we needed to speak to Massimo, and the only way to do that was to have him come to Italy.

"As I said, the only way he'll come here is if someone gets married," Ben said.

"He'd come if, say, Enrico's daughter married, would he?"

"He'd only come if it was the daughter of a family head he respected, and yes, he respects Enrico very much. But who is going to marry her? And there has to be a guarantee we will be invited as well."

"More importantly, Rocco, I don't how things are done in America, but you can't just walk up to the girl and tell her you're getting married," Mario said.

"I know that, thank you for the explanation. I know it sounds so far-fetched, it was an idea. Come up with another way to get Massimo here, or me there."

"I dated her for a little while. She was desperate to leave Sicily," Alex said, quietly.

We looked at him.

"You dated her?" Ben asked.

"I just said that, didn't I? Yes, I dated her, just a few times. She's a great girl but not one to settle down. However, as I said, she's desperate to leave Sicily. I wouldn't be surprised if she'd *agree* to marry someone just to facilitate that," he said.

"Then it has to be you," Ben said, I could see the smirk, and I knew he thought it the worst idea but worth a little fun.

"She hates me, I think," he replied with a laugh.

"Then make her *unhate* you," I said with a wink.

"Okay, let's get serious. A funeral would be the other reason Massimo might come here," Ben said.

"So we have a choice, a wedding or a funeral," I said.

"Enrico didn't look too good," Ben said.

"We can't orchestrate a death, unless…" Mario said.

"There's no guarantee Rocco would be invited to a funeral. In fact, there's no guarantee he would be invited to a wedding, unless it was one of us," Ben said. "And it won't be me, I've got a wife."

"All down to you, then," Mario said, looking at Alex. "You'll get a say on the guest list."

I wasn't sure if the whiskey we were drinking was the source of our idea, or if it really was a good idea. It was that crazy, though, it might just work. It was important that I spoke with Massimo to secure the route, as it was the largest income source, according to Ben, that Sal had. If I took out Sal, the first thing that would happen would be that the other families came after his business before I had a chance to establish myself.

One week later we had a breakthrough, but it wasn't the one we were hoping for.

"Enrico wants to meet with you. Why you?" Sal asked, before I'd even managed to close his office door.

"I don't know, what did he say?"

"That he wants to meet with you privately. I want to know what the fuck is going on Rocco. You belong to me, remember that."

"I don't *belong* to anyone," I said, taking a seat without waiting to be offered one.

Sal's response was to throw an envelope across the table as a reminder. At first, I ignored it.

"Open it, Rocco, remind yourself. Those were taken recently, I think you might enjoy them."

I didn't want to, but I couldn't help myself either. I shook out two photographs. One was of Evelyn and she was laughing with the dark-haired boy. He had his arm around her shoulder, and although much younger than she was, he was looking down at her. At first glance she looked happy, but I knew better. I saw the lines around her eyes, the dark circles not quite concealed by her makeup, and I noticed the lack of sparkle to them. Nearly a year and she was still hurting. I made a conscious effort not to rise to Sal's smirk but my heart hurt in my chest.

The second photograph was of my sister, and how I was able to conceal my shock had to have been a miracle. She held her hands, protectively, over a small but noticeable bump in her stomach.

"Want to know who the father is?" Sal asked.

I slid the photos back into the envelope. "Not really," I replied.

"I'm not sure your sister knows, though. I hear terrible things about her, Rocco. It's a shame you're not there to protect her from herself."

"If I was a free man, Sal, I would be in America anyway. She is not my responsibility."

He laughed. "So, you see, you belong to me. Now, what does Enrico want?"

I leaned forward, placing my forearms on the desk, my hands splayed, and my fingertips just brushed the envelope.

"I have no fucking idea what he wants. But it's interesting that he didn't feel he could tell you, isn't it? Want to pass back a message? Tell him I'll see him in a couple of days."

Sal's face colored, the usual redness spread to his cheeks before anger turned that puce. I sat back in my chair.

"You're not going to deny him his request, are you? He's a very important man, Sal, and does, after all, control the families in Sicily, as well as head the Commission. He wants to meet me, I suggest you set that up."

His vitriolic response had me wanting to chuckle. There was a shift in power that day, a little earlier than I would have wanted but a shift nevertheless.

Once Sal had spewed his curse words and spittle over the desk, he sat back gasping for air. I slid a glass of water across the desk to him and his eyes watered as he started to cough. At that point, I began to think something was very wrong with him. I stood and walked around the desk. I held the glass to his lips.

"Drink," I said. He pushed the glass away but continued to cough, grasping at his chest as he did.

"Drink!" I said, again. He took a couple of sips before he was able to get his breath back and slumped in his chair.

He waved his arm to dismiss me. I picked up the envelope and walked to his fireplace.

"This doesn't work anymore, Sal. You've made me immune, numb, and that's something you should worry about. Set up the meeting so I can find out what Enrico wants." I threw the envelope into the fire.

I lit my cigarette the minute I walked from the house and paced the driveway. I wasn't going to show my agitation in front of him, but I fucking wanted to know who had gotten my sister pregnant. She wore no rings on her fingers, no sign of a husband. I also wanted to know who the boy with Evelyn was. I'd seen him in a few photographs. On average, Sal, *reminded* me weekly. There were times I wasn't sure when the images were dated, other times, I knew they were current.

"Can I get one of those?" I heard. I turned to see Felisia walking toward me.

"No," I said meeting her halfway.

"I want you to fuck me, Rocco," she purred.

"I asked you not to curse, Felisia." I threw my cigarette to the ground.

I took hold of her hand and led her to the shed I'd called home for a while. She laughed as she stumbled along behind me.

"Did Papa upset you?" she asked, as we walked through the door. "I've told you time and time again, I can do something about that."

She placed her hands on my chest, her fingers undoing the buttons of my shirt. She slid the shirt from my shoulders and then reached down for the buckle of my belt. It was as she lowered to her knees, dragging my pants down with her that I realized I had been fooled. I laughed as she wrapped her hand around my cock and her tongue darted out to wet the tip. She swirled her hot tongue around me, squeezed gently before opening her lips, and sucking me in. I grabbed the back of her head and I fucked her mouth, she took it all, like the pro she clearly was.

Not once did she gag, not once did her eyes water. The harder I fucked her mouth, the more she took it. When she looked up at me, eyes hard and cold like coal, I came. Her lips formed a smirk as she slowly released me, swallowing down my cum as she did.

"You fucking lied to me," I said, pulling her up by her hair.

She gently shook her head. "No, Rocco, you made an assumption, a wrong one."

I turned her from me. Before I had a chance to react, she had lowered her panties and pulled her skirt to her waist. She placed her hands on the cot bed and leaned forward, shoving her ass high in the air, she looked over her shoulder at me.

"Fuck me, Rocco. I don't care that you hate me, I hate you as well, but we both need this. We both want to fuck my father as much."

It was the start of a mutually agreeable relationship. I felt vindicated to a degree, we didn't like each other, there was no emotion, so it was okay. Or I was fucking kidding myself.

Enrico had decided I was to meet him at his home. After a short flight and an even shorter drive, Ben and I were driven along a dirt track of a road to a sprawling villa nestled among fruit trees. Nostalgia washed over me, it was accompanied by sadness. The entrance to the villa reminded me of home. A fleeting image of my father and brother walking through the trees with wooden crates full of olives came to mind. I blinked to rid myself of the image. I had successfully forced those memories to the soles of my feet so when they surfaced, they often took me by surprise.

I took a deep breath as the car came to a halt. The citrus scent that permeated the air brought yet more sadness.

"Rocco, I'm glad you came," I heard. I looked over to see Enrico walking toward the car. Beside him was his son.

I smiled at their warm welcome. "You have a wonderful home, Enrico," I said.

"Let me show you around before we have lunch."

We walked, Ben trailed behind, and Enrico pointed out a hidden fountain, his prized olive grove, and his secret garden. He liked to garden, he told me, to cultivate plants that wouldn't otherwise survive the harshness of Sicily. He had a row of sweet smelling roses. He told me of the hours he spent tending to those plants and how he likened them to a woman.

"They are so sweet, and so deceptive, Rocco. See how they tempt you to smell them? The flower is open and inviting. But when you touch, how sharp the thorns?"

I wanted to tell him it was just a plant but he was so engrossed with his garden.

"This one…this one is called Rosina," he said.

I glanced to Ben.

We watched Enrico and he ran his fingers up the stem, the thorns catching his skin, tearing it, causing him to bleed. He ran his fingers over the head of the flower, staining the white petals with his blood. Then he closed his hand around the flower and scrunched it.

"He seduced her, against her will, I believe. She felt she had betrayed me and left with him. I would have killed him had she not begged me to let him live. She doesn't love him, but she stayed with him. Why?" He had whispered most of his sentence and I didn't believe that he'd asked the question wanting an answer from me.

"She would love to come home," Ben said from behind. Enrico let go of the flower head and turned toward him.

"She isn't welcome here. Now, I'm sure lunch is ready, shall we?"

He was a complete contradiction. I wasn't sure he was still in love with Rosina, it was more he didn't want Sal to have her. I decided I'd make an effort to get to know her more when I returned to Rome.

A table was set outside for lunch, a checkered tablecloth wafted slightly in the breeze. Enrico indicated toward a chair and I sat. He poured some wine from a carafe into small glasses and raised his to me.

"Drink, Rocco, we have much to discuss after," he said.

Before I could take a sip, the chair beside me was pulled out. I smelled her perfume before I saw her. Chiara sat, and as she did, her hand brushed against my arm. I thought it was deliberate.

She tapped her finger on the table, just in front of the glass, and when I finally looked at her, she raised her eyebrow and smiled at me.

"I'd like some wine, please," she said.

I nodded and reached for the carafe to fill her glass.

A woman fetched dishes from the kitchen and by the way Enrico addressed her, I assumed her to be a housekeeper.

For a while talk was of Sicily and the villa's similarity to my village. Enrico Jr. joined us and I saw the look he gave his sister. I guessed he wasn't as pleased as I was that she had joined us. We ate and chatted some more.

"Papa, before you start your meeting, I'd like to walk with Rocco for a moment," Chiara said.

Enrico waved his hand, permission granted. I placed my glass on the table and stood, I pulled out her chair. She rose and thanked me. We walked, initially in silence, until we were far enough away from the prying eyes of her brother.

"I'd like a cigarette, please," she said.

We had paused before the rose garden I'd visited earlier that day. I pulled a pack from my shirt pocket and tapped the bottom. I extracted one and placed it between my lips before I struck a match and lit it. Once the tip was glowing, I handed it to her.

"Thank you," she said. "I asked Papa to invite you for lunch, was that wrong of me?"

"Is there a meeting with your father?" I asked.

"No, well, sort of. I know that he does want to talk to you and I took the opportunity to ask for a meeting myself. I have spoken with Alex, I was a little surprised by his proposal."

I wasn't aware Alex had made contact and thought that most of our 'let's get someone married' conversation was fueled by alcohol and not taken seriously.

"Ignore what Alex said, Chiara. It was an evening of too much whiskey and loose tongues." I wasn't sure exactly what Alex had said, so I measured my words.

We walked a way into the rose garden.

"That's a shame, Rocco, because I would have been interested in your proposal…your proposal, not Alex's."

She hadn't looked at me when she spoke. She paused beside the rose that Enrico had crushed, and I could see her brow furrow in question at the destroyed flower.

"What did Alex tell you?" I asked.

"Let's sit for a moment," she said, heading toward a bench.

I watched as she took one last puff of the cigarette and then looked around as if unsure where to put it. I took it from her, pinching the end to extinguish it.

"Drop it in that flowerpot, Rocco," she said.

"What exactly did Alex tell you?" I asked, repeating my question.

"You want to meet someone and one way of doing that is to hold a wedding, or a funeral. He asked if I'd like to marry him as a way of escaping this godforsaken place. You've no need to worry, he was vague enough, but since I am aware of your situation, Rocco, I can only assume this *meeting someone* is important to your plans."

She hadn't looked at me all the while she had spoken. Before I had the chance to answer, she turned slightly to face me.

"Could you ever love another woman?" she asked, and her question completely threw me.

"No, I don't think I could," I answered, honestly.

"Could you be kind to another woman?"

"Yes. I don't understand your questions, Chiara."

"I'll marry you, Rocco. I'll live in Rome for a period of time then I'll move on. My heart belongs to another, like yours. If we can help each other, then I'm happy to do so."

"Does your father know?" I asked, referring to the 'another.'

"He didn't approve. My father is a wonderful man, Rocco. He loves me, he is overprotective, of course, but after what happened to him with Rosina, and then the death of my mother, he wants to keep the family here —stuck in the past."

"What if Rosina returned?"

"I'm not sure I, or my brother, would be happy for that. My father never loved my mother, he was kind to her, he enjoyed her company, but she knew he had never given his heart to her. She died loving him with every fiber of her being and knowing that wasn't returned. She died of a broken heart, Rocco. I don't want to waste my life here. If I only get a short period of time with the one I love, then that will be enough for me. I think maybe you understand what I mean."

"What do I have to do?"

"We marry, I would imagine my father would expect that to be here, of course. I move to Rome with you, you do whatever it is you have to; I don't expect to live a poor life, Rocco. Maybe a year, then I leave and you help me disappear."

"You'll break your father's heart if you just disappear," I said.

"He sent Philippe away when he saw how much we loved each other, he decided what was right for us. When he did that he shattered mine."

"Are you in touch with Philippe?"

"It's hard for him. He's now in Turin, Enrico was told. He wanted to get to Switzerland and that's where I hope to meet him. We had always said if we got separated, that's where we would meet. I believe he'll be waiting for me."

"I don't understand, Chiara. You're old enough to leave here, you have money, I assume. Why aren't you with him? And why wait a year?"

She smiled at me. "Because he isn't the same as us, Rocco. He doesn't want to be part of this life, he's an artist, and I love him. As for the year? Papa knows I want to be with him, that's why I'm on a tight leash. Philippe will wait for me, I know it." She finished her sentence quietly; maybe she wasn't as sure as she wanted to be.

I chuckled a little. "You don't want to be poor, but you're in love with an artist?"

"Who said he was poor? My father will cut me off, financially, as soon as he realizes my plan. He'll make sure that Philippe and I can't be together. That is why I need to stick around for a little while."

I nodded my head as I lit another cigarette. Chiara was a nice woman, someone I was drawn to anyway. It wouldn't be any hardship to marry her, live with her as husband and wife for whatever time it took for her to arrange to meet with Philippe.

"And I wonder what your father will do to me when he realizes it was a scam?" I said, more to myself.

"He doesn't need to know. You just play the grieving husband whose wife has left him for another. I'm sure, given his situation, he'll have every sympathy with you."

I smiled as I looked at her. Her angelic features, her sparkling eyes that falsely showed innocence, belied her deviousness; she made my adrenalin race, my heart pound a little harder. Not because I loved her, but she did intrigue, and she reminded me of myself. She had a mission, a plan, and she'd used whatever resource was necessary to achieve that. I admired her. A small village woman, the daughter of a powerful man, was willing to risk it all for love.

"Deal," I said.

"So, no funny business like falling in love, are we clear?" she said with a smile that could melt icecaps.

"I'm not capable of loving another, I've told you that. But I have to say, Chiara, I do admire you, I respect you, and I am intrigued by you."

"Because I look like her?"

"How do you know what she looks like?" I asked.

"I've met her, a while ago. My father travels to the U.S., Rocco. He admires her father and, of course, her father has a friendship with the man you're trying to reach."

For the first time in a very long while, I felt like I'd made a friend. The expanse of loneliness that consumed me didn't feel so isolating anymore.

"How do we start this then?" I asked as Chiara stood. She reached out to take my hand.

"I already told Papa that I wanted to spend some time with you, so he knows I'm interested," she said with a laugh.

"After just one meeting?"

I wasn't convinced Enrico would fall for that at all.

"Why not? Perhaps Papa sees an alliance with you, a marriage might not be the worst thing that could happen between the two families."

We walked back toward the villa. Enrico Jr. stood outside the kitchen door, smoking a cigarette. I dropped Chiara's hand before he noticed. He looked over to us.

"Chiara, you're wanted inside," he said, a little roughly. I needed to be sure not to make an enemy of him.

Before I could walk in behind her, he placed his hand on my chest.

"A minute, Rocco, if you don't mind," he said.

I nodded and stepped back out.

"I know what she wants. I don't agree with her methods. Treat her well, Rocco, she deserves it, because she won't get to Philippe. I don't think Philippe is around anymore."

"Maybe you'll tell me what you know and we can find out. She believes he's in Turin, heading for Switzerland. Is he?"

Enrico gently shook his head. He looked over my shoulder toward the kitchen door. "It will break her heart to know the truth, and I can't bring myself to tell her. Take her to Rome, let her fly, have fun for a while, but don't ever hurt her."

"I don't intend to. I take it your father doesn't know?"

"Of course not. This will stay between us. I liked Philippe, it was a shame they were not to be. Now, don't keep my father waiting any longer."

I walked into the house and Enrico Jr. showed me into his father's office. I took the seat that was being offered and waited.

"How are your plans?" Enrico Sr. asked.

"I only left you a couple of weeks ago, they are still in the 'plans' stage."

He laughed. "I have spoken with my friends here, you'll have all the support you need."

I rested back in my seat and stared at him. "This all seems a little too convenient, bearing in mind you don't know me. I'm sure most families have been 'challenged' before, but to have your support immediately is a little strange, don't you think?"

"You are an astute man, Rocco," Enrico said, laughing again.

Enrico poured two glasses of whiskey; he slid one toward me. I picked it up and raised the glass to my nose. I inhaled the earthy oak scent.

"We know Sal is losing his own trucks. We knew the senator was involved in that, he was playing both sides and he paid the price for that. We know that Sal is causing problems and if it isn't sorted, we will lose our hold in the U.S. and that is very lucrative, we don't want to lose it. So, you come along, all guns blazing so to speak, and you're offering to do the job for us. Of course we're going to back you."

He took a sip of his drink, looking over the rim of his glass at me. There was a sparkle to his eyes and his honesty had me warm to him further.

"And when I've done your job for you, do you believe that you'll be able to cut me out?" I asked.

"I'm sure that will be the discussion among some. I like you, Rocco. My daughter likes you, I believe, although I'm not so sure I'm in agreement there. Before Sal became greedy, it all ran smoothly. We'd like to get back to that. You sort it so that we can get back to where we were, and I'll ensure you have no trouble as long as you understand that I have helped you."

I understood only too well. I'd be swapping one 'master' for another. However, I had to weigh the odds. Once Sal was out of the way and I took over some of his operations, I'd have more substance to be able to then stand up to Enrico. I nodded my head. I would not shake his hand on that and he didn't offer his either.

"I understand my daughter would like to spend some time with you?"

"So she said."

"I will allow her to come to Rome, with a chaperone, of course, for a couple of days."

We chatted a little about Sicily, my village, and my experiences in Rome. The more we chatted, the more I realized how much I was being played, but what he didn't realize was it worked in my favor as well. Men like Enrico didn't just allow their daughter to travel with a man he'd met once before. But it served a purpose he was unaware of, I hoped.

Chiara walked around my apartment, she placed her bag on the bed in the bedroom.

"It will do," she said with a smile, when she laughed I realized she was teasing. "Oh, Rocco, you really need to relax a little. It's a great *little* apartment."

"If this ends up being a long-term thing, then we'll have to move someplace else."

She walked around again, familiarizing herself in the kitchen area, opening cupboards, and switching on the coffee machine. The apartment door opened again, Enrico Jr. walked in dragging a suitcase behind him.

"How long do you intend to be staying here?" he asked, huffing and puffing.

He left her suitcase in the middle of the room.

"Coffee?" I asked.

He nodded before slumping into the sofa. It had been arranged that Enrico would take the empty apartment in the loft of the building. We hadn't told Sal he was accompanying Chiara, and it was Ben that managed to get the key.

"Will you take me to the Vatican?" she asked, as the coffee machine gurgled away.

"You make a list of where you'd like to visit, and I'll organize that for you. I do have to work as well, though," I said.

She patted my arm as she walked past.

---

For the next couple of days, I showed Chiara and Enrico around Rome. I enjoyed their company. At times when Chiara shopped, Enrico and I sat at a coffeehouse and talked 'work.' I told him how I came to be in Rome and my situation in the U.S. It was clearly news to him and his level of disgust was evident on his face.

"I don't know what to say, Rocco. How can I help? I can get word to Evelyn, if you want me to."

"I can't risk that, Enrico, someone in Joe's family is helping Sal. If they found out word had gotten to her, or even Joe, she's dead. My sister is dead. It has to be this way for now. Once I know who my enemies are, believe me when I tell you, hell will unleash."

He looked at me. "Then you can count on me by your side, regardless of my father's wishes or desires. This is what they did to Philippe," he said, quietly.

"Tell me about him," I asked.

"Chiara had been in love with him for years, long before either confessed to that love. It wasn't right, it wasn't approved, and the minute it was public, despite them believing they'd kept it a secret, he was 'moved on' in the middle of the night. She looked for him, for days she searched, but he had disappeared and no one seemed to know where, or how."

"I understand, Enrico, when the heart loves, it's devastating to lose that." I said.

Chiara walked toward us, she raised her many bags and cocked her head to one side. Dramatically, she slumped into a chair and the waiter was quick to her side. We ordered more coffee and she detailed all her purchases. She reminded me of my sister and a pang of sadness had to be tuned out. Adriana would have loved to spend a few hours shopping for clothes and shoes in Rome. There was very little that she, or Chiara I imagined, could purchase in their villages.

"Rocco?" I heard.

I smiled. "Sorry, I was miles away."

"I was saying, we shouldn't waste too much time before we organize this wedding," she said.

"Let's just make it a small, family, but with the necessary *family,* affair," I replied.

"I don't know how Papa will feel about that, of course."

"You could tell him that it would be unfair to have a grand wedding since I can't invite one member of my own family."

It had been an *off the top of my head* comment but one that had me torn apart inside with its truth. I lit a cigarette as a means to distract myself. I felt Chiara reach over; she placed her hand on mine for a moment before sliding my pack of cigarettes toward her. When I looked up and struck a match for her, she smiled at me.

As much as I had been intrigued with Chiara, I decided then that I really liked her. She was kind, considerate, and I wondered why she was single. Whichever man she decided to settle down with would be extremely lucky. I worried for Chiara. To marry me for one reason only, then divorce at a later date, might ruin her chances of finding a love for herself.

---

The cursing, screaming, and shouting echoed around the house, and that was just from Felisia. Sal was fuming, his body shook with anger when I told him I was marrying Chiara and handed him a wedding invite. I smiled as he took a call from Enrico, detailing all the plans, and how excited Enrico was to welcome me into his family. It was all too perfect. It was all too rushed, and I knew there was a reason beyond what I was doing for that.

Enrico wanted me to marry his daughter. He believed that would give him a little control over me, and once I took over Sal's businesses, maybe he thought there would be an alliance. We'd be a powerful force, for sure. I liked the idea. I further liked the idea that—one day—I might rule *his* empire.

"Why, Rocco?" I heard.

I'd decided I'd had enough of Sal's rants and left his office for a smoke. I turned to see Felisia. It was clear she had been crying.

"Felisia, we hate each other, isn't that what you said?"

"But you don't love her, do you?" she asked.

"No, I'll never love another woman but I admire her, I like her, even," I replied gently.

I didn't want to hurt Felisia unnecessarily, I had in the beginning, but that was the selfish part of me. Felisia couldn't offer me what Chiara did. Although, I would never tell Felisia that, I didn't trust her at all, a pang of regret hit me.

Sal was beside himself; he didn't know what to do with me. I wasn't allowed to return to Sicily and meet with the Commission; I think he knew his grip on me was lessening. He decided to play dirty.

"Rocco, I've received word your mamma is in trouble. Or rather, the farm is. I decided that I'll buy out the farm so she could retire," he said.

I swallowed the spew of hate that rose to my throat.

"I think that's a great idea. I'm sure she'd be up for retiring by now," I replied, refusing to rise to his bait.

The last time I'd spoken to my uncle, he'd told me that he might negotiate a sale of the land; I only hoped he had already managed to do that and this was a bluff from a desperate Sal.

"Yes, I think I'll do that. It isn't worth anything, I'm sure she'll take any pittance just to be rid of it. It's not like she has anyone to leave it to. As for your sister and her bastard child, I'm sure someone will take them in."

I picked at some imaginary lint on my trouser leg. "Yes, I'm sure they will. Now, this wedding. I was going to ask Enrico Jr. to be my best man, what do you think? I mean, I'd like to stay close to that family."

He didn't reply and I felt just a small amount of joy at my slight. I walked from his office. I heard my name being called in a soft voice.

"Rocco," she said.

I turned to see Rosina wringing a towel in her hands. Her eyes darted between Sal's office door and me, she looked anxious.

"Maybe you'd like to join me for a walk? Perhaps you could show me your herb garden," I suggested. She nodded her head, her gratitude palpable.

Until we arrived at her herb garden, we walked in silence. We passed Alex and one other security, both nodded to me.

"How is he?" Rosina asked quietly. She didn't look at me; she'd bent to pluck a weed from a raised bed.

"He is well, Rosina. I suspect that he still misses you," I replied, knowing full well who she meant.

"I live every day with regret, Rocco. Can you tell him that?"

"I think he knows. He didn't speak much about your situation, but I do think he believes you didn't walk away from him because you fell in love with Sal."

"He is correct. I walked away from him to save his life, but he can never know that."

She weeded some more. I lit a cigarette and thought.

"Rosina, if there was ever a chance for you to return to your village, would you take it?"

"In a heartbeat," she replied. She stood and rubbed at her lower back.

"I was pretty once, I was young and in love. I've been beaten, abused, raped. I've given birth to two children who dislike me because they are their father's, yet I love them unconditionally. In a heartbeat," she repeated.

It was only when I studied her as she'd spoken that I realized: the distortion to her features were scars and lack of love, neglect, even. She didn't care for herself because she didn't care about her life. I wanted to embrace her. I wanted to tell her that she'd soon be free, but I also knew that returning to Enrico might not be as easy as she thought.

"One day, not now, will you tell me what happened?" I asked.

She sucked in a deep breath. "I don't know, is the honest answer. It's not really a time I want to relive. I just want you to know that you and I are very similar, what brought us here, I mean."

"I thought as much, and I'm sorry that you've had to endure this life longer than I have, than I will."

She stared at me until she understood. She patted my arm.

"I look forward to that day, Rocco," she said, and then she turned and walked away.

I sat for a while and smoked. I thought of the life I imagined she had led.

She said she had been raped, was that by Sal? Bile rose to my mouth and I spat it out onto the ground.

---

Exactly one year after my kidnapping—one year after my *death*—I stood at the altar of a small church in Sicily, waiting for my bride. I scanned the pews. Enrico and his family occupied the front, just behind him sat a man who stared intently at me. The hair at his temples was a little gray and prematurely, I thought. He wasn't as old as I imagined he was going to be, but he was certainly commanding.

"Massimo Gioletti," Enrico Jr. whispered.

I had guessed as much. Before I could acknowledge him, the organ started to grind out a tune. I watched the wooden doors open and my breath caught in my throat. As beautiful as she looked, as elegantly as she glided up the aisle, I wanted to shed tears. It was the wrong woman.

She reached out to take my hand and leaned forward.

"It's okay, we know why we are doing this. No falling in love, that was our deal," she whispered, she then gave me a peck to my cheek and squeezed my hand.

I didn't hear one word of the service, I sang when I was expected to, I knelt, I stood, I offered my vows, and we exchanged rings. It was a blur. Even accepting congratulations went over my head. Chiara was perfect. She smiled; she held my hand all the while introducing me to her family and friends. She gushed about our whirlwind romance and how happy she was. At some point during the photographs, I began to fall into the fantasy. We walked hand in hand back to Enrico's house for the celebrations.

We took our seats and we dined on course after course of food prepared by the local women. As the day wore on, the fantasy began to wear off and reality crept in.

"She'll forgive me," I said to myself, and I took a sip of my drink.

Perhaps I'd said it a little too loud, I looked up to see Chiara staring sadly back at me.

Our guests started to tap their cutlery against their glasses, a sign they wanted a display of affection. I stood and reached out to her. I helped my bride to her feet and I wrapped my arms around her. I closed my eyes, pictured another, and I kissed her.

When the guests were satisfied, I whispered to Chiara that I was going to chat with Mario and Alex. I stood and walked among the tables set out in the courtyard.

"Take a walk with me, Rocco," I heard. I turned to see the man the whole charade had been orchestrated for.

We left the wedding party to their drinks and walked to the front of the house. I noticed Sal, who had attended without Rosina, of course, begin to rise from his seat as we passed, but like Massimo, I ignored him and he sat again.

"This was a little elaborate, don't you think?" he asked.

"Elaborate?"

"If you wanted to meet with me, you didn't have to marry her. She's a good girl, Rocco, and you'll ruin her."

I chuckled, knowing different. "I'm sure she'll ruin me first. But this was the only way I could have the opportunity to meet you."

"You could have just used a telephone. I'm pretty sure the last time I was here there were such things, and a call to America isn't beyond the realms of your salary I take it?"

I laughed, and he smiled at me.

"Okay, maybe it could have been that simple, and maybe there is another reason for me to marry Chiara, one she has instigated."

He waved his hand to a bench under a metal canopy by the front door. We walked toward it and sat.

"Tell me what you want," he said.

"You know that Sal loses one of his trucks each shipment, and you suspected the senator was involved in that, which is why you asked the Commission for him to be taken out. I got the job of delivering him to his demise and Sal got pissed. Now I'm here, against my will. The love of my life is in Washington, D.C. with a death threat hanging over her and everyone thinks I'm dead."

He pursed his lips, cocked his head, raised his eyebrows, and nodded. "Yes, I think that's an accurate summing up."

"I need your help," I said.

"I gathered that."

"Sal loses his trucks deliberately, you want control of his route, the families here suspect that, no one is actually telling it as it is, and I'm going to kill Sal."

Massimo looked at me with a smile on his lips. Finally, he laughed.

"You are exactly as I was told and, Rocco, it would be a pleasure to work with you. But we have much to discuss, and here isn't the place for that. I'm intending to stay for a few days, I suggest you get rid of Sal, so to speak, and we meet tomorrow."

So it was set. I returned to my wedding, I danced, I drank too much, and when Chiara had to wrap an arm around my waist to steady me, I was led to her bedroom.

There would be no consummation of our union that night. I don't recall actually arriving at the bedroom, but I know I woke the following morning still dressed in my shirt and trousers, minus my shoes and with a mouth that tasted like sandpaper.

Chiara sat in a chair in the bedroom with a cigarette and in her underwear. She had one leg crossed over the other.

"We will fuck, Rocco, I'm sure we'll both want that, but we won't be betraying anyone. Can you do that?"

I shuffled up the bed a little.

"If you mean right now, probably not. If you mean we start our *married* life in…about an hour's time once I've had coffee, then absolutely."

She laughed, rose, and walked toward me; she offered me her lit cigarette.

"I'll be the good wife and fetch you a coffee," she said.

"You'll cover up first, won't you?"

She laughed as she pulled a robe from the back of her bedroom door.

"Bathroom is that way," she said as she left the room.

While I waited, I stripped off my clothes and took a shower. I had a towel around my waist when she returned with two coffees. Without a care, she slipped off her robe and adjusted her stockings. I felt a stirring; I wouldn't be a man if she didn't arouse me. I tried to contain that. She watched as I dressed and then I sat beside her, taking my coffee from her hand.

"What do we do now?" she asked.

"I have a meeting with Massimo arranged for this morning, we have lunch with your father, then the afternoon is ours. Maybe you can show me around," I said.

"Sal has suggested to Papa that you're *escorted*," she said with a laugh.

"I'm sure he is beside himself right now."

"Why do you let him control you so much?"

"I don't, Chiara. Don't mistake my actions with weakness. Everything I have ever done from the day I was kidnapped has been because I have an end goal."

I sipped on my coffee while she dressed. "I like you, Rocco. I think we'll make a great team."

I walked her downstairs where we were greeted by aunts and cousins and more aunts, and food. A table was laden with food for breakfast.

Sal sat at one end glaring at me. Enrico sat beside me, and I was sure he was enjoying Sal's discomfort as he called me his son and welcomed me to his family. It was a game, I knew that, but his cheeks reddened as his anger increased.

"Rocco, I'd like you to walk with me before Chiara whisks you away," Enrico said. "A father of the bride talk," he added with a wink to Sal.

We walked through his garden until we reached a path that weaved through lemon trees. I plucked a leaf, scrunching it between my fingers to release the bitter scent. My heart missed a beat as a pang of hurt born from a memory hit my chest. I dropped the leaf.

We arrived at an outbuilding made of local stone. He opened the door to an area set out like a gentlemen's lounge. I laughed. Massimo was already seated with a pot of coffee on a small table.

"My escape. I like to come here to get away from the family," Enrico laughed.

Massimo rose and held out his hand. "I take it you are alone?" he asked.

"Of course, although I think Sal is about to bust his gut with curiosity and anger right now," I replied.

Massimo laughed. "Then we need to get down to business quickly."

Massimo and Enrico had clearly had previous chats about Sal and the missing drugs. They had come to a conclusion long before I'd come along, and from what I could tell it was fortuitous. I stumbled into their, 'what do we do about Sal?' discussions right at the opportune time for them. Massimo gave me an ultimatum.

"You take out Sal when, where, and how we say. We will allow you his businesses, except the routes into the U.S. Enrico is to take those back," he said.

"And if I don't agree with your when, where, and how?" I asked.

"Then you do not have our backing. You have our blessing, but not the physical support you need."

I sipped on the coffee that had been poured for me.

"If I do it your way, I want one favor from you," I said, looking at Massimo. "I want you to get word to Joe that I'm alive, but someone in his family is working with Sal. Someone is taking those photographs and that someone is close to Evelyn, they have to be."

"Joe and I are distantly related, through marriage. As soon as I return, I will let Franco know. He's closer to Joe, he should be able to find out who is working with Sal. He will also tell Joe when the time is right."

It was the best I could have hoped for and a mixture of relief, happiness, and extreme sadness washed over me.

I sat and listened to Massimo as he outlined his plan.

"Can he do it?" Enrico asked, speaking to Massimo. I felt myself getting riled.

"He can do it. I watched him in America and, Enrico, I don't think you've given him the credit he deserves. As for Sal? He has a surprise coming his way, for sure." Massimo chuckled at the thought, and I appreciated what he'd said.

"I suspect my daughter would like your company, and I won't spend any time on that father of the bride chat, but hurt her, Rocco, and I will kill you."

I had no doubt he would. I nodded respectfully and left them. Sal met me halfway back to the house, I imagined he had been bouncing on his toes with frustration at not knowing where I was or what was going on.

"Where have you fucking been?" he said, keeping his voice low.

"Being threatened with death if I hurt my bride," I said with a laugh.

"You're up to something, Rocco, and I'm fucking on to you. Mark my words, I will slit your fucking throat if you try to cross me."

I stepped closer to him. "Sal, I saved your arse today, so don't push me."

I walked away to him shouting, asking what I meant by my lie.

"I'm spending the afternoon with my wife, then we arranged to head back to Rome," I called over my shoulder.

For the first couple of weeks, I showed Chiara around Rome, took her to the Vatican, and all the other places she insisted on seeing. We spent evenings dining out, when we decided on a night in, she cooked and we fucked. The guilt I felt at my betrayal settled in my gut like acid, it constantly bubbled away. Over time that settled, it calcified inside me and I found myself numb. Numbness wasn't the greatest start to a marriage, even though that marriage was fake.

I met with Sal on the morning I decided the plan was to start. I had been told to wait until Massimo gave word, but I didn't want to. Since returning to Rome, Sal, and Felisia had been unbearable. I wasn't willing to take their shit any longer.

"From what we know, Massimo gave the order to take out the senator because he'd discovered, somehow, that Massimo was diverting your truck," I said. I watched him squirm.

"No, I don't think it would be him…"

"It's looking very much that way, Sal," Ben said, interrupting him.

Sal squirmed further; the last thing he wanted was any kind of war or incorrect accusations against the Gioletti family.

"Yes. We believe the senator was going to either bribe Massimo or come to you and tell you. Massimo asked the Commission for backing in his decision. We have to remember, Sal, that backing was given, so the Commission is on Massimo's side here."

I wanted Sal to know he had no standing in the U.S. Part of what I'd told him was correct, of course, part a lie.

"So, here's the plan. I've spoken with Enrico, he will gather the families and also investigate, but he trusts me, obviously. We all go after Massimo," I said.

Sal didn't speak for a little while, although his mouth flapped open and closed like a fish landed on a dock.

"I think Sal is pleased," I said to Ben, smiling.

"Pleased! Are you fucking mad? You are. He is. Where the fuck were you when these conversations were going on? In fact, when did this conversation happen?" Sal fired his questions between Ben and me.

"You asked me to find out who ordered the killing of your senator. I have. It's taken this amount of time, but come on, Sal, Massimo is someone we've suspected for a while. This isn't news," I said.

"You starting a fucking war with him is." He shouted so loud I was sure the whole household would have heard his words.

"Isn't that what you want? Think about it. We have the backing of the Sicilians. The Giolettis are not only in New York, but Sicily, as well. We are well-placed to deal with both."

"How the fuck can we deal with them in New York?" he screamed at me.

"I can cover that end."

"You think you're going to America? Is that what this is all about?" He slumped back in his chair.

I sighed. "Sal, let's get real here. I can walk out of here tomorrow and head to the U.S. Regardless of the fact that I've just gotten married, I still do not want to see anything happen to Evelyn, and until I know who your man over there is, I have no choice but to stay here. But I am not your fucking puppet anymore, do you understand that?"

He raised his eyebrows in disbelief.

"This is what we are going to do. We'll call a meeting with the Commission, and you will ask for the sanction to arm all our drivers in the U.S. When the truck gets pulled, our driver will take them out. We also get backing to take out whoever masterminded this. So, if that's Massimo, then we ask for a hit to be put on him," I said.

I sat back and watched all the emotions a man has, once he realized he was in serious trouble, cross his face

I checked my watch. "I'm off duty for the afternoon," I added. I rose and before Sal could gather whatever words he had lodged in his chest, I left the room. Ben would bring me up to speed later.

That acid that had calcified in my stomach at my betrayal to Evelyn started to break down a little. I could see the end. I could taste victory, and

I could smell the revenge. I still had to figure out who was taking the photographs before Evelyn would truly be safe, but for now, I was getting closer to freedom.

"Can you call your dad?" I asked Chiara, once I'd returned to the apartment.

"I can, what do you need him to know?"

"I need that invite to the meeting with the Commission brought forward."

I unbuttoned my shirt and walked to the bathroom, no matter how little time I spent with Sal, I always needed to shower off the hatred that coated my skin like sweat afterward.

When I returned Chiara handed me the telephone.

"You could call me yourself," Enrico said.

"I was taking a shower."

"How did he take it?"

"He's not happy, of course." I repeated the conversation.

"Okay, I'll get a meeting set up. You make sure you are ready at your end, Rocco. If you fuck this up, it won't be just him being carried out, and there won't be anything I can do to stop that."

I sighed, I was done with the threats, but I played the game. I was well aware that both Enrico and Massimo thought they were using me to do their dirty work. I was also well aware that they thought they'd be getting most of Sal's businesses, leaving me with the shit. They were wrong, so very wrong.

---

Sal knew something was going on, I was sure of that. He kept me at the house and away from any of his businesses. What he didn't understand was that gave me time with Ben to learn exactly what he did. Sal ran drugs into the U.S., as well as distribution around Europe on behalf of the Sicilian families, that I knew. He owned houses of prostitutes that he hired out to rich men and exclusive parties. He distributed his own drugs through a team of dealers. He owned underground gambling dens, fight rings, and illegal parlors betting on horses. There was a property portfolio I found interesting, it seemed he owned a rather expensive hotel, which was often frequented by members of the government, and, I suspected, some of his women.

Money laundering, extortion, protection services, and smuggling were his everyday activities and where he earned a steady stream of cash. Ben ran through the kind of figures and it surprised me that Sal's businesses weren't as lucrative as I'd originally suspected.

"Has someone taken over some of his businesses?" I asked.

"Yeah. Over the past couple of years, Sal has isolated himself more and more from the other families. It goes back to the days when he *stole* Rosina. He doesn't have their backing for much, and so when another family moves in, he can't do anything about it. He doesn't have the muscle anymore, Rocco."

"Why do you stay with him?"

Ben sighed. "I'm a loyal man, I guess. He wasn't always like this. There was a time he was a fair man, a liked and respected man."

"What happened with Rosina?"

"I don't know the facts, what I was told was that he plied her with drink and then he…well, you know what I mean."

"She was engaged to Enrico at that point? I'm surprised he didn't fucking kill Sal for that."

Ben shook his shoulders. "If I had to speculate, Sal has something on Enrico, what? I don't know."

"So why did she end up with Sal?"

"Because she got pregnant and I don't believe Enrico was, or still is, the saint he paints himself to be. He couldn't accept that the child could have been Sal's. Again, not that I know this for fact, but he beat her, she lost the child, and that's when Sal stepped in and took her away."

"It sounds a little fucked up," I said.

"I think it was, this was over twenty years ago now, before my time."

I didn't doubt Enrico was a ruthless man, but to beat his fiancée because she had been raped and possibly gotten pregnant from that? Either he wasn't the man I thought or that wasn't the truth. It wouldn't be beyond the realms of Sal making that story up himself. Still, it wasn't my concern. I had grown to like Rosina and I'd be doing her a favor. Once Sal was out of the picture, she was free to do as she pleased. I suspected she'd return to her village to live a quiet life.

Over the period of a week, Ben had not only filled me in on all Sal's activities, but we had decided which ones we'd keep and which ones we'd let go. I wasn't into the prostitution, but I understood the women were better cared for in the houses than left to their own devices on a street corner. We'd keep that. The drugs? That was lucrative as was the laundering. The extortion could go; I wanted respect not fear. I wanted to walk into to a store and be offered goods for free because the shop owner wanted me to taste, not because he was terrified I'd put a bullet in his skull.

All we had to do was to wait for the invitation to a meeting.

---

Despite Enrico's belief that Philippe was 'gone' I decided to see if he had indeed made his way to Switzerland. Chiara spoke about him often and I learned a lot about him, as she did about Evelyn. We'd sit in the evenings with our wine after a meal and talk about the people we loved, we'd then head to a bedroom and share a bed—it was surreal, as well as guilt-ridden, for both of us.

I was given scant details about Philippe, his name and the fact that he was an artist, I also discovered he was black. That was the reason Enrico had forbidden his daughter that relationship, so she believed. It wasn't something I could get confirmation of, and although I hadn't known Enrico Sr. that long, I suspected she was correct.

A man like Enrico would want his daughter to marry within her race, and would especially want his daughter to marry someone within the *community*, or from another family that was beneficial. It was the only reason we had his blessing, I was sure.

I spoke regularly with Enrico Jr., who delved as far as he could and the news he came back with wasn't good. He didn't believe Philippe had made it to Northern Italy, that in fact, he hadn't made it far from the village where he and Chiara had been caught. I sat on that information until I was sure it was correct, and I was sure Chiara was in a position to handle it.

Like me, Chiara had a photograph of Philippe; it sat next to Evelyn on a shelf in the living room. I'd see her staring at it wistfully, and I wanted to know what she was thinking. I never asked, of course, I'd hate to divulge what I thought about when I was staring at Evelyn. It was those two people, that situation, which bound us, really. We had a mutual respect for each other, we liked each other, and over time we grew to love each other, but not in the depth it should have been. We both knew we were 'second best' and we accepted that.

---

"A meeting has been called," Ben said one morning. "Sal is doing his nut about it. He thinks this is not necessary and, obviously, he's panicking about it."

"Good, I want him to panic. When is it?"

"Tomorrow."

I turned to face him. "Why so soon?"

"I guess they don't want to wait any longer, and it's not the easiest to get the Commission all together."

"Fuck! Okay, so we know what we are going to do, right? You back out, or you betray me, Ben, and I don't care if you have your *insurance information*, it won't save you."

He nodded his head. "I don't think Sal was going to tell you. If he does, it will be last minute, but the meeting is being held in his village. Is that relevant?"

Enrico had decided on the where and the when, and to kill Sal in front of the people that knew him the most, in front of the Commission, and ironically in the place he had held me like a dog, amused me. I approved.

It was the how I was about to divert from. I smiled as I walked back to my apartment. Enrico favored old style assassination, a bullet to the back of the head. Not me. I wanted to make a statement and look into his eyes while I did so. This was more than personal for me.

It was late that evening Sal told me he was invited to a meeting. I could see through the bravado to the sweaty palms and the slight stammer in his voice.

"Sal, this is good. We get the ball rolling to get everyone on the same page as us. We tell them everything we know, and what we plan to do about it."

"Exactly what the fuck do we plan to do about it?"

"We take Massimo out of the equation. I mean, he's not directly involved, but he earns from the heroin for no input other than he runs New York."

"*Other than he runs New York*," Sal mocked. "That's the point, you prick, he runs New York!"

"You're missing the point. If all the families are together on this, tell him that you know he is responsible for wanting your senator dead and for stealing your trucks. If that is done in front of the other families, he will have to stop, won't he?"

Sal blinked rapidly, he opened his mouth to speak and then closed it again. If he had any sense, he would have noticed my slip up. Massimo was based in New York, he might have family in Sicily, but he never sat in any Commission meetings in Italy. I'd told him, in other words, that Massimo would be in attendance.

If I could see inside his mind, I'd see it whirling. He was in trouble, he was about to accuse one of the major players in the U.S., a man who could, with the click of a finger, shut down Sal's routes and take them over himself. I wondered why he hadn't.

The following day, I slid into the passenger seat of a car being driven by Mario, Ben sat in the rear with Sal. Ben fidgeted the whole journey, to the point that Sal asked him a couple of times if he was okay. I wanted to smack the nerves out of him. Mario sighed and shook his head as subtly as he could. Alex had been left behind, well, he had a mystery illness that prevented him from traveling to which Sal was most annoyed. I needed Alex back at base to settle things as soon as news spread. A second car with security followed.

The closer we got the location, the more distressed Sal seemed to be. His viciousness escalated.

"Remember being here last time, Rocco?" he asked, as we entered the village and climbed the hill to a villa.

I had been held for a few days in an outbuilding that bordered my mother's farm. That farm had been sold and my mother had moved on, so I'd discovered. I assumed, hoped, that it was to look after my sister, but since I was *dead* I had no way of knowing. When it was time, I would contact my uncle and pave the way to a meeting with my mother.

It was ironic that we pulled into the courtyard of the villa Sal owned. I wondered if Massimo was aware of my incarceration there and the venue was a little reminder to me as well. It was beginning to look a little like Massimo wasn't the ally he portrayed himself to be. One to add to the list maybe.

Cars began to arrive and Sal took on the role as perfect host. He was rude and doing his best to belittle Mario and me, which surprised us. Mario was his underboss. I heard Mario grumble under his breath beside me.

"Not long now," I whispered, as I smiled and held open the villa door for a very distinguished man to arrive.

I expected the stares and the whispered conversations, they knew I was the one who killed Aldo, and if Enrico was to be believed, they knew why. Whether they all agreed was another matter, of course.

When the last of the Commission had been shown into the villa and to a room that housed a temporary large table, Mario and I took our place standing against the wall behind Sal.

It pleased me to see the sweat roll down the back of his neck and the shake to his hands as they came into view.

Enrico opened the meeting. He explained that Sal believed Massimo responsible for the missing trucks and he had a plan to put forward to remedy it. I put my hand in my pocket and felt for the weapon I intended to kill Sal with. I smiled as my fingers closed around it.

For a while, I listened as each person detailed any problems they had and a discussion was had on how to solve it. Votes were taken and agreements given. The closer the conversation got to Sal, the more nervous he became. I could see him shifting in his seat, wiping his brow with a handkerchief repeatedly. He drank his glass of water and asked for more. When it came to his turn, Enrico glanced at me. Sal made to stand and muttered that he didn't feel well.

As the door to the room opened, I stepped forward on the pretense of helping Sal; he leaned on the back of his chair and one hand reached out to me. I wondered, for a brief moment if he really was ill. That was until I saw the evil glint in his eye; his acting skills hadn't quite obliterated that.

I pulled out the corkscrew I'd carried around with me since Sienna, and I plunged it into the side of his neck.

His eyes grew wide as realization occurred. I twisted the corkscrew, catching his carotid artery. His blood spurted out, coating my hand, my wrist, and splattering over my face. I twisted more, digging deeper, all the while I smiled at him. I pulled the corkscrew from his neck, it made a satisfying squelch as his fat and skin released it. He covered the wound with his hand to no effect.

Men jumped to their feet, Mario and Ben moved to stand beside me, as rehearsed, and for protection. There was stunned silence, other than the gurgling from Sal and the thump as he finally fell to the floor.

Using my foot, I pushed him as far as I could and then I pulled out his seat. Enrico handed me some tissues and I cleaned my face and my hands, before sitting at the table. I placed the corkscrew on the table as Massimo entered. He stood behind me, placing his hand on my shoulder.

"Friends, let us welcome Rocco Sartorri to the Commission," he said.

Chairs scraped as room was made for Massimo to sit one side of Enrico, I was the other. I wasn't sure if positioning was significant or not at that point.

"Friends, let me explain what just happened here," I said.

I made eye contact with all that sat around the table. I made sure to let them know Sal was responsible for their missing heroin, and I would ensure all drugs were received. I would take over Sal's operations, and I had the full support of both Massimo and Enrico.

I watched frowns of suspicion on brows and narrowing of eyes with disbelief. I knew I'd have my work cut out; I'd just killed someone they may have held in high regard. I was only still sitting there because of Massimo and Enrico. I had to earn their respect, and I would.

"Can you remove him?" I asked, looking over to security by the door. Sal was starting to stink.

Two guys came forward and dragged the body out, leaving a trail of blood in their wake.

"Why should you be trusted?" I heard. I looked to the end of the table; a younger man sat twirling a glass of whiskey in this hand.

"Because I'm asking you to. And I know you, you also know me, Darius, isn't it?"

The man sitting at the end of the table was the same that had accompanied the mayor to the Palio over a year ago. Mr. Not Important, I think I'd renamed him.

Darius smiled and slowly nodded. He stood and walked to where I sat. I rose as he got close.

"Rocco, I wasn't sure you'd remember. You and I need to talk privately." He held out his hand for a shake. I took it.

"I have something I need to do when this meeting is over. After that, then yes, we should talk."

He nodded to Massimo and then left the room. I wondered where he fit in with the Commission, as far as I was aware, he had nothing to do with the four families. I wanted to ask, but I didn't want anyone to know I hadn't a clue who he was. It suited me to have them think I knew him, though.

"Rocco, this is all rather unexpected. We need a further meeting. Enrico, I would have thought a little warning would have been forthcoming from you, since you and Massimo appear to be in on this."

I turned to face an elderly gentleman, who had walked with a cane from one end of the room.

"Carlo, my apologies. You were in America visiting Franco when Rocco first came to us. I can assure you, we will tell you everything," Enrico replied.

I had heard the name Franco mentioned before, but it was a common name. I held my breath though as he approached me. He placed his hands on my upper arms and stared at me. For an old man, he had a strong grip.

"You will speak with my son, he has moved to America, but he will be of use to you. Massimo will arrange it."

Before he left, he kissed me on both cheeks and chuckled. He patted my arm as he released his grip and shuffled to the door. Massimo bowed his head in deference to him. It was obvious Carlo was a respected man and I looked forward to meeting his son. There was only one Franco in America that Massimo had already mentioned, someone close to Joe. My heart raced at the prospect of being that one step closer.

"I want this villa," I said, as I turned and stepped over the pool of blood.

"Sal never owned it, he just rented it when he wanted to. You'll need to speak to the Contessa, but you need to deal with Rome first," Enrico said.

"I need to deal with one other person, then I need to deal with my family as well as Rome."

We walked from the room. A housekeeper stood outside with a bucket and mop, as if it was completely natural that she cleaned up the blood trail. She tutted as we walked over her wet floor.

In the courtyard, I looked to the brick building I'd been housed in. Mario stood to one side and Ben to the other.

"Make arrangements for me to buy this villa," I said to Ben.

I knew I'd be needed in Rome, but I wanted a base more akin to my roots. I hated the city, but could I live on the edge of my parents' farm?

"And we need to find out where my mother is, where my uncle is."

I walked to the car and they followed.

"Do you know where he is?" I asked, as I climbed into the back.

"Yes, there is a butcher's shop in the village, he's in the apartment above, hiding."

Lou had traveled to the villa from Rome in a separate car. I wondered how he'd heard about Sal's demise already, but I didn't care. He'd know I would be coming for him. What I'd do would depend on what he said when I got there. But it was a nice feeling to know he was hiding from me. I liked that tingle of power as it traveled through my body.

I walked into the butcher's in the square. News had sure traveled fast. I was greeted as if I was already head of the family. I had yet to see if any of Sal's men would join me, or whether I had to start my family from scratch. I had the businesses, but that meant nothing without the men.

I was offered cuts of meat, and I thanked the butcher but refused his kind offer. I explained he owed me nothing, but I would like to taste his ham. I assured him we would purchase some of his products once we were settled back in Rome. Although my village had been a neighboring one, it wasn't much different. Each resident supported the other with buying local or trading goods. I wanted to help that.

I picked up a cleaver, running my finger down the blade to check its sharpness. The butcher ushered me to a door in the back of the store, he gestured up the stairs. I nodded and made the slow, noisy, ascent.

Lou was cowering in a room, which, had the apartment been occupied, I imagined would have been a small bedroom.

"Rocco, I'm so glad to see you. I heard about Sal. What can I do to help you?" he said with false sincerity.

I walked toward him holding the cleaver by my side. "Why are you hiding out here?" I asked.

He stammered but held his stance, not that he really had anywhere to go.

"Rocco, I just follow orders, you know that. I know nothing and I get paid peanuts to listen to his shit."

"Who is taking photographs of my family?" I asked, not expecting him to know anything at all.

"Like I'd know that," he said with a dramatic shrug of his shoulder. "He'd know though," he said, pointing to Ben.

I nodded slowly. "Yes, I know he knows. Now, Lou, what to do about you?"

He didn't respond initially, in fact I heard his sigh of resignation. He took a step forward.

"I worked for him, so did you, so did they. You gotta do what you gotta do, Rocco. I just ask one thing."

"Which is?"

"My kid sister is ill, like, not right in the head. Something to do with having an older mamma. I've been saving my money, it's in the house, will you make sure it gets sent to my mamma?"

I smiled and started to nod, then I raised the cleaver and I brought it down on his face. I heard the gasp from Ben, who had probably witnessed more carnage in the short time he'd been aligned with me than he had his whole life in the family. I pushed the cleaver into Lou's face, slicing through his cheeks so he looked like his smile really was from ear to ear. He stumbled back and fell. I stood over him, blood dripping from the cleaver in my hand.

"People who lie to me lose the ability to speak," I said, as I leaned down and cut out his tongue. I shoved that down his throat then left him to die.

"He doesn't have a sister, and his mamma died years ago," I said, as I walked past Ben who looked about ready to faint.

I handed the cleaver to Mario, hoping he would remember our conversation on the correct disposal of a murder weapon, and walked down the stairs. The butcher was standing at the bottom. He held out a towel before I was even able to ask for one.

"I'll have someone clean that up," I said, as I handed back his towel.

"Signore Sartorri, it is a pleasure to have you in my shop," he said.

My mobile vibrated in my pocket, I pulled it out to see Alex.

"Yes?"

"News has arrived here. Felisia threw herself down on the floor for about a minute, and Rosina said to tell you *thank you*. I've secured the office as instructed and told Rosina to stay put until you return," he said.

"Anything from the guys?" I asked.

"Nope, all on board. Half don't care as long they're still getting paid."

"Get rid of those ones."

The only people I wanted on my *team* were ones who wanted to be there. Money made people greedy, needy, and not loyal.

I spent the rest of that day meeting with Enrico and Massimo. I told them I wanted a period of time to get to know what elements of the business I wanted to keep and what I was willing to let go.

It took me the best part of six months to reorganize the business. In that time, I was desperate to contact my family and Joe. But the delivery of another set of photographs put a stop to that. I had thought with the death of Sal that would stop, and I'd be able to get my family back, but whatever measures he had put in place were there even in his death. Of course, Ben was keeping quiet, and I began to doubt he actually knew who in Joe's family was taking those images. However, he was useful so I kept him close.

Rosina stayed in the house for a short period of time. Once I'd cleared out Sal's office and taken all the paperwork that was relevant, I'd emptied his safe, his bank, and the small room in the basement that resembled La Banca d'Italia, then I moved out and bought a house of my own. I gave her some of Sal's money and she sold the house. She and Felisia returned to her village.

It all soured soon after when I was told that my mother had died. My uncle had sold the farm some time ago and he had retired himself. I had someone tell him that I was alive and I wanted to meet with him. I needed for him to keep my existence a secret still, but I was distraught my mother died believing her husband and her two sons had died before her.

I never got that meeting with my uncle; he was killed in a car crash no one seemed to want to investigate fully. I knew I had some work to do to find out who authorized that and to make sure that I was never treated with such disrespect again.

Even though I was free, I wasn't. The only way to ensure my freedom was to take everyone out and not just run my family, but the largest organization in Italy, the deadliest, most corrupt, and one that I was already on the rung of the ladder with, thanks to Enrico.

I set my sights on 'Ndràngheta: the most powerful crime organization in Italy.

*Letter from Rocco*

*It was a few years later that I finally got to America. I stood on the side of the street, and I watched Evelyn with her beau. She looked happy, I saw the glint of an engagement ring on her finger, and I knew she was doing okay. I had been keeping track of her via Franco for years. I still received those photographs, once a month a brown envelope would arrive addressed to me, until one day they stopped.*

*Many times Chiara had asked me why I hadn't left to be with her, I was in a position to protect her, she'd say. I would smile and tell her that I loved her. Not in the way I loved Evelyn, and she didn't love me in the same way she had once loved Philippe, but we had children, a boy and a girl, and my life was in Italy.*

*The day I finally told Chiara that her father had killed Philippe had been the day she'd shut down. Despite our opulent lifestyle, our many homes around Italy and Europe, despite the millions in the bank and the many businesses I owned, she was perpetually unhappy. She started to drink and it pained me. She neglected our children—she was lost, not just to me, but also to herself as well.*

*As her habit increased so did her hatred, for her father and for me. She blurred the lines, drank herself into oblivion, but it was when she started to snort the cocaine I sold, but never touched, I decided enough was enough. I sent her home to her family to see if they could dry her out.*

*That proved to be the only mistake I'd ever make where Chiara was concerned.*

*I took a call one day to say Chiara had killed herself. Not before she had killed Enrico. I held myself responsible for many years for that. I should have told her when I knew that Philippe was dead. I should never have let her believe I was searching for him. I should never have sent her home; I should have helped her myself. I failed her and that lived with me for years. It hardened me; it tainted me further.*

*I took over Enrico's business, his son not ready for that challenge, the day we buried him.*

*I raised my two children myself and as best as I could. I was sure I made many mistakes. They had the best education but they never really had the best of me. I was lonely, I was heartbroken again, and I had built an empire that had taken on a life of its own. It constantly evolved. I both loved and hated my life.*

*I killed Ben, as I said I always would when I finally discovered the traitor in Joe's family. I thanked God Joe was already dead by that time, and I prayed Evelyn would never discover that her brother had been the one to sell his family out. From an early teen he had been taking photographs to send to Sal. When Sal was no longer around, that relationship had continued with Ben. I wanted to know why he had betrayed his family. I wanted to beat the information from him, but that opportunity was taken from me when Roberto killed him instead.*

*All I was able to discover was Joey had decided he wanted in with the heroin. He sold the drug that started life as a missing truck for Sal. He was his man, or kid, for that was what he was in the beginning, in the U.S. I never told a soul about Joey. It would be information I'd take to my grave.*

*I shot Ben in the back of the head in the square of the village that had adopted me, and then I walked to my villa for dinner with my very good friends, Enrico Jr. and his secret boyfriend, Darius, who has just been elected Prime Minister of Italy. We toasted with wine and we dipped bread in oil from my farm. I didn't give Ben another thought.*

*I only told my son, Roberto, about this short period of my life, yet there had been many years way more colorful. There were things that were just too painful to recall so I glossed over them, there were things that were just too complicated to detail. I needed him to know mainly about those three locations, and to tell him that, I needed to tell him why as well. I killed three men in three different locations, two within hours of each other, one many years later, yet those three locations were the same his family had been photographed in. Was it coincidence? Maybe. Was it ironic that my life had been shaped by a series of photographs and now his was? Perhaps. Someone knew my life and me, and someone knew my son. Now it was up to us to discover who and why.*

*Rocco Sartorri*

Present Day: Robert & Rocco

The sun had begun to lower over the horizon. We had moved to the terrace to stretch our legs, eat, and drink some wine. Brooke and Evelyn had been successful in keeping everyone away, and I was thankful for that.

Rocco looked exhausted. Telling us his story, the missing years, had taken its toll on him.

"How much of this does Evelyn know?" I asked.

"Some of it. She knows about Felisia and Chiara, the reasons and the whys. It was important I gained her forgiveness for betraying her," he said.

"It wasn't exactly betrayal, you did what you needed to survive," I said, gently.

"No, Roberto, I betrayed her because there came a point when I enjoyed my time with other women."

"You thought Evelyn was lost to you, forever. You thought she was happily married, I think you can forgive yourself for that," I said.

Rocco sighed and leaned back in his chair. He raised his wine glass to his lips and took a gentle sip. I watched as he inhaled at the same time, closing his eyes as he savored the taste. He nodded as he swallowed, as if in approval of that sip of wine.

"So what to do about our small problem?" he said.

Rocco had spent the last few hours telling Travis and me about the time he was kidnapped and what he'd done to survive that, but he hadn't quite told us why he thought his past was connected to our photographs. I got the reference to the locations, but that still didn't connect enough to an individual in his past.

Even after hours of listening to Rocco, we were no closer to understanding who had wanted those pictures taken, and who had sent them to me.

"Travis is going to head home tomorrow, I'll stay on another couple of days, but then I'll leave as well. Brooke is keen to get home and get Gerry settled in time for the new term at school. Maybe you and Evelyn should move up your visit," I said, as I sat beside him.

In the few hours he'd spoken, I imagine he'd been taken through a range of emotions, unwanted memories, and he looked exhausted. I didn't want him to dwell anymore.

"Let's sleep on it, Rocco. We'll chat some more tomorrow. I'd rather you stayed here tonight, I'm sure Evelyn would like to spend some time with you alone," I added.

He nodded and I noticed the strain on his face as he pushed himself from his chair. Evelyn had long since made her way over to her side of the villa. She wouldn't have headed to bed without seeing Rocco before he left, though, and I accompanied him as far as the fountain in the courtyard. I watched her open her door and welcome him in.

I stood looking out over the valley and the village below, just inhaling the night air. I liked the night; it was the quiet I enjoyed the most. I had been lying to everyone. I wasn't as in control with my emotions as I said I was. I was confused and there were times when I wished I hadn't learned my parentage, and moments when I was so overwhelmed with it. My internal conflict was a little more complicated though.

As I looked out over the village, I felt at home. The language rolled off my tongue as if I'd been speaking it my whole life. The heat, the smells, the sounds, felt so natural that I wasn't looking as forward to returning the U.S. as my family was. It confused me.

"You okay, Boss?" I heard.

I turned to see Gary. "Yeah, I thought you were off shift tonight?" I said.

He laughed. "Am I ever off shift? I don't trust Vinny, or those idiots on the gate, so on, or off, shift, I like to take a walk around."

"Are you looking forward to going home?" I asked.

He frowned at me; I imagine he was thinking through what he thought should be the right answer. "I am. I miss Pat, obviously, and it would be nice to get out of this humidity."

Late October in Italy wasn't often as warm as it was then. I was informed that the winters could be quite harsh sometimes, but I wondered on the definition of harsh.

I sat on the low wall and Gary joined me. We looked across the courtyard and up the hill where the old building stood. It was the location of one of the photographs.

"Rocco was held captive there for a short while. And just beyond was his family farm. They believed him to be dead. Can you imagine how fucked up that would make you feel? To know your family just *buried* you and you can't do a thing about it," I said quietly.

"I don't know much about him, obviously. I understood he was the *can of snakes* that Franco referred to, and it can't be easy for you," he replied.

I looked at him. I didn't have any 'friends,' I'd never wanted any. I had family, and I had staff, of which he was one. In that moment, though, maybe it was my state of mind, the confusion I was feeling, or just the need to talk to someone unconnected, I confessed.

"It is. For most of my life I believed one thing, then I'm faced with another. It hasn't been easy to absorb, it still isn't. I'm a little tired of it all right now, Gary."

"You need a holiday," he said with a laugh.

I chuckled. "As if," I said with a sigh.

"I'll leave you in peace, and if this is completely out of turn, I'm going to say it anyway. I wouldn't want to be you, not with all the pressure and stress you have on your shoulders now. However, if I can take a little of that from you, I'm more than willing to."

I watched as he walked away. Was it that obvious? The past months had been like no other. The business I commanded was also like no other, and it was taking its toll. I was about to head into the villa, and hopefully spend a little time with my wife, when I saw the sweep of headlights come up the lane. I stood at the same time as Gary made his way back to me.

"Do you want to move inside, Mr. Stone?" he said, the informality gone.

"We're not expecting anyone, are we?" I asked.

"No, which is why I think you should move inside. I've messaged Travis, he's getting his pants back on," he said with a soft chuckle.

"Go check it out, I'll wait in the kitchen," I said, as I walked away.

I poured myself a coffee just as Travis came into the room.

"What do we have?" he asked.

"No idea yet, Gary's in charge. Want one?" I said raising my cup.

"Sure. We're not expecting visitors are we?"

"No, I asked the same question."

It was a couple of minutes later that Gary walked into the kitchen.

"Vinny maybe isn't such an idiot, after all. Sitting in the office over there is the man who took the photographs. I'm yet to establish just how Vinny came across him, he's all chest puffed and that shit right now."

I raised my eyebrows. "Okay, so what do you know so far?"

"Nothing other than his name. Dominic. He's refusing to speak at the moment, he looks terrified, so I don't think he was expecting to visit with you tonight. I've left him secured to a chair to contemplate."

I looked over to Travis, who smiled at Gary. Travis was scary when he smiled. I'd told him many times over the years, violence turned him on way more than pussy.

I slapped my brother on the back and we walked into the courtyard.

"Do you want me to call for Rocco?" Gary asked. I looked toward that end of the villa. Despite the noise of a car arriving, there were no visible lights.

"No, let him sleep. We'll find out what we can first."

Maybe there was just a little piece of me that didn't want Rocco involved, I was in charge of this family now, and although I shouldn't have, I resented Gary even asking that question.

I strode toward the office, leaving Travis and Gary following behind.

Blood splattered across my face as I threw the last punch, and I wiped my cheek with the back of my hand. I'd felt my knuckles split and that angered me. The bloodied face in a head that reeled back gave me no satisfaction. I kicked at the chair he was tied to, sending him spiraling to the floor. He cried out, sniveled, and tried to spit his broken teeth from split lips.

"Now, do you have something you want to tell me?" I asked, as I crouched beside him.

He nodded.

"Vinny, right his chair," I said.

Dominic was brought upright and I paced while I brought myself under control. Travis stepped in front of him.

"Last time, okay? Who put you up to this?" Travis asked.

The crying started then and it annoyed me further. I'd only punched him two or three times. He was lucky I hadn't cut his fucking fingers off. I shouldn't have had to punch him, but I was making a statement to Vinny as well. He was getting a little too *comfortable* and needed reminding I was the boss; I was in charge. He had fucked up in accepting that envelope, and I wanted to show him what happened when you fucked up.

"He's going to kill me," Dominic whispered.

"*He* is going to kill you if you don't speak. Either way, you're pretty fucked," Travis said pointing to me.

I stepped beside my brother.

"He isn't going to kill you because he won't know you've told me, until it's too late for him to do anything about it. That's as long as you keep your mouth shut, of course," I said.

"I'll write it down," he whispered.

Travis looked at me with raised eyebrows. He turned back to Dominic. "Why?"

I placed my hand on Travis' shoulder. "Vinny, get me a piece of paper and a pen."

Whichever way the prick wanted to tell me, I'd take it. I just wanted a name. Perhaps he had some misbelief that if he didn't say the words out loud it would absolve him of the worst crime he could commit—giving up his boss.

Dominic's hands were untied and the paper and pen thrust in front of him. His hand shook so much I was doubtful I'd be able to read the name. He handed it over to Travis. all the while looking at me. The fear that crossed his face was evident. His eyes began to water, a tear rolled down one cheek. I felt no remorse, of course; I was incapable of that. No matter what, the minute Dominic spied on my wife, took photographs of her, Katrina, and Evelyn without their knowledge, and then sent them to me in an unmarked package, he'd sealed his fate. He deserved the fear I instilled.

I held out my hand for the piece of paper. At first, Travis was reluctant to pass it to me. I took a step forward and snatched it from him. I stared at the name and had to grit my teeth to quell the expletives that were about to explode from me. Dominic didn't need to see a *very* angry version of me. I liked to keep that side of my character for those that truly deserved it.

I looked for a second time at the name. I felt my breath quicken while my heart pounded in my chest. I screwed it up and threw it at Dominic. I pulled the revolver from the waistband of my pants, and I pressed the barrel into his forehead. He started to pray.

"You fucking lied to me," I said, pushing harder.

He prayed louder, all the while trying to shake his head. "No, no lies. I swear on my mother's life. It's the name he gave me," he said between sobs.

I pulled the gun away. I wasn't into killing just for the sake of it, and I wanted a battered face, a bruised forehead, to send back as a message.

"Get him out of my fucking sight," I said.

Before I walked from the room, I turned to look at him.

"You speak one word of what happened here, your mother will be staring at the bottom of the river with no way up. Understand?"

He nodded and I walked away.

"What the fuck?" Travis said, once we were out of earshot.

"I don't believe it. Well, I don't think I believe it."

"What are we going do?" he asked.

"Nothing right now."

We came to the fountain in the center of the courtyard. I paused beside it, dipping my fist in the cool water to wash away the blood.

"Fucking prick," I muttered, as I inspected the broken skin.

I wiped my fist on a handkerchief Travis held out and balled it into my trouser pocket.

"Come on, Bro, let's deal with this in the morning," I said.

I stripped off my clothes and stepped under the shower. I scrubbed my skin clean and wrapped a towel around my waist. I stood beside the bed, watching my wife sleeping. She was naked and lying on her stomach. Her perfect ass was begging for my touch, but I was conscious of the nights I'd kept her awake with my insomnia. I threw the towel on the floor and slid under the sheet beside her.

"Hey," she mumbled, as she shuffled into my side.

"Go back to sleep, baby," I said. I doubted I'd gotten to the end of that sentence before she had.

I lay for ages, thinking on the name I'd been given. It wasn't possible, but then I had no reason to think Dominic had lied. I closed my eyes, hoping sleep would come. My body was tired, but my mind just wouldn't shut down. I climbed from the bed and walked to the balcony. I stood, naked, and let the cool air chill my body.

"Robert," I heard. I turned to watch my wife walk toward me. "Can't you sleep again?"

I shook my head and sighed. She stood beside me, placing her hand on my back, and rubbed gently. "Do you want to talk about it?" she asked.

I placed my arm around her shoulder. "No, I'm fine."

"Fine like your sister says," she said, looking up at me. I smiled back at her.

"Yes, fine like your sister says. Give me some time, yes?"

She nodded.

"What did you do?" she asked, picking up my hand and inspecting it.

"A little boxing, didn't strap my hands, that's all," I said. It wasn't an out and out lie.

"Doesn't look like a *little boxing*. Don't let Gerry see, will you?"

"I won't, pack a bag in the morning. Let's go home."

As much as I was well-known in Tuscany, in my region, the one I controlled after merging my father's businesses with mine, I wasn't taking any risks.

Brooke wriggled her naked body until she was in front of me. I had her pinned against the balcony. She gently kissed my chest, concentrating around the tattoo I had with her and Gerry's initials.

"Let me help you sleep," she whispered against my skin.

Her hands ran down my sides, her nails gently scraped against my skin.

"How, Brooke?" I asked.

"I'd like to suck your cock," she said, looking up at me with a smirk.

"And what else, that won't make me sleepy."

As I spoke, I stepped back. I wasn't about to fuck her mouth on the balcony. I continued to walk back until I was in the middle of the bedroom. Brooke stood in front of me, and I placed my hands on her shoulders. I gently pushed her to her knees. I wrapped one hand in the hair at the back of her head, and without having to guide her, I felt her wrap one hand around my hard cock and her tongue gently teased the end. She licked all the way from the tip, down my shaft, to my balls. Her tongue circled back up before she opened her mouth and closed her lips around me. Her hot mouth felt so good, I could feel the tension leave my shoulders.

She hummed as she sucked and the vibrations caused my stomach to tighten with want. I tightened my grip on her hair and gently rotated my hips. Brooke slid her hands around to my ass, she gripped, digging her nails in my skin. That was her cue to step up the pace a little. I complied, of course. She gripped harder as she felt me tense, she sucked faster as she felt my cock pulse, and when I came, she swallowed every last drop.

I pulled her to her feet and before she could take a breath, I kissed her. I bit down on her lip, tasting myself, and her blood as I broke skin. She moaned as I devoured the mouth that had devoured me.

I walked her back to the bed and when we were close, I turned her around. She bent at the waist, sliding her hands across the edge of the bed and gripping the sheets. I placed one hand on her hip. She looked over her shoulder at me and smiled. I guided my cock just inside her and stilled. She pushed back against me, wanting more.

"How do you want me to fuck you, Brooke?" I said.

She mumbled into the bedding.

"How?" I asked again.

"Hard," she said. Again, I complied.

I fucked her until sweat rolled down my forehead and dripped onto her back, until there was a sheen of perspiration on her skin, and until she cried out my name when she gave in to her orgasm. I reached beneath and ran my fingers over her clitoris. I pumped faster when I felt her legs begin to shake and she slid farther onto the bed.

I pulled out of her and before she could catch her breath, I rolled her over. She lay with her back to the bedding and her legs hanging over the side of the bed. I fell to my knees and sucked her clitoris into my mouth. I needed to taste her, to inhale her scent. I licked, and at the same time, I wrapped my hand around my still hard cock. I slid my hand up and down using the wetness of her to lubricate myself. When she came again, so did I. My hot cum spurted over my fist.

"Oh, God," she said quietly. "That didn't go quite as planned."

I laughed as I stood and reached for some tissue. Brooke slid completely onto the bed.

"What didn't go as planned?" I asked.

"I was supposed make you come, help you sleep."

She shuffled over and I climbed on beside her. I pulled her into my arms and wrapped the sheet around us.

"Why are you struggling to sleep?" she asked.

"I just have too much on my mind right now."

She pushed herself up until she was sitting crossed-legged beside me. She wrapped the sheet around herself before she spoke.

"Talk to me, Robert. I don't want to know about your business, but we don't talk so much anymore. What can I do to help you?"

"You're already doing everything I could ever ask of you. I feel unsettled, Brooke, misplaced, I guess. I feel very much at home here in Italy, speaking the language as if it's what I've done my whole life, but I know I have a life in the U.S. I feel conflicted right now."

"You don't want to go home?" she asked, although she tried to hide it, I could hear the surprise in her voice.

"Yes, I want to go home. You want to go home and I want to be wherever you are. Like I said, I just feel very unsettled. I don't like it. Travis isn't feeling great, either. He feels out of place here, as if he doesn't belong in my life anymore. And I think that's part of the problem. I've created this empire and it's a little lonely at the top right now."

It was about the most honest I'd been with her in a long time.

"Oh, okay. Well, Travis we can do something about. He's in a panic about life and Katrina, and I don't know if he told you, but she's pregnant. We both know he isn't going to deal well with that. Remember how he was with Caroline?"

I sighed and stared at her. With her hair tangled around her head, her cheeks still rosy from her orgasm, she'd never looked as beautiful.

"Okay, Travis we can deal with. I told him if he didn't want part of this, I'd walk away."

"You could no more walk away from this, Robert, than you could stop breathing and still survive. This village, this language, the people, they make up who you are and it's only now that you've discovered that. I want to go home, I'm longing to be in our house with my friends, but I also love it here. For me, it's different. I get bored because there isn't a great deal for me to do here. At home, I can meet the girls, we can go for lunch. But you need to understand, I want to be wherever you are," she said, echoing my words.

"How can this be? How can I feel so at home in this environment when I haven't experienced it in forty odd years of life?"

"Because it's inside you. You have experienced it. You were brought up by Joe as an Italian, no matter that was in America. You spoke this language for so many years until he died, and then you didn't anymore. With everything that's happened, it's no wonder you feel misplaced, and how amazing that you can recognize that," she said.

"Recognizing an emotion, and doing something about it are two different things. Now, sleep," I said, wanting to finish the conversation.

Reluctantly she settled beside me again. I knew she felt that I was getting insular again, she'd mentioned that to Evelyn. When we'd first met, I'd internalize rather than open up to her. In fact, I'd beat the shit out of something, or someone, rather than try to understand what was going on in my head. I knew I was heading back that way.

# Robert - Chapter Six

Flying back and forth between the U.S and Italy wasn't as arduous for us as it could have been. We had a private jet and a nonstop comfortable journey. Brooke was quiet to start with; she was leaving Evelyn and Rocco behind. It had been Evelyn's choice not to return immediately to the U.S., the day Rocco walked back into her life. They had, however, both promised they would spend Christmas with us, which was only two months away. She was happy, and that made me happy.

I watched Brooke close her eyes and rest her head back. She'd sleep for part of the way. I envied that in her. Gerry had his headphones on and his iPad open on the table in front of him. He was nodding along to some tune or other, while his fingers worked furiously over the screen to keep up with a game he was playing.

The older he got, the more complicated my life became. When it was just me and Travis it was easy. Then it was me and Brooke, and for a while I struggled with that. Now it was the three of us, and the need to protect them from harm often felt so overwhelming. I'd look at them and feel a punch to my gut, a physical pain at the thought I could lose them because of my lifestyle. But it was a lifestyle I hadn't chosen; it was one I had been thrown into, and one that had saved my life in the beginning.

"Can I get you another drink, Mr. Stone?"

A stewardess brought me out of my melancholic thoughts. I pushed my glass toward her.

"Whiskey with ice...please," I said, only adding the 'please' when I saw Brooke stir. A ghost of a smile formed on her lips.

"Is Mr. Curran traveling with you today?" she asked, as she poured my whiskey.

I looked behind me, at the empty cabin. I craned my neck up front, staring at the empty seats, other than the one Gary sat in. He made to rise, assuming I wanted him. I turned back to her. I opened my mouth and before I could speak, I felt a sharp kick to my shin.

"No, he'll follow on with his wife and child, of course," Brooke said, straightening herself in her seat.

My wife had a tongue that could cut glass when she wanted it to.

"Of course. Mrs. Stone, can I get you some tea?" a chided stewardess asked.

"Yes, please."

I watched as she walked away.

"She came on to him once," Brooke said.

"How do you know that?"

"A woman's intuition."

"So why the kick to the shin?"

"She may be on the prowl, but Mr. Sarcastic isn't always as controllable as Mr. Forced Polite."

I shook my head. It had been within hours of us first meeting, if I remembered, that she had decided I either had multiple personalities, or was just an asshole most of the time. I suspected it was the latter.

The stewardess returned with Brooke's tea and was rewarded with a bright smile.

"Are you happy to be going home?" I asked, as I picked up my glass of whiskey.

"I am. Although, it's a little rushed, isn't it?"

I shrugged my shoulders.

"You know me, baby, I make a decision and I act on it."

"Mmm, okay." She sipped on her tea while keeping eye contact with me.

I placed my glass down on the table and leaned forward. I took the cup from her hand and placed it back in the saucer.

"Did I tell you today that I loved you?" I whispered.

"Yes, but you can tell me again, if you like," she replied.

"I'll show you, later."

"You make a lot of promises, Mr. Stone."

"And I keep every single one of them."

"You do, I'll give you that. How long before we get home?"

I laughed, causing Gerry to glance over. Perhaps his music wasn't as loud as I'd initially thought.

Brooke settled back into her seat. I studied her face. To me, she'd grown more beautiful as she'd aged. Although still in her late thirties, with just a few lines gracing her forehead and beside her eyes, she had that playful look about her, which had me willing the plane to up its speed.

As the hours wore on, Gerry got bored and the captain allowed him in the cockpit for a few minutes. He came back with plans of how he was going to be pilot. My son was always full of enthusiasm, until he was with his friends. Then the 'nearly teenager' emerged and the battles commenced. Brooke often had to mediate. Maybe I was too tough on him, but he knew a little about the life he was in, yet not enough to stop taking stupid risks. He'd slipped away from his security one time, causing that guy to lose his job, and for me to nearly have a coronary.

Losing one, or both, of them was my biggest nightmare.

I thought on the photographs Travis would be bringing back with him, and I was anxious for news. He'd hung back until Vinny had found out a little more about Dominic, and I wondered how Katrina felt about that. She'd been the one to want to leave early, I believed.

Brooke and Gerry chatted, watched a movie, and I was content just to sit back and watch them.

Gerry had fallen asleep by the time the plane made its descent. Brooke gently woke him and fumbled with his seat belt to buckle him up. The time difference played havoc on his body, and it would often take him a good few days to go from super grumpy to just grumpy. By the time we had landed and the steps were lowered, we were at the super grumpy stage.

"Buddy, come on," I said, as Gerry took forever to pack his iPad and earphones in his backpack.

He mumbled under his breath. Brooke placed her hand on his shoulder and guided him to the door. As we descended the steps Mack greeted us.

"Welcome home," he said, and then opened the rear door of the car.

Brooke slid in first, Gerry second, and then I joined them. Gary took the passenger seat. Mack glanced at me and gave a nod, just before he closed the door. I took that to mean he'd had word from either Vinny or Travis.

"How is everyone?" Brooke asked.

"All good here. Is Evelyn definitely coming back for Christmas?" he replied.

"She said she was. I'm looking forward to it. I need to get together with the girls so we can coordinate our diaries," she said.

"Taylor has missed you, she'll be calling as soon as it's morning, I bet."

It was a little under an hour before we arrived home. The gates opened automatically as we approached and security stepped in front of the car. Despite knowing the car, they still checked through the windows before waving the car on. The lights to the house were blazing and I could see Patricia at the front door. She would have ensured the fridge was full and the heat was on.

"Hey, I've missed you," she said, as she pulled Brooke into an embrace.

"We've missed you, too. How are you?"

"We're good, everyone sure missed you at the Old Wives Club. I have so much gossip," she said, mimicking Taylor's accent.

Brooke laughed as she walked into the house with Gerry in tow.

"Any news?" I asked Mack, as we watched Gary park the car.

"Something interesting has come up, and I doubt very much you're going to like it," he said.

"Okay, let's get in."

The sun had long since set and the garden was lit, but it was October and chilly. We walked up the stairs to the living room and while Patricia and Brooke chatted, we made our way to the home office. I closed the door behind us.

"What happened out there?" Mack asked.

I explained that I'd received a plain envelope with just my name written on the front and the *interrogation* of the photographer.

"After a little coercion, he told me who had instructed him to take the photographs," I said.

"Who instructed him?"

"Matteo DeLuca."

Mack stared at me, then frowned.

"Not possible, he's dead."

"I know. I watched him being killed. Someone thinks it's fucking funny to use his name, or…"

"He has a son, or whoever, with the same name," Mack finished. "Why now?"

Matteo had been the man who had instructed the kidnapping of my son. He'd paid a very heavy price for that.

"I don't know why now. I'll arrange a gathering here to see if any other families have an answer."

Matteo's family had been Sicilian. All his businesses had been redistributed to the other families in that region, on the instruction of my father, as a punishment. He'd lost his life, of course, but his family had been weakened so retribution wasn't possible. Or so I thought.

"What do you want me to do?"

"Go through security measures here, Mack, make sure there isn't a weakness anywhere."

It was a waste of time really; Mack was constantly reviewing our security measures. As the children in the family grew older and moved into their own apartments, hooked up with partners, or left for travels abroad, our security measures were constantly evolving to keep up.

I stifled a yawn. I rarely suffered with jet lag, unlike Gerry and Brooke. I guess it was because I never kept regular sleep times, so my body clock was as fucked up as the rest of me.

I checked my watch and at the same time my stomach grumbled.

"So what's this thing I'm not going to like?" I asked.

"There is an organization who wants to buy some of our properties. The interesting part is they are Russian and they want to pay in cash."

I frowned. We dealt with many nationalities but we never dealt in cash, it was too risky and smacked of laundering.

"That's not the part you're not going to like, though," he said.

"Go on."

"The organization is a front, obviously, and I can't find much on them at all. They are seriously underground, other than one name. And the fact I've been able to find this name suggests I was meant to."

"The name is?"

"Volkov."

I stared at him. "Are you sure?" I asked. He nodded.

"That is very interesting. Who is negotiating?"

I didn't deal with the day-to-day running of Vassago anymore, and the team I had around me, now had their own teams. I struggled sometimes to remember names of key workers.

"Richard is dealing with this himself."

"Good. I need to eat. Let's meet again in the morning at the office. Travis will be returning tomorrow, once he's seen Rocco and Evelyn off."

"How are they?" Mack asked, as we walked from the office. "It seems odd not having her around."

"They're good, I'm pleased for her, but yeah, I'll miss not having her here. I don't know what's going to happen there. I don't think Rocco will come here permanently, and it's handy having him in Italy. It means I don't have to be there so much. I'm not sure Brooke is as keen on all the travel, though."

"She did say to Taylor that the novelty had started to wear off a little."

I smiled at him. I wished my wife was as honest with me as she was her friends. I knew it was because she didn't want to upset me. She'd follow me anyway, but I needed to know how she felt about everything I did. Well, everything I let her know that I did.

"Tomorrow then," I said.

Mack walked from the room. I waited until I heard the front door open and close, and then I walked down the stairs to the bedrooms myself. I stood outside a partially open door. I could hear Brooke speaking softly to Gerry who, I imagined, was tucked up in bed.

"Sweetheart, your body is going to change, and when it does so will your moods. It's okay to feel sad, angry, happy, it's okay to feel all those things at once. Your dad and I understand, darling, and we will always love you, no matter how sad or angry you feel. But, right now, this is jet lag. We've flown a long way, we have a different time on the clock, and our bodies can't cope with it. You ignore what Harley says and you come to me if you ever want to ask those questions, okay? Now, settle down, shut your eyes, and see if you can get some sleep. I love you," Brooke said.

"Love you more," Gerry replied. I smiled at the sentiment.

I was about to push open the door when Brooke walked through, she gently pulled the door closed behind her.

"What was that all about?" I asked.

"Harley was teasing Gerry about his mood swings, telling him he's going through puberty."

"He probably is," I said.

"I know, but what does Harley know about puberty? Anyway, Gerry was upset that he'd upset us with his grump. I told him it was jet lag. Which reminds me… Let's go and get a glass of wine. I need to talk to you," she said.

She smiled as she walked past, she reached out and let her hand slide down my arm. I followed her back up the stairs to the kitchen.

"Do you want something to eat?" she asked, as she opened the fridge door.

"I'm hungry, but what do you need to talk to me about first?"

While she poured two glasses of wine, I studied her face. Worry lines crossed her forehead.

"I think it's too much for Gerry at the moment," she said, sliding the glass toward me.

"What is?"

"The traveling. I'd like for us to stay here for a while, he has some real changes coming up, Robert, and I'm worried that he's missing out. He's not settled at school anymore, and you know he hated school but he had a nice circle of friends. I don't think he has those anymore."

It wasn't that I didn't want my son to have a circle of friends, but I was wary of who was in that circle. The smaller, the better, as far as I was concerned.

"We're here for next couple of months, at least. Baby, I see how tired you are; I know you're bored out there and I understand. I need to travel and I need to be with you. Let's enjoy the next couple of months, we have a family Christmas to prepare for, and then we can decide what happens after, is that okay?"

"It's not that I'm bored, well, I am, but this isn't about me. It's about Gerry. I want a little more stability for him. And if I'm also honest, we don't get to spend much time on our own anymore, Robert. I miss that. I miss you. When we are in that villa we have a house full, always. If it isn't security it's family, which is great, but it's never just us anymore."

I reached out and pulled her toward me. She rested against my chest and looked up at me.

"We're nearly there, Brooke. It's all very nearly settled and we can go back to normal," I said.

She chuckled as she wrapped her arms around me.

"There was never, and will never be, a normal where you're concerned. It's okay; I just want to stay home for a little while. If you need to rush off to Italy, you go. We'll be okay here," she said.

I smiled, not trusting myself to speak. I kissed her forehead, choosing not to respond.

"Now, do you want something to eat?" she asked.

"I do. I'm also thinking that I might like to feast on you."

She laughed as she moved away. "Food first, I'm hungry as well."

Brooke laid some meat and bread on the breakfast bar. It was too late to cook a meal and I was happy just to snack. She sat beside me and I refilled her glass. I watched her stifle yawn after yawn. Eventually, I slid her glass away and cupped her chin.

"Go to bed, you look shattered," I said.

"I think I might have to. Come with me?" she asked.

I gently kissed her lips, tasting the wine.

"Soon. I have a couple of things to do, then I'll be down."

She smiled but barely concealed the sigh. I watched her walk away. She smiled one last time as she disappeared down the stairs. I picked up my glass and sipped on my wine.

---

His screams echoed around my mind. I had watched in utter fascination as Rocco slowly sliced from neck to navel. The blood didn't rush, pour, or gush from his skin, it seeped, creating rivers that weaved through his chest hair and down his stomach. The scream escalated as that knife then sliced from nipple to nipple. But it was the tightening in my stomach, a sensation similar to what I felt when I was about to come, at the sight of Lucia, her tears and quiet begging as a bullet ripped through her skull, that had disturbed me the most.

"What the…." I said. I jolted forward and it took me a minute to realize I was sitting on the sofa and I must have dozed off.

Thoughts of Matteo still whirled around my mind and I closed my eyes, taking in a few deep breaths to calm myself.

"What the fuck?" I said, again.

I understood why Matteo was in my mind, but not the sensation I felt as I dreamt of Lucia's killing.

I screwed my eyes closed tight and pinched the bridge of my nose to hope-fully quell the tension headache I could feel brewing. I looked at the empty bottle of wine, the glass with a mouthful of red wine still left in it. I stood and stretched; I needed a coffee. I walked to the kitchen and switched on the machine. While I waited for the coffee, I stood and stared at the memory wall Brooke had created for me. There was no more space left for any more photographs. We'd have to start another wall somewhere. I looked at images of me as a young man with Joe. I smiled at a picture of Travis with his black biker jacket, matching jeans, and studded boots. All he needed was black nail varnish and a little eyeliner and he'd look the rocker I think he was trying to pull off. The problem with Travis was he always looked ten years younger than he was, in that photograph he looked like a pretend rocker. I chuckled quietly.

At the thought of the biker jacket, I knew what I needed to clear my mind. I grabbed whatever coffee had already filtered through; it amounted to half a cup, and walked downstairs. I swapped my shoes for boots, grabbed a jacket, and quietly left the house.

I crossed the drive activating all the security lights, which caused men to appear from the shadows. One called out, I raised my hand to indicate that I was okay. I opened the garage door and standing to one side, unused for a while, was my Ducati. It was probably deemed a classic now, there was certainly a more up-to-date version on the market, but I loved that bike. I wheeled it out, narrowly missing Gary.

"Robert," he said.

"Can you ride a bike, Gary?" I asked, swinging my leg over the saddle.

"I have, nothing that powerful, though."

I looked toward Travis' bike. "Want to go for a ride?"

"I'm going to have to if you are. Although, I'd rather take the Range Rover."

I laughed. Gary was just doing his job but if he wanted to keep up with me, he'd need to take the bike. It was past midnight and I knew the lanes through Great Falls would be empty, but the Range Rover would be much slower.

"Truth time, Gary. I need to clear my head at the moment. I can't sleep; I need to do something I always used to do when life was troubling me." I pushed the button for the engine to come to life and prayed that I wouldn't wake Brooke.

As I slowly drove down the drive, I heard Gary behind. I chuckled doubting Travis would be overly pleased to know someone else was riding his bike. He was very possessive over that machine. I'd often caught him running his hand over the seat or the fuel tank when he thought no one was looking. Security walked from the hut and stood in front of the gate, lights were angled toward me, and once they were satisfied, the gates were opened. I drove through and, for a moment, kept at a low speed as I turned onto the unpaved road. I dodged the holes and kept Gary in my line of sight behind me. I imagined he'd be terrified of damaging the bike.

When we made it off of the gravel road, I opened the throttle. Gary would know where I was headed if he couldn't keep up, and I was sure that he'd do his utmost to.

Was I being reckless? Absolutely, but I needed some space; I needed the solitude to think.

Gary kept a respectable distance when I pulled off the main road and into a parking lot for those that hiked to the falls. I sat astride the bike, just listening to the sound of water. The air was cold, damp, but refreshing. I breathed in deeply, trying to clear my lungs of the humidity of Italy.

I remembered bringing Brooke here when she'd had the misfortune of meeting Joey. We'd sat near the monument and I'd told her all about Joe. Well, I'd told an abbreviated version. There was so much, even after five years together, she didn't know, she'd never know. That added to the guilt and conflict I felt. So much had happened in the past year alone, she'd be fucking terrified if she knew it all. As the merger with my father's businesses had progressed, so the circle of those with knowledge got smaller.

Jonathan had retired, yet he was still my advisor, I decided I'd call upon him and talk through my feelings to see if I could make sense of them, unravel a little. I recognized I was coiled as tight as a spring, I felt it and I needed to unwind a little.

Having made a decision, I climbed back on the bike and gave Gary a small wave as I drove past him. We arrived back at the house together, stored the bikes away in silence, and then I watched him walk to the pool house.

"Gary," I called out after him. He stopped and turned toward me.

"Thanks, I just needed to clear my head. I think, also, that Travis will be building a house in the grounds, maybe you and Pat would like to take the apartment when that happens?"

Gary slowly nodded his head. He looked over to the apartment. "I'll chat to Pat about it, thanks."

Gary and Pat lived in one of my apartment blocks in Columbia Heights. Most of my employees rented my property. The one that Gary and Pat were in wasn't one of the nicest, and bearing in mind how frequently Gary was 'on call' with me now, it made sense to have him closer. Whether Pat would see it that way was another matter, of course. I wondered if we ought to entice Pat to work in our organization.

I walked into the house, closing the front door behind me. I sat on the bottom of the stairs and took off my boots. I hung up my jacket and made my way to the bedroom. Before I entered, I stood by Gerry's door. I peered through the gap and watched him sleep. I chuckled as I recalled Brooke's conversation with him. He was growing up way too fast for my liking.

Brooke was asleep, propped up against pillows and a book had fallen to her side. I picked up the book and closed it, then placed it on her bedside table. I wanted to straighten her neck; she'd be sore as fuck in the morning if she slept the night that way. I slipped off my clothes and climbed in beside her. I threaded my arm under her back and gently slid her down.

"You're cold," she mumbled, not opening her eyes.

"Shush, go back to sleep."

She didn't need telling twice. Within seconds, she was curled onto her side and back to her dreams.

I was dressed and sitting at the breakfast bar with a coffee when Brooke climbed the stairs. It was still early but I had a meeting with the team scheduled.

"Where did you go last night?" she asked, as she kissed my cheek.

"Just for a ride on the bike."

"Do you want more coffee?"

I slid my cup toward her.

"I'm worried about you, Robert. You're not sleeping."

I smiled at her. "Don't. I just have a lot going on right now. I've told you, a couple of weeks and things will settle down a little."

"I'm not sure you're telling me everything, but it's okay. I'm here if you want to talk things through, and if you want some company, wake me up next time. We don't seem to do anything just on our own anymore."

The sound of a car leaving the garage was the distraction I needed. Brooke was right in what she'd said; we didn't spend enough time alone. It was months ago that we'd been out on our own; I needed to rectify that. But my wife was like no other. I couldn't hide much from her anymore. She knew something was troubling me, she wouldn't push for information, and that made me feel guilty. I reached out for her, placing my hand on her cheek.

"Did I tell you today that I loved you?" I asked quietly.

She shook her head. "No, you haven't."

"I love you," I said.

"I know you do. I love you, too. And that was a nice diversion," she said, adding a wink.

She covered my hand with hers and turned her face. She kissed my palm.

"Will you be home in time for dinner?"

"I'll call. I don't know yet. Travis will be home this morning; they flew overnight. I'm sure he'll want a catch up."

"I have lunch with the girls today, and then I have some work to do here this afternoon."

"Okay, I'll send Gary back for you. Text him the time."

I slid from the stool and gave her a brief kiss before I strode to the stairs. I was about to take the first step down to the front door when I hesitated. I looked over to her.

"Maybe we need a couple of days on our own someplace. I just need to…"

"I know, you need a couple of weeks to sort things," she finished for me, except she added a sigh at the end, letting me know it wasn't quite what she wanted to hear.

## Robert - Chapter Seven

I exited the elevator and was immediately met by Gina and Mack. I liked the welcoming committee, especially when a cup of strong black coffee was thrust toward me.

"Thank you, Gina. Mack, everyone here?" I asked, as I walked to my office.

"Yep, downstairs, getting ready."

"Okay. Gina, what do you have for me?"

"Nothing that can't wait. There are two files on your desk. One with messages I've dealt with, but that you might still want to follow up on, and the other with calls and letters that you need to instruct on. I have some documents for you to sign later as well," she said.

I nodded just the once and pushed open my office door. I would never tire of the view as I walked over to the floor-to-ceiling glass windows. D.C. was spread out below me, the White House in the distance. I took a moment to reflect, drink my coffee, before I sucked in a breath and Robert Stone, the businessman, was back.

"First on the agenda. What the fuck is Volkov doing?" I said, as I took my place at the conference table on the floor below my office.

"And a good morning to you, as well," Jonathan said with a laugh.

I gave him a smile and wink. My team, my family, was sat in seats they had occupied for over twenty years now. Prior to that, they had sat around a broken table in a shithole office that Travis and I regularly cleaned.

"You weren't fucking starting without me, were you?" I heard. My brother walked through the door.

"Thought you might catch up on some sleep," I said as he took his seat.

"I'll sleep later. I have news."

"So do we. Richard, want to bring us up-to-date?" I said.

Richard opened his glasses and placed them on his face. I hadn't seen him wear glasses before, and by the way he fiddled with them, they were clearly new. He stared over the frame at me.

"Getting fucking old, my friend," he said.

"I think you *got old* some time ago," Travis replied. Richard was only ten years older than us.

"We got a call a week ago, an agent working on behalf of an organization abroad wanting to buy up some empty apartments. Sean dealt with them initially. There was nothing untoward, nothing to flag suspicion, at first. They were interested in ten apartments in the same block, Project Cable, the one…"

"We know which one is Project Cable," I said. Richard would have given us the fucking coordinates had I not interrupted.

"Of course. Anyway, as I said, nothing suspicious. Agents deal all the time, but Sean handed it over to me when there was no negotiation on cost and they seemed in a rush to complete."

"What do you mean, no negotiation?" Jonathan asked.

"No negotiation. They were willing to pay our advertised price per apartment. For the ten, that's a little over nine million dollars."

Homeowners didn't negotiate. Well, they tried, but they never got far. Corporations or organizations buying property for investment always negotiated. Agents acting on behalf of them negotiated even harder.

"How did the agent check out?" I asked.

"We've dealt with them before, a New York deal. A couple of years ago now, but straight forward, no fuss deals. However, this was different, obviously."

"In what way?" Mack asked.

"As I said, there was no negotiation. They wanted the apartments, their clients wanted a quick deal, and they were willing to pay cash, which was ready to be deposited in a bank of our choice."

I sat back. I knew what was coming, Travis didn't, but I let Richard tell his story.

"I did a little digging on the corporation and came up empty-handed so passed it over to Mack," Richard said.

"I did a little more digging and this is what I've found. Trav, I don't think you're going to like this." Mack slid a folder toward me.

"Tell me," Travis said.

"The corporation name is Global Properties, registered office is in Moscow. The only individual that I can locate as a shareholder for Global Properties is Dimitri Volkov."

He looked up at Travis.

"I don't get that. Why not just call, or something?" Travis said.

"I think I was supposed to find his name butn. And I'm guessing, I was supposed to find his name as security that this isn't a scam. Why your future father-in-law couldn't have just called, is what makes this very strange."

Dimitri Volkov was Katrina's father. He was unable to leave Moscow as he'd been arrested for various crimes. Although not incarcerated, his liberty had been severely stifled. The fact he wasn't in prison, or assassinated, suggested he was still a powerful man.

"Have you ever spoken to him?" Jonathan asked Travis.

"Once. Katrina called him when we were in Italy. She told him we were getting married and she handed the phone to me. I didn't understand a fucking word he said. He spoke in English, but with such a heavy accent it might as well have been Russian. You've done your checks on her, Mack, what did you find?"

"Nothing more that you. Mother still alive and in New York, father probably part of the Russian mafia but unconfirmed. There was a younger brother that died of cancer."

"And that's why I don't like this," Richard said.

"Neither do I. Go back and tell them the apartments are not for sale," I said.

"Hold on, why?" Travis asked.

"This corporation is a front for something else. That's fucking obvious.

They want to pay in cash, no negotiation. That smacks of laundering to me. Not interested. They want to buy those apartments, no problem, but the money trail has to be transparent. Unless your father-in-law wants to speak to me directly, of course," I said.

"He's not my father-in-law yet," Travis said, and I was immediately reminded of his issue back in Italy.

"Okay, sit on that for a little while, see what happens, Richard. Now, let's get to this," I said, opening a second folder and sliding out the photographs I'd received in Italy.

I placed them side by side.

"Rocco believes each one of these pictures was taken from a location he'd killed someone in. He believes this is, possibly, revenge for something he did. We were given a name of the man who wanted the pictures taken. As you know, that man is dead. So, where does that leave us?" I asked. "Matteo's businesses were divided up among the remaining families in Sicily. Enrico, Alberto, and Soli were at a meeting I attended before I came home. Enrico is someone I believe we can trust, but not so much the other two."

"Could one of those be using the name Matteo as a way to freak you out?" Mack asked.

I shrugged my shoulders and sighed. "Alberto, I don't trust and he knows it, but that's just too obvious. Soli? I don't know so much. Perhaps I'll talk to Enrico, he is going to manage the families there while I'm here."

"Do you trust Enrico?" Mack asked.

"Rocco does. They've known each other since they were in their twenties. We have to start with someone," I said.

"In the meantime, security has been assessed. I think we're at the right level already, short of locking those three up, there's not much more we can do. Evelyn will be back in the U.S. soon, right?" Mack asked.

"She's in London right now, back here in a couple of days," Travis said.

"Okay. Let me chat with Enrico and see if we can get some information on Alberto and Soli," I said, gathering up the photographs. "In the meantime, let me know the minute you get contact from the agency on those apartments, Richard."

I had no doubt the agency, or Dimitri himself, would make contact once we'd cut off communication, if they were that desperate to buy them, of course. If we didn't hear another thing, it was our loss. The property side of Vassago had been one of the first to be legitimized many years ago, and I wasn't about to get caught up in any shit, regardless of who was involved. I owed Dimitri Volkov nothing; I'd never met the man, never likely to, either. Just because he was Katrina's father didn't mean we had to deal with him.

The guys left the conference room and I hung back.

"Trav, can I have a word?" I said.

He sat back down beside me.

"Did Katrina say anything to you?" I asked.

"Of course not. She doesn't get to speak to him that frequently. To be honest, I'm not sure she really knows what he does, or did, other than he's not in prison but on some kind of house arrest and has been for years. I think her mother got her out before she was really old enough to understand. I will say, though, she's only spoken to him in front of me that once, and I don't recall her talking to him when we've been at home."

"What do you mean?"

"When she's here, home, D.C., I've never heard her mention that she spoke to him. She talks about calling her mother all the time, but never him. Yet, in Italy, she had no hesitation in calling him."

"Did she use her own cell?"

"No, I got us a couple of throwaways. And, of course, we were on an Italian network."

"If he's under arrest, then it's possible his calls are being monitored. We need to find out what we can about him. There was a reason his name was the only one that came up when Mack did a search on that corporation. I want to know what it is."

"I'll do some digging. What can I tell Katrina?"

"I'll leave that to you. I don't want her to know too much because when we tell them to go fuck themselves, I don't want her, or you, left in an awkward position."

"Will you? Tell them to fuck themselves, that is," he asked.

"Certainly. There's only one reason, in my mind, why there is secrecy, cash, urgency, and that's because there is nine million dollars that needs to be spent, hidden, or cleaned, and it won't fucking be in my company or my bank."

I stood and buttoned up my suit jacket. Travis slowly nodded as he followed me from the room. We stood by the elevators waiting for the next car.

"I told Richard to speak to one of the architects about some drawings for a house," he said.

"That's great news. There so much fucking land, Trav, you can build a house the other side of the chapel and still be close enough if you want to be, of course," I replied.

"Katrina wants for us to live away."

"How do you feel about that?"

"I don't. I'm banking on a fucking amazing drawing of a house to sweet-talk her to coming around," he laughed.

"Bro, if she has any idea who we are, and I think she might, she'll come around. Don't worry about it."

I'd said it a million times before. We were safer as one unit and Katrina, just because she was marrying into my family, didn't really get a say in dividing or separating us. Perhaps it was time for her to be told that.

We took the elevator down one level. Travis headed to the security office and I slowly walked to mine. Gina hovered until I indicated that she could come in. She took the seat opposite my desk.

"How was Italy?" she asked.

"Good, hot for the time of year," I said.

"I need you to sign these letters. There is a senator that seems quite anxious to meet you. He's called a few times, I'm assuming, as it's reelection time, and he wants your support." She sighed, "I've told him that he has to write in to request a meeting, that might put him off for a little while longer."

Gina rambled on, getting me up to speed on things I had no interest in. I needed to either give myself a kick up the ass or get a grip on what was unsettling me.

"Gina, I'm sorry. Can you give me a half hour?" I asked, interrupting her mid-sentence.

"Of course," she replied. She closed her folder and left the office.

I stood and walked around. I stared out the window for ages, long enough for Travis to walk into the room. I guessed he would have seen me on the camera and wondered why I was standing for as long as I had.

"You okay, Bro?" he asked.

"No, Trav. I don't think I am."

He didn't answer; I guess my honesty had taken him by surprise.

"Fancy a hit?" he asked.

Eventually, I turned and nodded. We walked in silence to the elevator and rode down to the basement.

Instead of heading to the changing room, I walked through the gym door. It was empty; the staff wasn't allowed to use it on kids' day. My footsteps echoed on the wooden floor as I walked to the boxing ring at one end of the room. I sat on a bench and smiled. I had some great memories of being in a boxing ring. Not that one, of course, but many others over the years.

"What's wrong, Rob?" Travis asked quietly.

"I don't know. I feel very unsettled right now. Do you remember our days in the old gym?" I said, changing the subject.

"I do. I remember when you put Mack on his ass, it was the talk of the gym and office for weeks," he said with a laugh.

We reminisced for a little while; sadness mixed with warmth flowed through me when I spoke about Joe. Maybe it was because we'd just returned from Italy. Maybe it was all the upheaval and revelations that had been discovered, but I was feeling very nostalgic. I had a yearning for the old days, the old ways, and that surprised me.

"Anyway, I need to get back to work, I guess. Let's go over what we know about these photographs again. Put that to bed and I might feel a little more settled," I said.

We made our way back to my office. I spread the photographs over my desk.

"Three locations. Three murders over thirty years ago. I wonder if it's just coincidence. Rocco can't be sure those pictures were taken from those exact locations, and as much as I agree the one of Brooke was taken from up high, the others really could have been from anywhere," Travis said.

"The question mark is what worries me. I doubt there is any significance in the color pen but, to me, that's telling me he's deciding who to deal with first," I said.

"I agree with that. You know, something has come to me. Who else knows Rocco's story? Could it be that someone is playing us all?"

"I've no idea. I mean, most of those who were around at the time he killed those guys are dead themselves now. Whoever used the name, Matteo, knows us as a family and what we did to him. That ties us all together anyway, since Rocco was the one that actually killed him. So I think this is more likely to be revenge for that and, as you say, someone knows Rocco's life story, so they used those locations to fuck with us," I said.

"Dominic was frightened of him, so whoever this is has kept himself hidden for a while but is powerful, scary even. I mean, Rocco would have…" Travis stopped talking and we stared at each other as realization hit.

"He's not in Italy," I said.

"He's American, maybe," Travis said.

"So maybe he's here and not there after all. Dominic took the pictures after being instructed to by this Matteo. He didn't say that Matteo was ever there, did he?" I asked, trying to recall, word for word, the conversation.

"No, he just said he'd kill him, nothing more. That means fuck all."

I picked up the phone and called through to Mack. I asked him to come and join us. When he did, I filled him in on our theory.

"Where is Dominic now?" Mack asked.

"We let him go. I wanted him to go back with bruises to his face and then see what transpired."

"If whoever asked him to take the photos is here, that was a waste of time, really," he said with a chuckle.

"My mind was on other things, more important things. I didn't take too much notice of him or what he said, other than wanting a name," I said. I wasn't overly happy with his comment.

"Okay, can Vinny pick him up again? Ask him if he has ever met Matteo, and why he thinks he'll kill him?"

"I'll get on that," Travis said.

Annoyance flowed through me. I'd been too distracted by Travis and the comments he'd made to focus on Dominic. For sure, I'd punched him, and I guessed that was more out of frustration than anything else. I hadn't been on the ball; otherwise I would have been asking the same questions Mack had.

A thought ran through my mind. There had only been one individual that had an idea who Gerry's kidnappers were. Although Matteo had been manipulated by Lucia and helped by Paul, Franco understood a saying that had been used and how that related to Matteo's family. He knew the family way more than any of us. I reached for my phone to call him.

'Franco, it's Rob," I said when he answered the call.

"Roberto, it's good to hear from you. Did you remember the time difference?" he asked, or perhaps it was a rebuke.

"I did, I'm sorry. Is it late?" I asked, checking my watch.

He chuckled. "I'm having a coffee before I retire."

"I wanted to ask you a question about Matteo's family. What are they doing now?"

"He had a daughter, an illegitimate one. She is still in Italy, I believe. He had a son, who took over his father's diluted business. He isn't a problem, or hasn't been until now. Is there anything I should know?"

I told him about the photographs and Dominic, and the fact I had been given that name.

"I wish you'd come to me earlier with this. I might have been of use," he said.

A layer of guilt was added to the many other layers I carried on my shoulders.

"I didn't want to worry you, Franco. I wasn't sure what it all meant, and to be honest, I just wanted to get the women home."

"I can understand that. Now tell me about this Dominic. I don't know of a Dominic in the village."

I cursed myself for a second time in not consulting Franco. He knew everyone, and no matter that he had lived in America for many years, he was a highly regarded man in our village.

"From his look, Dominic could have been from Northern Italy," Travis said. I stared at him. "Light eyes, they have blue eyes, fair hair, don't they?" he added.

"Travis just said something interesting, he had light-colored eyes, possibly blue. Fair hair."

"Ah, maybe Northern then. The closer to the Swiss border, the fairer the hair and eyes."

"Do you know any families that far up?" I asked.

He took a deep breath in and released it slowly.

"Not really. I'm sure there are some nowadays, of course. I could ask around."

"Whoever it is knows what we did to Matteo. I don't believe this is Matteo's family. I think they used the name just for effect."

"I agree, if this had anything to do with Matteo's family, I'd know about it, Rocco would know about. This is from outside, Roberto."

"We think maybe whoever asked Dominic to do this also knew Rocco.

The locations are relevant."

"I wish you'd shown me, Roberto," Franco said, sighing.

"How about I copy them over to Vinny. He can bring them down to you."

"Yes, do that now. Let me look, and why are the locations relevant?"

I explained Rocco's theory, agreed to send them immediately, and promised to call Franco again the following day.

"Fuck," I said quietly as I replaced the handset.

"We should have consulted him, shouldn't we?" Travis said. I nodded.

"Yes, what we did was a knee-jerk reaction and that's not good."

"Send those over to Vinny," I added, sliding the photographs to Mack.

"What do we do now?" Travis asked.

I consulted my watch, "I'm going to head home. I think I need to take my wife on a date, she's missing time with just me."

"Want me to watch Gerry?"

"He's grumpy as fuck, and I'm sure you're jet-lagged and wanting an early night, don't you?"

"No, he's good. He can be grumpy as fuck with Harley. It's times like this I sure miss Evelyn," he added with a laugh.

Not only had Evelyn been our resident housekeeper, a permanent child sitter; she was the master at dealing with grumpy boys.

"She'll be here soon enough," I said.

I sent a text to Brooke.

**Dinner, 6pm, you and me. R xx**

**Sounds good, I'll look forward to it,** she replied.

Travis left with Mack and I got on with some long overdue work. I signed the documents Gina had placed on my desk after a scan through each one. I went through each slip of paper that detailed a call, screwed most up, and threw them in the bin. I then started to look through the long list of emails I had mounting up. Gina would attend to my emails, normally, but these were sent to my private account. The majority was junk and quickly deleted, one or two were asking for donations, I forwarded those to Gina to be dealt with, and when I'd had enough, I logged off.

Brooke would often laugh at my lack of technological enthusiasm. I even hated the basic cell phone I carried. One of the perks in having the connections I had, was also knowing how easy it was to track someone. I'd sit and look at the camera on my laptop, although it was covered over, and wondered just who the fuck was watching me.

Over the years, Travis had had loads of fun fucking with the system. We had discovered a bug in the office one time. He was able to hack into it, fed cheap porn back to wherever it was being recorded. He chuckled for days about that one.

"Hi, you're home early," Brooke said, as she stepped out of the shower and wrapped a towel around herself.

"Yep, where's Gerry?"

"Already with Katrina. He wanted to play with Harley because he's got a new Xbox something or the other."

"I don't like him on those games, I saw one the other day."

"He's a boy, there's nothing too nasty. I'm sure Katrina, of all people, would monitor what they watch."

I watched Brooke sit at her dressing table. She had tied her hair to the top of her head, not wanting it to get wet, I guessed. She ran her fingertips under her eyes as if wanting to straighten out the faint lines. I walked behind her.

"You're so beautiful," I said, quietly.

"So are you, Robert. Inside and out."

"You might have to keep reminding me of that." I laughed, as I slipped off my jacket and slid the tie from the collar of my shirt.

She watched me, watching her, as I pulled my shirt over my head. I saw her moisten her lips as I threaded my fingers in her topknot. I gently teased her head to one side and ran my tongue down the side of her neck, inhaling the scent of her skin as I did.

"Mr. Black-eyes is with us," she mumbled.

"That's a new one, what does it mean to you?" I asked, as I kissed along her shoulder.

"Either you are angry, or sexually aroused. Your eyes darken with both. I'm hoping it's the latter."

"I'm always sexually frustrated when I'm near you." I grazed my teeth over her shoulder.

I felt her reach up and grip the back of my hair. She tugged and I chuckled. She was already sore in that spot. I ran my tongue over the area, gently blowing on her skin to raise it. I reached forward, slipping the towel from her chest and cupped a breast. Her erect nipple grazed my palm, and I felt her take a deep breath before a gentle moan left her lips. I kissed back up her neck, taking her earlobe into my mouth. I pulled my head back and when she opened her eyes, I gave her a wink and walked into the bathroom.

"Bastard," she called after me.

"Been called a lot worse, baby," I replied with a laugh.

By the time I was showered, she had on the fucking sexiest, midnight blue-colored lace underwear; high-heeled shoes, and was applying her lipstick. My erect cock pushed through the towel at my waist. She stood with one hand on her hip until I was close enough for her to reach forward and pull the towel away. She wrapped her hand around my cock and squeezed before sliding it, just the once, slowly from tip to base and back up again. As she looked at me, she started to lower to a crouch, I parted my legs slightly and closed my eyes. I felt her tongue run up my shaft and swirl around the tip. Then she stood and walked away.

"Bitch," I whispered.

"Been called a lot worse, baby," she replied with a laugh.

"It's okay, you know we have an empty house. I'm going to fuck you wherever I want tonight."

"I look forward to it, now get dressed."

I watched her slide a dress over her head. She pulled her hair to one side and without needing to be asked, I walked to her and raised the zipper. She slid her hands down her sides, smoothing out the material. She turned and held her hands out.

"Like?"

"Love," I said.

"So you won't rip it then?" she said.

"I didn't say that." I walked into my closet to dress.

"I just bought this and it's a one off. I'm going to pour a glass of wine, do you want one before we go?"

"Sure, why not."

I heard her make her way upstairs as I selected a shirt and trousers. I grabbed a fresh tie and jacket and dressed.

Brooke had two glasses of red wine sitting on the countertop by the time I joined her. She slid one over to me and raised her glass.

"A toast to our date," she said. I clinked my glass against hers.

We'd taken no more than a couple of sips before the lights of the car swept across the living room.

"Shall we?" I asked, standing and taking her hand in mine.

We walked down to the front door and out to the waiting car.

---

The club was busy as we walked into the foyer. We were immediately shown through the restaurant and, as usual, I was stopped multiple times by diners. Brooke kept her hand on my arm, smiled, and greeted people she knew. When she could feel I'd grown bored of businessmen or politicians disturbing my evening, she gently squeezed my arm and excused us. Our table was in an alcove, kept specifically for us. The waiter pulled out her chair and she sat.

"You were very well-behaved there," she said with a smirk.

I raised my eyebrows. "I'll make sure not to be next time."

She laughed as she picked up a menu. I ordered wine and a bottle of water from the hovering waiter.

"Tell me about your day?" I asked.

"I met with Taylor for lunch. She said Patricia isn't doing too well at the moment, and she's worried for her. Patricia didn't mention it when we arrived home and I didn't notice anything wrong. Did you?"

"Jonathan said it was her hip playing up but you know her, she'd play it down and be annoyed if we were all discussing something she didn't deem important," I said with a laugh.

"I'm just annoyed with myself that I missed it."

"Maybe you should encourage her to visit a doctor. I know Jonathan has tried, but she may listen to you. They're all getting old and I guess I've only just noticed it, really."

"Maybe that's part of why you feel unsettled. The people you had surrounded yourself with for so long are now taking a back seat, the younger generation are coming through, and you have to go through that process of trust again," Brooke said. I raised my eyebrows at her not wanting to acknowledge how right she was.

The waiter showed me the bottle of wine before pouring a little into my glass. I sniffed before taking a sip, and then nodded my consent for him to pour. Brooke lifted her glass to her lips and sighed.

"I don't know that she'll listen to me if she isn't listening to anyone else," she added.

"Try, for me, will you?"

She smiled at me. "For you, anything."

"Anything?"

"Within reason," she said with a laugh.

I reached over and threaded my fingers through hers. I didn't often do public displays of affection, but Brooke always grounded me. I needed her touch like I needed air to breathe at times.

"Are you okay?" she asked, as I knew she would.

"Can't I hold my wife's hand now?" I replied with a smile.

"Anytime, I just want to be sure you're okay."

"It's all good. I've missed this," I said, quietly.

Brooke could have come back with her cutting wit. Not only did I avoid public displays of affection, it had taken me a long time to convey my feelings to her. We might have been together for a few years, but it was something I still had to work on.

"So have I. You've been so busy lately…" Her sentence trailed off and as much as she forced the smile, I could hear the sadness in her voice.

"I've neglected you, haven't I?"

"You've done what you've needed to do. I guess…I guess I don't feel as settled because we're always on the move. I know you won't like this, but next time you fly to Italy, I'd like to stay here."

It was on the tip of my tongue to deny her that request. I kept that tongue firmly rooted in my mouth, for the moment.

"I love it out there, I really do. And I love spending time with Evelyn, but when I'm home, I realize how much I miss it," she added.

"Let's talk about that when we have to. For the next couple of months, at least until the new year, I'm staying put," I said.

Brooke wanted me to order for her while she visited the restroom. I only had to glance over to the maître d' who, whenever I visited was packing a revolver, for him to subtly follow her. She'd be seriously pissed off if she knew I had her followed to the ladies' but I wasn't taking any chances.

"Mr. Stone, it's good to see you. May I?" Senator Hunter stood beside my table with his hand on Brooke's chair.

"No, you may not. My wife will be sitting there as soon as she returns, and I'd rather she wasn't left standing. That would be considerably rude, would you not agree?"

He bowed his head slowly, not in deference but agreement, I hoped. I stood and he held out his hand.

"My apologies for interrupting your evening. I left a call at your office, I was hoping we could talk."

"About what?" I asked, knowing exactly what his call had been about.

"I thought it might be nice to meet. We have some exciting bills to present to Congress that you'd find beneficial. I wanted to check on your support to the party."

"I don't get involved in politics, Senator, as you well know."

He chuckled. He was an arrogant fucker, like most politicians, slimy as well.

"It's not so far removed for your world, Mr. Stone."

"And you're aware of *my world*, are you?" I wasn't sure I liked his comment.

"Business, was all I meant, business. The party would be overjoyed to know they have your support."

"Then the party will have to be disappointed, I'm afraid."

I watched Brooke as she was escorted back across the restaurant. I leaned forward a little.

"Now, if you don't mind, my wife and I would like to enjoy a private meal. If you want to talk *shop*, Senator, don't fucking do it on my very limited downtime."

I plastered a smile on my face as Brooke was led back to her seat. I glared at the senator until he stepped away.

"What did he want?" she asked, as she placed her napkin over her lap.

"Some bullshit about wanting my support."

She laughed. "Let me guess, you told him you don't do politics?"

"Baby, I do you, I do my work, but that's all. That lot on Capitol Hill can go fuck themselves, for all I care."

I had no idea what the senator actually wanted. I didn't care for his party, or any of them to be honest. Years ago, he would have been sitting just inside my back pocket, but I had no need for that. He wasn't high enough up the food chain for me to worry about. He might have been a senator, but he didn't wield the power he thought he did.

As I'd said, I didn't do politics, but I did do politicians when it benefited me.

Brooke and I ate, we chatted about her day, and we talked about Gerry. I loved to watch her when she spoke of our son. She came alive; a protective fierceness glinted in her eyes, exactly as a mother's should. It hadn't been that long ago that she'd longed to birth a child; it wasn't to be. As much as I'd have loved to father that child for her, we were content with just Gerry. I had no doubt he'd be a handful as he grew older, though.

"Do you want dessert?" I asked, once our dishes had been cleared from the table.

"I do. Perhaps not here though, I'm sure we'd be arrested. Do you know what I'd like to do? Something we haven't done for years."

"Tell me."

"Let's drive out to the falls. We haven't just sat and talked or watched the stars for a long time."

"We talk," I said.

"Not really. We're always surrounded by security, and I understand, I do. I just don't seem to get you to myself without interruption anymore."

I stared at her. There wasn't anything I could say, she was right but to argue that would also mean to tell her why. My life since Rocco was very different to the life I'd spent years cultivating. I'd sworn I'd given up on a life of crime before Brooke, but I was very much back in the middle of it. In fact, more so, since most of what Joe did was minor compared to Rocco.

I took her hand and encouraged her to stand. I led her from the restaurant. At the sight of us, Gary had the rear door open. I gently pulled him to one side.

"Give me your gun," I said. He stared at me.

"Brooke and I need a little time alone."

"I don't think…"

"I know, but my wife needs this and what she needs, she gets."

"I'm not giving you my gun, I'm sorry. But there's a spare in the trunk. I can't do my job if I don't have the tools," he said.

I walked Brooke around the car to the passenger side. I opened the door for her and she climbed in, giving me a broad smile. I closed the door and returned to the driver's side.

"Mr. Stone, I don't like this. Can you at least tell me where you're going?"

"The falls. Speak to Luigi, he'll have a car. I'll wait ten minutes or so before we leave."

He walked to the rear of the car and opened the trunk. It contained a small metal box and I knew, spare firearms. He checked one before handing it, subtly, to me. I wasn't wearing a holster, so slipped it into the pocket inside my jacket.

Gary wouldn't leave the sidewalk. He waved to Luigi, who left his post as front of house in the club. I watched them chat and then Luigi reached into his pocket for a set of keys. He pressed the fob and the lights of a car a couple up flashed.

"I'm following, Mr. Stone. You'd be fucking pissed if something happened and I wasn't there. So would I," Gary said, and the fact he'd used my full name meant he was serious.

I smiled, it was the first time I think he'd stood up and spoke his mind. He was as protective of Brooke as I was and I nodded. I admired him for his stance. He waited until I got behind the wheel and closed the door. The glass was bulletproof and through it I could see the anxiety cross his face. He half sprinted to the car he'd use to follow us.

"Are we in trouble?" Brooke asked, with a giggle.

"I think we are. He's not pleased. We might be able to escape, but he will follow us."

"I don't mind that, I just want a little time without worry about people overhearing us."

I started the car and pulled away from the sidewalk. As I did, Gary was immediately on my tail.

Brooke reached over and took my hand.

"Do you remember that day you took me to the falls on your bike?"

"I do. We'd escaped that day as well."

"I miss those days. Well, I don't miss *those* days, but I miss the days when it wasn't as complicated."

"Are you unhappy?" I asked. She turned sharply to face me.

"No. You don't think that, do you? I wanted an hour of just us. I know we have the house to ourselves, but it never really is. I hear them prowling around outside and…I don't know. I just wanted to play hooky, isn't that what you say?"

"No idea, I was born in England, remember?" I laughed.

I hadn't driven a car in ages, but I loved the feel of the wheel in my hand and the power under my foot. We made our way out of the city and I hoped that Luigi's car had a decent engine under the hood. As we hit the more rural roads, I slammed my foot on the gas.

Brooke screamed and then laughed as the car shot forward. I checked the rearview mirror and noticed the gap widen behind. I wasn't being fair to Gary, who was probably on the phone to Mack and Travis organizing a backup should I lose him. I slowed down a little.

I pulled off the road onto a small lane that took us to a parking area on top of a hill. As we climbed from the car, I pulled the revolver from my pocket and tucked it in the waistband of my trousers then untucked my shirt to cover it. I slid off the jacket. Brooke didn't have a coat, so I placed it around her shoulders. We didn't walk anywhere, just rested against the front of the car and looked out. In front of us were waterfalls at full force because of the time of year. We didn't speak at first; I pulled her in front of me so her back rested on my chest. I wrapped my arms around her, keeping her warm.

"This is nice. I feel like I can breathe," she said, quietly.

"Why can't you breathe, Brooke?" I asked. I felt her shrug her shoulders.

"Talk to me, baby." I said.

"The last few months have been such a whirlwind, travel, new people, more security, secrecy."

She turned in my arms to look up at me.

"I love you and I'd follow you anywhere, but it's just been a little exhausting. I know I said I didn't want to know anything, but it makes me anxious. I guess, I still need a little time to adjust. I don't like walking in the garden and having the sound of footsteps behind me. I feel like every word I speak, I'm being overheard, listened to. It all sounds so paranoid, doesn't it?"

I sighed. "Brooke, a lot has changed, but it will settle down. I promise you that. After...what happened, I can't take any risks with you or Gerry. I know I'm suffocating you, but give me some time as well. I won't compromise on security, but I don't want you to feel this way, either."

She smiled at me, she knew I'd never lessen up with the security issue, and this wasn't the first time she'd felt this way.

"I know, and I love you for that. I want to ask you one thing. Have you ever sat down, taken some time to reflect on what has happened to you?"

"I don't do reflection," I said and then winced. "Maybe that's not accurate. I have been thinking, but it's all a mess in my mind right now. When I've got it straight, we can talk again."

"You're very unsettled back here, aren't you? I see such a difference in you when we're in Italy, and I think that's what scares me."

"Why does it scare you?" I asked.

"Because you'd live there tomorrow if you could, and I think you know I'd struggle with that."

I tightened my arms around her.

"This is all talk about things that might not happen and which are way in the future. We're all unsettled, fuck me, Brooke, we're entitled to be. It's been a whirlwind few months. I want us to have a nice family Christmas, and then we can worry about the future when we get to it."

She laughed gently, knowing I'd shut down a conversation I wasn't ready to have. She rose up on her tiptoes.

"Did I tell you today that I loved you?" she asked, using my words.

I kissed her gently on the lips. "No, you can tell me now if you want," I said.

She laughed, "I love you, Robert. I think Gary is probably having a heart attack right now, so shall we be grown-ups and go home?"

"I guess we ought to. Come on."

We climbed back into the car, and I winced as I remembered the gun in my pants. It had dug into my back. I reached around and pulled it free, depositing it in the pocket in the door. I raised my hand to Gary as we passed and I drove slowly back to the house.

"That was fun, irresponsible, and I'll apologize to Gary," Brooke said, when we'd pulled up in front of the garage doors.

"You don't need to apologize to anyone. I think we both needed just five minutes to *breathe* as you said."

"Thank you."

I didn't want her to thank me for taking her to dinner and then granting her wish for a few minutes alone with me. It stung that she felt she had to. I picked up her hand and kissed her knuckles.

"How about dessert?" she whispered.

Dessert was extremely satisfying and as Brooke lay sleeping beside me, I climbed from the bed. I pulled on some jeans and walked upstairs. Knowing it was probably the worst thing for my insomnia, I ground some coffee beans and filled the percolator. The room was mainly in darkness, just the under counter lighting gave a glow over the open plan space. Once my coffee was brewed, I poured a cup and walked to the windows. I stood and sipped on the rocket fuel strength while I looked out. Small lights lined the driveway from the gates to the house. I could see the security hut lit up, and every now and again the red embers of a cigarette would be visible.

I left my spot by the window and walked to my office. Sitting in a new envelope were the three photographs. I pulled them out. It was the red question mark on the back of each one that had my adrenalin spiked.

I took a plain piece of paper from a pile beside the printer and I wrote what I knew.

*Matteo De Luca – dead*

*Known family – daughter: illegitimate, might have grievances. Son not a problem according to Franco*

*Dominic is possibly Northern Italian – maybe there is someone masquerading as Matteo there*

*Three locations – Rocco killed Ben in the village, Sal in villa, Lou in the apartment*

The more I read my words, the more convinced I became it had nothing to do with Matteo or his family. Like Franco had said, any unrest and he or Rocco would have known about it long before it presented itself.

That left us with the long shot that, just because Dominic was possibly Northern Italian, so was the imposter. My mistakes in not asking the right questions were eating me up inside. I rarely fucked up. I could blame Travis all night, but the fact was, I didn't do enough to get the information I needed. I only hoped Franco would be able to learn what I had missed. I sent a text message.

**Vinny, I want you to find Dominic again. Bring him to the office and leave him with Franco.**

I didn't expect an answer immediately. I also sent a message to Franco, letting him know what I had instructed Vinny to do. I tried hard not to think about the fact Dominic was long gone. I slammed my palm down on my desk. I needed to be in Italy. I needed to be at home.

"Fuck this shit," I said, and then stood. I wasn't used to being so far away from a problem.

I wondered if I could get Brooke back to Italy, even if just for a week, but then shook my head. It was a stupid idea at that time. I would have to go and leave her behind. But then the thought we'd had earlier surfaced. Whoever this 'Matteo' was might be in the U.S. My frustration grew. I left the office needing to walk to calm the thoughts whirling in my mind. I paced the living room, walking alongside the glass frontage. I contemplated turning on some music, but there were speakers all around the house, and I wasn't sure which were switched on or off. I didn't want to be fumbling to silence sound at…I checked my watch. It was nearing one in the morning and I had an early start to come.

I walked downstairs and gently opened the bedroom door. Brooke was asleep, as I expected her to be. I cursed myself for allowing the insomnia to take control, for my ability to clear my mind easily to have left me, temporarily, I hoped. I lay on the bed and closed my eyes, hoping I could just take some deep breaths and focus my mind on one thing.

It was Joe that came to mind. The early years of sitting in his garden room and chatting, and the later years when he was poorly and he'd handed the business over to me. I heard his voice in my head, counseling me, and I was too frightened to open my eyes for fear of losing the memory. I needed it; I needed him. The loss that hit me was physical and it took my breath away.

It hit me then. The unsettledness I felt wasn't the overload of work; it wasn't the having to be in two countries. It was the fact I'd had Joe as a father for so many years, and then I'd discovered Rocco, my biological father. I felt guilt, as if I was betraying Joe in some way by accepting Rocco. I knew I had no choice, of course, and I knew Joe would be pleased for me, had he still been around. I needed to reconcile my feelings and I knew of a place I could do that.

The following morning I was up earlier and out long before Brooke woke. I knew she'd be upset about that. She liked to see me off each morning, but she was still getting over her jet lag, and I needed to be someplace before I headed into the office. Travis met me on the drive.

"Ready?" he said.

I nodded as I climbed into the rear of the car. I looked out the window as we cleared the gates and drove down the lane.

"How are you doing?" I asked Travis.

"Okay, better now we're home, to be honest. I don't know what was wrong with me out in Italy, I guess it all got a little too much for a while."

"Did you speak with Katrina about building a house?"

"I did, she was hesitant, said something about me not wanting to separate or some physcobabble. I told her that was the plan, no argument."

I chuckled. "She'll come round, don't worry."

We drove into Colombia Heights, slowing past some of our many apartment blocks.

"It's sure different to when we first came here, isn't it?" Travis said, as we slowed at our destination. "Ready?" he added.

I opened the car door and slid out. I stood looking up at the building that held so many memories for so many people. We walked around the side and along the gravel path. We came to a halt at a grave.

"Do you feel guilty that we don't visit that often?" Travis asked.

I slowly shook my head. "No. I don't think we need to be beside his grave to think about him."

"Why are we here now then?"

"I don't know, Trav. I just needed to today."

For a moment we stood in silence. Travis bent down to pluck a weed from around the base of the headstone. I just read, and then reread, the inscription.

"I feel guilty. That man there was my father for a long time and now I have another. I'm not sure how to deal with that," I said quietly.

Travis looked up at me. He slowly stood but didn't speak.

"I think Rocco would like for me to acknowledge him more as my father, but I don't seem to be able to. I respect the man, but I can't shift the 'father thing' from Joe to him. I don't know how to explain that."

"Just the same way as you have now," Travis replied.

"He refers to me as his son and I publicly call him Rocco. I wonder how he feels about that."

"Rob, I doubt he's expecting you to fall into the role of his son any more than he's expected to fall into the daddy role. I mean, that's a fucking lot of allowance he has to catch up on, isn't it?"

I chuckled, grateful that Travis could always lighten my mood slightly.

"I wonder what he thinks about Rocco's return, and whether he can see how happy Evelyn is?" I said.

"Honestly, I think it was a pretty shitty thing of him to do, to keep Rocco a secret from Evelyn."

I shrugged my shoulders; I wouldn't completely disagree with him.

"I guess, for a long time, he had no choice. It was to protect his family, but I'm not sure I would have done the same thing."

We stepped away from the grave and to the small bench on the path where we sat. There was a definite chill in the air and I saw Travis shiver beside me. My internal thermostat was set higher than the average person, I was sure. I could be out in a T-shirt in October and not feel the cold.

"Why don't you talk to Rocco about all this?" Travis asked.

"Maybe it's still too soon. I haven't met his children yet, and I wonder what the fuck they are thinking. One minute they have each other, the next there is an older sibling."

"His daughter is excited to meet you, according to Evelyn."

'That may be the case, but I'm not sure how I feel about meeting them, and that makes me feel...I don't know."

"Normal. It makes you feel normal, Rob. Fuck me, we've lived a life of not knowing if we, you specifically, have family, whether they are alive, coming for us, or whatever. You haven't taken one minute to sit down and absorb everything that has gone on, have you? You've just shelved it and thrown yourself into the task."

"Brooke said something similar."

I stood and smoothed down the front of my pants, I walked over to the headstone and crouched.

"Joe, I'll figure it out, but if you have any advice for me, I'd sure appreciate it," I said. I raised my fingertips to my lips and transferred that kiss to his name.

We drove into the office and straight to the boardroom for a meeting.

---

Franco was on video link, something he wasn't particularly keen on.

"Roberto, can you see me? Why am I in a small box?" he said.

"Franco, it's all fine. Just talk as if we are sitting in the same room as you," I said.

He huffed and raised a coffee cup to his lips.

"Elvira makes a good cup of coffee," he said with a smirk.

"She sure does. Now, what did you manage to discover?" I asked, wanting to get to the point.

"Okay, Dominic is long gone. He was seen arriving in the village the same day as he asked the boy to deliver the photographs, but no one can recall him being here before. No one knows him, or any family related to him. He confirmed to you that he had taken the photos, didn't he?"

I nodded. "Yeah, he did. Could he have been lying? Covering up for someone else, maybe?"

"That I can't answer. What I can confirm, is there are no families in Northern Italy that would be involved in this. I have spoken to a few contacts, most of the crime is by the Albanians," he spat the word, as if highly offended by the nationality.

Internally, I echoed his sentiment. I hated the Albanian criminals: they had no morals, no ethics, and no code. They were primarily involved in prostitution and child trafficking. They were the scum of the earth as far as I was concerned.

"So the Northern link is a no-go really?" I asked.

"I don't think there is any real connection, just coincidence that Dominic happens to be from there, if he really is, of course."

"So where does this leave us?" I asked.

"For now, back at square one. Roberto, you know you didn't get enough information from him for us to work with this. I think that we will have to wait to see what happens next, unfortunately."

Only Franco could chastise me, and only because he was so much older and I respected him. I didn't reply, obviously.

"Could this 'Matteo' be here?"

"Maybe, but I doubt it. I don't see any value in taking photographs of the girls in Italy, when it could have been done so easily there. And remember, whoever instructed for these photos to be taken knew of Rocco's history to link the locations. That has to be an Italian."

"You don't think it's just a coincidence?" Mack asked.

"No, I don't."

Franco sat back and sipped on his coffee. I could see a shadow in the background and eventually Vinny came into view.

"Mr. Stone, can I add something?"

"Of course."

"The kid was paid ten euros to deliver the envelope, that's a lot of money for a kid in this village. He was just playing when he was asked to cycle up to the gate. It was the kid that remembered what Dominic looked like and what car he was driving. The car was out of place, a brand new hire car. No one in the village, other than you, has a brand new car, most don't drive full stop. That's how we were able to intercept him as he was leaving. He had a holdall of camera equipment on the back seat. It's the camera equipment that had me thinking."

"About what?" Travis asked.

"If he worked for a family, would he be a photographer in his spare time? That wasn't the kind of thing you'd take on a holiday, it was professional gear. Could he just have been employed by someone?"

"Why would he have thought he'd be killed if he divulged the name?" I asked.

"I don't know, but it just seems strange to me. Maybe it's nothing," he said before stepping behind Franco and sitting in a vacant chair.

"Dig some more, Franco. There's more to Dominic, and maybe Vinny has a point, but he knew who paid him, who sent him, and he's scared of them. So, maybe he's not part of a family, but he sure knows one," Mack said.

We said goodbye and I chuckled as Franco complained about modern technology before Vinny leaned over to cut off the call.

"So I guess we are still no further ahead," I said.

No one had anything more to add. It wasn't often we were stumped like this. Dominic seemed to have snuck under our radar both before and after delivering that envelope. I didn't like that at all.

Something started to niggle at the back of my mind. I ran my hand through my hair, and rubbed at my temples, hoping to bring whatever it was to the forefront. I watched some of the guys rise from their chairs and leave the room, readying themselves for their day. Jonathan stayed put, as did Travis and Mack.

"What's bothering you, Rob?" Jonathan said.

He had a tone of voice that was instantly calming. There was a reason he had been Joe's consigliere and my advisor. It wasn't that he had the best advice in most cases, it was that he had a calming manner about him.

"Something, it's just out of reach," I replied and closed my eyes.

Jonathan didn't interrupt me, he sat in silence. Travis fidgeted and I wanted to tell him to either leave or sit still.

I placed my palm on the table.

"This isn't an outsider. This is someone inside, Jonathan. Someone close to home, a member of our family."

"Tell me why you think that?" he asked.

"No one saw this coming. It isn't a disgruntled family, otherwise Rocco or Franco would have heard about it. Rocco is so fucking powerful in Italy, no one would have done this without another tipping him off. But if it was one of us, how easy would that have been?" I wanted to fucking laugh.

"That's why Dominic was so scared. It's why he knew that name, but what about those locations?" Travis asked.

"When I say *our* family, I mean his. Ours now, of course."

"What's happening to Rocco's guys?" Jonathan asked.

"Alex and Mario are in charge in my absence. Well, that's when Rocco finally steps down," I said with a sigh.

"You don't see him doing that, do you?"

"No," I said with a chuckle. "But him staying in Italy will suit us. It means I don't have to travel back and forth so much."

"Rob, what do you want to do?" Jonathan asked.

There was a period of silence. The one thing I admired most about Jon was his ability to know the answer, yet tease it out of me at the same time. It was as if he was able to plant his idea in my mind and coax it forward.

"I think we need to reassess all the guys in Rocco's family, without him, or them knowing, of course."

"Will he be pissed with that?" Travis asked.

"Maybe, but I don't want him to react; he is still so fucking hotheaded. He's an *act before he thinks* type of man. I'll smooth it over with him when he needs to know."

I had met with Mario and Alex many times, I trusted my instincts more than anything else, and my instinct was telling me they were safe. I had nothing to worry about where those two were concerned. They had been with Rocco from the beginning and instrumental in his rise through that family.

"We'll start a little investigating, Rob. We've upped security, I don't think there is much more we can do until we know what level of threat we are at," Mack said.

That was the most infuriating thing. We didn't know the enemy or what those pictures actually meant. It could be something; it could be someone just trying to cause a little trouble. It was never 'nothing' though.

Mack and Travis left the room, leaving Jonathan and myself alone. I buzzed for Gina to bring us some fresh coffee.

"How are things with you?" I asked.

I missed having Jonathan around.

"Patricia isn't too good. Her hip is bad but she won't do anything about it. She seems to think she has to be on her feet all day to care for me," he said with a laugh.

"Has she seen a doctor?"

"Of course, he wants her to have a replacement, but that means a hospital stay and time out of her busy schedule. She simply can't fit it in right now," he said, mimicking his wife.

I laughed. Patricia was the first of the wives and around before my time. She was the mother hen, as Brooke had called her, and I admired her greatly. I hated the fact we were all getting a little older.

Gina brought in a fresh pot of coffee, and we fell silent while she gathered a tray of dirty cups. I refreshed Jonathan's and mine while I waited for her to leave.

"It's someone on the inside, Jon," I said, pushing the photographs across the table.

"Yep, that's my instinct as well. I can't be as confident it's someone from Rocco's side as you are, though."

"What makes you think that?"

He sighed. "Rocco's family, their methods, everything about them is so very different to us, Rob. They are the fucking *mafia*," he said with a laugh.

I frowned at him.

"They are the *let's not fuck around* type. If they wanted to send a message, would it have been something so obscure as three photographs of three women with three red question marks? I don't think so. If they wanted to send a message, I doubt it would have been a threat to the women, it would have been a bullet to someone's head."

I stared at him as I sipped my coffee.

"You have a very valid point there."

He leaned forward to pick up the first photograph, it was of Evelyn.

"This, you think, is taken from your boundary wall, near that outbuilding. A boundary, which is regularly patrolled in the middle of the day, from a distance where he could have easily been spotted. Either you have a fucking shit team out there, or it wasn't noticed because it wasn't out of place."

"I have a fucking shit security team here, as well, if it takes my consigliere to think that up and not them," I replied, cursing not only Mack and Travis but myself as well.

I glanced up at the camera in the corner, so well concealed most wouldn't notice it. Everything that went on in this room, and each floor of my office block was recorded, mainly for security.

"What else is wrong, Rob? You've been distant since you returned."

I drained my cup of coffee before slowly putting the cup back on the saucer.

"Have you got a spare hour?" I asked.

Jonathan leaned back in his seat and loosened his tie. I smiled at the gesture; it was what he did when he thought he has in for the long haul. The next stage would be to roll his sleeves up. I chuckled gently as I watched him undo his cufflinks.

When he was ready, when I was ready, I told him how I felt.

Over the following week, I started to feel a little more settled. I fell back into a routine of traveling to work with Travis, who spent the whole journey moaning about Katrina, wedding plans, babies, and buildings. Time after time, I told him to call the whole thing off, and he'd change track pretty quick then. I'd smile to myself as I sat in the back of the car and listen to him. He couldn't wait; he just couldn't let anyone think he was excited. Why? I had no idea.

"What time do Rocco and Evelyn get in?" I asked, as we pulling into the office parking lot.

"Just after midday. Want to come with me when I pick them up?"

"I can't, I've got a meeting. I'll see them when I get home."

"Brooke is taking Katrina to lunch with the girls today," he said.

I was pleased. Katrina wasn't necessarily one I thought would slot into our world seamlessly. She would need a little 'teaching' from the girls. She was too independent and way too strong-willed. I knew from Mack that she resisted security. Back when she counseled Gerry and Harley, we'd had one of those 'roundabout' conversations. She'd hinted at her father's situation, of course, we already knew about that.

I'd spoken to Travis a few times about Katrina and how to ease her in to the family. However, I had no doubt the girls would do a better job.

"What's on the schedule today?" he asked.

"Michael needs some training courses. Ted won't fully step down until he's satisfied the kid, as he calls him, is up to speed," I laughed.

Michael had been a *kid* in the home Travis and I owned. Ted, who ran the home, had decided Michael would be a suitable candidate to take over from him. Not that Ted would leave the home, but he was getting seriously old, and I wasn't sure he was in the best of health. I expected to receive a call one day to say he had died overnight and lung cancer would be the diagnosis. He had been to a doctor about the persistent cough, one he seemed to have had for years, but he refused to talk about it and no amount of bribery had gotten me his records.

"Talking about Ted, you did try to hack into his doctor's records, didn't you?" I asked.

"I did, and it was fucking easier to get past the security in the FBI than his doctor. No-go, I'm afraid."

I saw Travis glance in the rearview mirror at me. "Rob, we know what's wrong with him, we don't need confirmation. He wants it this way, play dumb with him, give him that, at least."

I rolled my eyes. It wasn't often Travis was right, or rather, it wasn't often that I acknowledged Travis was right. That day wasn't going to be one of them.

Thoughts of Joe, who also died of cancer, flooded my mind. I remembered the discomfort he'd been in toward the end, and I just didn't want that for Ted. I'd go along with it for a little while and then intervene whether he wanted me to or not.

---

"Rob, I'd like to take Evelyn to Fredrico's. Is it still there? It's where we had our first date," Rocco said.

We were walking around the graves by the chapel on the grounds. Rocco felt that he needed to stretch his legs after his travels and wanted some fresh air. He also wanted to see where Joey was buried which surprised me. I didn't think he would have been that close.

"It is, although I haven't been there for a while. You know we own it, don't you?"

He waved his hand. "Yes, of course I do. I *negotiated* that deal," he said. He had turned to me and his eyes were full of mischief. There was a story there, I was sure.

"How different is it all?" I asked.

Rocco and Evelyn had arrived the previous day. It was the first time he had stepped foot on U.S. soil for thirty odd years. One of the first things he had wanted Travis to do was to drive past Joe's old house, and the house that he had rented. He shook his head with sadness, he'd said, at the change in the environment.

"It's very different. You have done well with the neighborhood but there is no atmosphere now. Where are the people?"

I stopped walking. "They moved on, Rocco. Times are different. In your day, women didn't work, kids played safely in the streets, and neighbors sat on their doorsteps and chatted. They don't now."

"They don't because it's all high-rise blocks. Modern times, huh?" he said, giving me a smile.

"Modern times," I echoed.

"So this is where it happened?" he asked, more to himself than me as he pushed through the chapel doors.

"Here have been the best and the worst times of my life. I got married here. My *brother* betrayed me here by kidnapping my son, throwing Evelyn to the floor," I said.

Rocco had walked down the aisle. He stopped under the window and looked up. "Which came first?" he asked.

"The tattoo. I remember seeing a drawing in my aunt's house. I think it might have been in one of her Bibles she preached from, or beat me with, I can't be sure. I copied it and I kept it for years. It's coincidence, or fate," I said. We had taken a seat in the front pew.

"I turned my back on God many years ago, but do we really?" he asked.

"We do. For me, anyway. I don't believe at all, Rocco."

"Were you avenged, Roberto?" he asked, quietly.

It occurred to me then that he knew very little about my childhood. I shifted in my seat.

"I killed her. As for the priest that could have saved me, that encouraged the beating and the sexual abuse of other children? Joe dealt with him."

He gently nodded his head and patted my hand. "I wish I'd known. I ask myself many times, Roberto, what would I have done? I would not have left you there, had I known about you. And I would have avenged you had Joe not."

Those were words I needed to hear and also words that I knew to be true. Rocco was very much a family man, an *honorable* man.

"I wonder what our lives would have been like had you known about me."

"I think, maybe, not much different to now. We were always destined to be where we are, my son. Cosa Nostra isn't a choice, it's in our blood, whether we resisted, as I did, or fell into it, as you did. My blood runs through your veins, Italy runs through your heart. She cannot be denied, no matter how hard you try."

I was immediately taken back to a conversation I'd had with Joe. He'd said something similar and a bond was formed with Rocco in that moment. Joe, Rocco, they were both instrumental in my upbringing whether it was purely genetic or physical. I felt a little of the burden and guilt lift.

"Can I tell you something? Something I'm struggling to come to terms with?"

Rocco turned to face me.

"I feel unsettled here, in the U.S., I mean. I feel at home in Italy, I find myself speaking the language so fluently that I resent anyone speaking in English to me. Yet I was born in the U.K. How is this?"

"It's your heritage. What do you know about your mother? Where was she from? You don't, and I can't apologize for this. I don't remember her. I wish I did, but back then forty-odd years ago, Roberto, my village was a new destination for tourists, and I wonder if maybe your mother had some Italian heritage herself. What drew her to visit that country, that village?"

I shrugged my shoulders. "I can't even remember what she looks like now."

We fell silent for a little while. I heard Rocco take a deep breath.

"So, Fredrico's? Is it still called that?"

We stood and walked the short distance back to the doors. "It is. It's managed by his son now."

Rocco chuckled. "Fredrico. He had seen some things. Is he still alive?"

"He is, in a nursing home, I believe."

"I'd like to call on him. I should tell you about the chef one day."

Judging by the look on his face, the twinkle in his eye, and the smirk, I wasn't sure I wanted to hear about the chef. I laughed.

"Rocco, I'm aware of what happened there."

"And Tony?"

"He is still alive, and still...*practicing*," I said.

Rocco raised his eyebrows in surprise. "He was scary, he must be an old man now."

"He's still a scary man, thankfully on my payroll. As for old, I'd say he was only in his seventies, still a very fit man, though."

We walked slowly back along the path through the woods. He paused at the gun room.

"Rocco, right now you have a forged visa, I don't think we need to add a forged gun license and a concealed firearm to that," I said, knowing what he was thinking.

"Roberto, my boy, I don't need a license, and your concern, although touching, is misplaced. I was concealing guns while you were in short pants," he said.

With a laugh we continued to walk back to the house. We found Evelyn and Brooke in the kitchen; Evelyn was regaling Brooke with stories of London. My stomach lurched when I overheard her detailing landmarks I had recently become familiar with. I decided that Rocco and I, a whiskey bottle, and a couple of glasses, should head to my office.

"Bring me up to date with the photographs," he said, as he poured us a whiskey each.

"We have nothing other than we believe it's someone close. It isn't another family because you, or Franco, would have heard about it. I think it might be someone close. Dominic has completely disappeared. Maybe he has fulfilled his purpose," I said accepting the glass from him.

"My guys or yours?"

I shrugged my shoulders. "If the person is here, then mine, obviously, but

I'm wondering if it's someone in Italy. I think, if it's someone on the inside, working alone, it would be easier to conceal who it is."

"You spoke to Franco?" he asked.

"I did. He did a little investigating for me. No one in the village knows of this Dominic, other than he was seen a day or so before in the square."

He gently nodded his head.

"What does your instinct tell you?" he asked.

"That it's someone closer than we think, someone working completely alone, who has a grudge for some reason. Maybe someone who has held on to the grudge for a while, or I've annoyed them recently. It's also someone who knows your past, Rocco."

"Which leads more to one of my guys, but there is no one here," he said.

"That's where we get stuck," I said.

"I can see that. Tomorrow, I'd like you to spend some time with me. If you can, of course," he added.

"I'd like that."

"I have…what do you say, nostalgia? There are a few people, and a few places I'd like to visit. Maybe just for the morning."

We were interrupted by a knock on the door.

"I wanted to know if you had made plans for dinner?" Brooke said.

"I'd like for us to go out, Brooke," Rocco said.

"Of course, do you have an idea of time so I can sort Gerry out?"

"How about seven, maybe he can sit with Harley?" I said.

"I'll ask." Brooke gently closed the door behind her.

I didn't doubt Travis would have Gerry sit with them, but I worried that he might think he had been excluded, again, although it didn't appear that Katrina was with him that evening. Her car wasn't in the driveway and her name hadn't been given to security to allow her in. He'd have to stay behind to watch Harley.

"Travis seemed a little grumpy earlier," Brooke said.

We were in our bedroom and she'd just taken a shower, she was sitting at the dressing table applying her makeup.

"What did he say?" I asked, as I tied my tie.

"Nothing particular, just seemed grumpy."

"I wondered if he felt left out this evening."

"Robert, Rocco is your father, he is also your business partner. It's okay to dine with him without Travis, sometimes."

"I know, but…"

"But, nothing. Travis needs to grow up if that's what he's feeling. Has he said anything to you?"

"He's just feeling a little pushed out, I think. He doesn't like the changes, and I think some of that comes from Katrina being pregnant."

"I imagine so, although, he's had Harley for a while now, so I don't really see the difference."

"I just think it's all moving a little too fast for him. I'll wait upstairs for you," I said, kissing the top of her head.

She smiled in the mirror at me and continued to apply her makeup.

I walked up the stairs and over to the glass windows, the lights outside were blazing. I could see Evelyn and Rocco walk, arm in arm, across the drive from her apartment. I heard her laughter as they came through the front door and my smile broadened at the sound.

"Wine?" I asked as they rounded the top of the stairs.

"Of course, just a small one for me, though," Evelyn said.

I'd uncorked a bottle of my favorite Merlot, two glasses had already been poured, I added a third and then a half. I raised my glass in toast and took a sip.

"I don't remember the last time we dined out as a family," Evelyn said.

I had to think hard, I didn't remember either. If Brooke and I were out, Evelyn usually sat with Gerry.

"We need to make up for that," I heard. Brooke walked across the room and reached for her glass of wine.

Her and Evelyn chatted about outfits and shoes, and what shopping was needed in the run up to Christmas. When the car arrived, we left our wine glasses on the counter and headed downstairs.

"Mr. Sartorri, Evelyn," I heard. Dean had the rear doors of one vehicle open.

Brooke and I headed to the Range Rover with Gary driving us.

"It would have been nice to have traveled together," Brooke said.

"We don't fit comfortably in one vehicle," I said, as I climbed in after her.

It wasn't necessarily the truth, of course. Like we didn't allow Harley and Gerry to travel together anymore for security reasons, Rocco and I didn't travel together. If someone took us both out, there wasn't a successor to our *joint* family, just yet. It was something that needed to be addressed at some point.

"It hasn't changed at all," Evelyn said as we stood on the sidewalk. She looked up the road a little way.

"We'll take a walk there after dinner," Rocco said. I guessed there was something up the road significant to them both.

The door was opened and Joseph greeted us.

"Mr. Stone, Mrs. Stone," he said, holding the door wide for us.

"Mr. Sartorri, my father speaks highly of you. And you, too, Evelyn," he added.

Inside, the bistro was as authentic as it had been all those years ago. As we took our seats, I learned that Rocco had brought Evelyn here for one of their first dates. I chuckled.

"Robert brought me here, too. Not for our first date, that was at the club, but soon after. If I remember we sat outside," Brooke said, laughing at the memory.

"It's a familiar place, very much like home," Rocco said.

A waiter placed a jug of water on the table with the menus. He told us of the specials they had that evening, and even the region in Italy the meats had been sourced from. He seemed very enthusiastic about his job and the produce on offer. Or perhaps, he was in awe of the famous, infamous, Rocco. I saw the waiting and kitchen staff peek around the door and whisper.

We ordered and wine was poured. We chatted and laughed. We ate and it was the first time the four of us had spent time alone together. I liked to watch Evelyn when she was with Rocco, she became a different person, younger somehow and more vibrant. She'd tell me that she hadn't totally forgiven him, she couldn't, there were just too many years of hurt for it to be wiped out in the few months he'd been back in her life. But she was happy, content, and for that, I thanked him.

"How about coffee?" I heard. A waiter stood beside the table.

Our dishes had been cleared away and a second bottle of wine consumed. The girls were chatting quietly, and every now and again I heard Patricia mentioned.

"Roberto, accompany me outside?" Rocco said, he had retrieved his pack of cigarettes from his pocket.

"We'll take our coffee outside," I said to a passing waitress.

Rocco pulled his jacket tight around himself. "I miss the Italian climate," he said as he lit a cigarette.

"I bet you do. You should wait for when the snow comes," I replied with a laugh.

We sat on old metal chairs around a rickety café style table. Rocco inhaled his poison and slowly let the smoke out.

"Evelyn wants me to quit," he said, and he stared at the lit end.

"You should, those things will kill you," I said.

"They probably will. I've survived my throat being cut and a bullet to the chest, it would be ironic to die from smoking a cigarette or worse, crossing the road," he said. His deep laughter was echoed by mine. "I'll tell you about those times one day.

"What a life, huh?" he added, as he stubbed the cigarette out.

"Are you ready to retire, Rocco?" I asked.

He took a deep audible breath in, releasing it slowly. "Am I ready to retire?" he repeated. "Do I need to?" he asked.

I shrugged my shoulders. "Only you can decide that. It was your decision to, initially, although I don't suppose anyone believed you really would."

He smiled at me. "Can you work with me, Roberto?"

"Can you work with *me*, Rocco?"

"Honestly? You are my son, and I know that's still something both of us need to adjust to. It works in our *business* world perfectly. I'd like it to work more on a personal level, but that's a conversation for another time. So, can I retire?" He rubbed his chin as if contemplating the question.

"No, Roberto, I don't think I can. And that poses a big dilemma for me, doesn't it? We have already broken down some of my *empire*, but it was time for that anyway. I'll be returning to Italy, I don't think I can stay here. I will run our operations there, while you run your operations here."

I noticed that he'd said *our* operations in Italy but stuck with my operations in America, I was thankful for that. There wasn't going to be a *power* struggle but we did need to set boundaries.

"Will Evelyn be happy to live permanently in Italy?" I asked.

Although it was a conversation I'd already had with her, and she'd told me she would be wherever Rocco was, I think, secretly, she hoped they would travel back and forth.

"No, she wouldn't. She tells me she would but I know her. She's American, and her heart is with you as well as me."

"What do we do then?" I asked.

"We'll muddle through for now. We'll find a system, I'm sure." He lit another cigarette while I sipped on my now cold coffee.

We sat in silence just for a few minutes, savoring the evening and enjoying each other's company. That was interrupted by the sound of running footsteps. I was half standing when I heard the window of one of the Range Rovers parked in front of us shatter. Had it been my car, we would have had more protection; it was bulletproof. I reached out for Rocco just as Dean got to him and threw him to the floor. Gary was beside me before I could even register the screams I heard from inside the restaurant, as machine gun fire rattled off and the windows exploded behind me.

Rocco was dragged closer to the car for protection; I was too far away.

"Can you make it inside?" Gary shouted.

"I don't know, but Brooke is in there."

"I'll cover you," he said.

While I ran, crouched as close to the ground as I could, he opened fire into the wooded area on the opposite side of the road. As I barreled through the door into a darkened restaurant, with Gary close on my heels, I felt the air move as a bullet flew just millimeters from my head. I could hear Brooke's screams but I couldn't see her. She was screaming out my name.

"I'm okay, Brooke," I shouted. I felt a hand grab the back of my jacket.

"It's only me. The ladies are out back, and they're safe. I've rang Mack," Joseph said.

"That's great. Who is with Brooke?"

"My chef, he's very capable, Mr. Stone."

The gunfire ceased and the smell of fear and the metallic tang of blood filled my nose. I crept along the wall to the window. I stepped over two bodies. Tables had been overturned. A waitress crouched behind one, utter fear etched into her face.

"It's okay, just stay exactly where you are. Joseph will get you to safety soon," I said to her.

I doubted she heard my words, she stared at the man whose face was unrecognizable and who lay at my feet.

I quickly peered around the window frame. Rocco was still beside the car with Dean to his side. He looked over to me.

"Evelyn?" he said, as loudly as he dared.

"Okay," I replied.

Gary had moved to the back of the restaurant, he pushed open the kitchen door. I could see Brooke and Evelyn huddled together. I raised my hand in indication to stay put. Gary returned to my side.

"I think they're good," he said. "The chef has a fucking arsenal back there."

"Go get me and Rocco something," I said.

He was back in less than a minute with a semi-automatic in one hand and a revolver in the other. He leaned out the broken window and slid the revolver to Rocco. I took the semi from him and headed back to the door. Gary was on the phone as I passed and scanned the street outside. I couldn't see anyone as the Range Rovers had obscured the view. No one moved and no further gunshots were heard.

My cell vibrated in my pocket. I pulled it out and swiped to take the call.

"Bro, what the fuck is going on?" Travis said.

"Someone shot at us, in fact, I think two people from the woods opposite. One with a fucking automatic, Trav." I made an effort to control the anger in my voice.

"Where is everyone?"

"Brooke and Evelyn are in the kitchen, Rocco is on the sidewalk shielded by the car. There are two dead, as far as I can see, and no movement or sound from the woods."

"Mack has got a team coming in from the woods. There will be a car at the rear of the restaurant in about two minutes; Phil's driving. Get the girls out then. I'll be there shortly."

"Okay, Mack is calling me now," I said, as I pulled the phone away to see the name of the second caller. I cut off Travis.

"Mack, give me an update."

"We have one. They ran, but we got one before they could drive off."

"Take him to Tony's," I said, and then disconnected the call.

I walked out of the restaurant and to Rocco. I held out my hand to help him to his feet.

"All clear," I said.

We rushed back into the restaurant and as I pushed through the kitchen door, Brooke ran to me.

"What happened?" she asked.

"There is a car out back, you need to get in it with Evelyn and get back to the house," I said.

I nodded to Gary, who went to check it was our car and the driver we were expecting. Phil was a relatively new guy on the team but a shit-hot driver. Prior to working security for us, like most, he'd been in the military, and like most, dishonorably discharged.

"I don't…"

"Get in the car, Brooke. No arguing," I said, placing my hand on her back and encouraging her to walk with Evelyn and Gary.

When I saw them safely drive away, I returned to the front of the restaurant. Travis had arrived and was bending over the two bodies, both waiters. Joseph was comforting the waitress.

He looked up and shook his head. I didn't need confirmation they were dead, one had half his face missing.

"We need to go," I said, as Rocco joined us. "Mack has one of them, the other got away."

It was only then that I noticed blood staining on Rocco's hand.

"You've been hit?" I asked.

"A graze. Let's go find out who this son of a bitch is."

We left Dean with Joseph and with a plausible story to give to the police. Gary drove Travis, Rocco, and me to a remote location in the middle of Great Falls.

As we bumped over the broken driveway toward a house, we veered slightly off and headed to the barn. I shivered as a memory from the last time I was in that barn and the ensuing fallout washed over me. We came to a halt, and in silence, we exited the car.

"My friend, it has been too long," I heard. Tony walked toward us with his arms outstretched, and he embraced Rocco as if it was the most natural thing to do in the circumstances.

"Robert, welcome, come in, come in, we are all ready for you," he said with a broad smile. He whistled as he turned away and walked back to the barn.

"That dude is fucking mad," Travis whispered.

I nodded as we followed.

"Here we are, all ready for you. We've been having a little friendly chat, haven't we?" Tony said, patting the knee of a man secured to a chair with tape over his mouth. I doubted he'd have been able to *chat* back.

Tony handed me the contents of the man's pockets, all contained within a small ziplock bag. I handed that to Travis.

The man sitting in the chair had beads of sweat on his brow but a defiant look in his eyes. I walked slowly around him and the room fell into silence. When I'd circled him, I stood and stared at him. He stared back, but the longer it went on, the less conviction he had in his eyes.

Beside the man was a gurney, alongside that was a metal operating table. It held an assortment of *tools*. I picked up what resembled a small hand-held drill. I held it in one hand and placed a fingertip from my other on the drill tip.

"That's sharp," I said quietly.

"I particularly like that tool," Tony said. "Shall I tell you what it's for? It's actually for inserting screws into bones, but it will drill through anything, I've found. Teeth. It drills through teeth as if they are butter."

I didn't dare look at Travis. The man secured to the chair, however, had eyes that had widened in fear.

"And this?" I said, picking up what looked like a meat cleaver.

"Ah, that is exactly what it looks like. I like to butcher in here as well. In fact, remind me, I have some amazing venison out back to give you."

Tony was, indeed, fucking mad.

I looked over to Rocco, who was staring intently at the man in the chair. He walked over to him and pulled the tape from his mouth. The man's eyes darted from me to Rocco.

I swung my arm around and pressed the trigger on the drill just as the bit touched the top of his knee. He screamed out as I ground down through skin, tissue, and bone. The chair rattled as he tried to move but it was bolted to the floor. I pulled the drill free and inspected the end. It was smeared with his blood and fragments of bone. I picked up a rag and wiped it clean.

"That is really sharp," I said. I placed the drill back on the small metal table.

The man whimpered, biting down on his lower lip to stop himself from crying out.

"What is your name?" I asked. He shook his head from side to side.

I picked up what looked like a long screwdriver. "That's for affixing the screws to the bones," Tony said with an excited voice.

I studied it, and then looked at the bloodied knee. I angled the screwdriver so the end was over the puncture wound, I pressed down, gently.

"Cody," he shouted before I could plunge the screwdriver further.

"Cody...?"

"Cody Martinson," he shouted.

I looked over to Tony who nodded. He'd already identified the man.

"Why were you shooting at us?" I asked.

Rocco was in the process of removing his jacket. He rolled up his shirt-sleeves and I could see a trail of blood run down to his wrist. The side of his shirt was torn but didn't look too bad.

"I can clean that up for you," Tony said, bustling around with a first aid box. I wanted to fucking laugh.

"I feel like I've stepped into the scene of a movie. You know, something like a fucked-up *Alice in Wonderland*," Travis said with a laugh.

He stepped forward and grabbed Cody by the front of his T-shirt. "Cody, friend, you were asked a question. Don't keep us fucking waiting for the answer. Do you know who we are?"

Cody nodded his head.

"I'll ask you one last time. Why were you shooting at us?" I said.

"We weren't supposed to hit anyone, just blow out the windows," he said.

"But there are two people dead; two people who were just going about their business in front of those windows. There could have been diners sitting there, Cody," I said.

I picked up the cleaver.

"Next question, and the most important one. You will lose a limb if you chose not to answer, Cody. Who paid you to shoot up the restaurant we just happened to be dining in?" I said. I gently ran the edge of the blade over his damaged knee.

"I never met him. Da…" He paused, looking at the blade.

"Continue, Cody," I said, pressing the blade into his jeans, just above the kneecap.

"Darren is the one who deals with him. I don't know his name, nothing. I got a packet of coke and a wedge of money. All I had to do was blow out some windows, so I was told. I didn't even know you were in there, Mr. Stone."

So he knew me; that was good. "And Darren is?" Travis asked.

"The other…"

I pressed the blade into his leg. It easily sliced through his jeans and then his flesh. He screamed out.

"Don't tell us Darren is the *other guy*. We fucking know that. Where do we find Darren?"

The crying had started then. He readily gave us an address. I placed the cleaver on the table and smiled at Tony, who was bouncing ever so slightly on his toes. I remembered back to the first time I'd met him, he was pretty scary, but now? Well, I don't think I'd like to be Cody.

I patted Rocco on the back and turned to walk away.

"Is that it? I can go now?" Cody called out.

"No, Cody. Now, you get to spend some time with our friend here. See, you lied to me. You said you didn't know who was in the restaurant but I was sitting outside, in full view. You know who I am, yet you still chose to shoot at us. At that point, you should have worried about what you were doing and understood the consequence of that."

I ignored his pleas for forgiveness as I walked away with Travis and Rocco in tow.

Gary stood beside the car and as we approached, he opened the door. I pulled my cell from my pocket and texted over the address for Darren, if it was indeed the address. I doubted very much Mack would find Darren at home, but I was hoping there might be something that would give us a clue as to who organized it.

"Now what?" Travis asked.

"Now we wait."

A piercing scream erupted from the barn, cutting through the night and so high-pitched, it hurt my ears.

"Let's get out of here," I said.

We drove back to the house to wait for news from Mack.

---

The lights were blazing and security patrolled both inside and outside the gate. As we pulled to a halt while we waited for it to open, three guys checked out the car, looking through windows, underneath, and even in the trunk. Once they were satisfied, we were waved through.

"Where the fuck did they come from?" I asked.

"Mack's new team, pretty impressive, huh? Mercenaries or something, waiting on another war to start and killing time here," Travis said with a laugh.

"I'm not sure I know what's funny," Rocco said.

"Travis finds most things funny," I said.

We pulled up outside the front door and were greeted by Evelyn and Brooke. Evelyn went into mother mode as soon as she saw Rocco's arm.

"Oh my God, Rocco. Come in, let me look at that," she said.

"What happened? Are you okay?" Brooke asked.

"Yes, we're all good. It's a graze, nothing more," I said, following Rocco and Evelyn into the house.

"You didn't answer my first question," she said, halting in the hallway.

"Some kids shot up the restaurant. They weren't intending to shoot us, I guess we were in the fucking way," I said. It wasn't a lie, or rather, it was the *story* Cody had given us.

"Just like that? Some kids shot up the restaurant?"

"Yeah. The police were called. One was caught and the other is on the run."

"The police caught one?" she asked, suspicion showing in her eyes.

"Yes, now, I really could do with a coffee. Is Gerry okay? Who is sitting with them?"

"Katrina came over to visit, which was handy."

"It was." I shrugged off my jacket and left it over a chair in the hallway.

As I walked up the stairs, Brooke followed slowly behind.

Travis was on the phone and I could see his smile broaden. He nodded his head and as I walked toward him, he indicated to the office door.

"Can you make some coffee?" I asked Brooke, she nodded her head. "We'll be in the office."

Travis continued to listen, and I assumed it was Mack on the other end of the phone when he said that he'd see the caller in a half hour.

"Mack?" I asked.

"Yeah. The address was right, although it's more a shack at the bottom of a garden belonging to Darren's mom. The mom thinks Darren is in prison. She hoped he was still in prison, anyway. She was more than happy to hand over any information Mack wanted. Seems she's a decent woman, fed up with her son's behavior."

"Great. Let's have a look at who Cody is," I said.

Travis pulled the ziplock bag from his pocket. It contained a driver's license, a set of keys, some coins, and a small wad of cash.

"Not professionals then," I said, holding up the license. No one would take on a job with identification in their pocket.

"I think he was telling the truth. Whoever is doing this is using these idiots, we need to know where they are being recruited from." Travis walked to my desk and fired up my computer.

Brooke came into the room, followed by Rocco. She placed a tray on the coffee table. "Is there anything else I can get for you?" she asked.

I gave her a smile. "No, thank you. We've got some work to do," I said.

She nodded and left the room, I wasn't sure her smile wasn't a little forced, though. I poured the coffee and watched Travis access every database he could for details of Cody and his friend, Darren.

"Both did time, probably where they met," he said.

"For what?"

"Cody was petty stuff. Breaking and entering, car theft, drugs. Darren, however, well, he's a little more interesting."

I heard the printer start; it's blue activation light flashed.

I picked up the first page that was churned out and scanned over it. It was Darren's prison record. He'd been in and out since teenage years. There was also a photograph of him. He was standing topless against a white wall. His torso was covered in tattoos. Some were circled and a line led to words blanked out.

"Can you find out what this is?" I asked Travis.

"I'm trying. Someone thinks those tats are significant."

"Why would it be blanked out?" Rocco asked.

"This record is juvenile. I'm guessing, when he turned eighteen some of his records were deleted," Travis answered.

"They look like prison tattoos," I said, studying his face. He wasn't a happy teenager that much was clear.

He had what looked like a very crudely drawn eagle carrying a child tattooed on his chest. I placed the page down on the coffee table. Travis printed off some more material; he worked the keyboard trying to find as much information as he could. Cody seemed to have met Darren in prison, probably was impressed and, being a drug user, likely to do anything for his next fix.

"What can you find out about the guns?" I asked.

Mack had recovered a rifle, but the other was presumed to be with Darren, and both were still missing.

"Not much, no identification marks, serial numbers, obviously," Travis said without looking up.

The office door opening without a knock disturbed us. Not even Brooke would do that. Katrina walked, uninvited, into the office with a fresh coffee pot. She smiled at us. Travis glanced at me and gave a very gentle nod of his head. He'd talk to her. As she placed the fresh coffee pot on the table, she picked up the piece of paper I'd left there. I reached out to take it from her.

"Russian guy is he?" she asked.

"Why do you say that?" I replied.

"That tattoo, typically a Russian criminal. Do you know what that means?" She visibly shuddered as she spoke.

"No, what?" Travis asked.

"He's a rapist, that's what the eagle means. And the fact the eagle is carrying a child…" She didn't need to finish her sentence.

"Who is he?" she asked.

I took the piece of paper from her. "Some kid that shot up one of our properties earlier," Travis said. I wasn't sure I wanted her to know.

"Well, he's a Russian kid, if that helps," she said, as she picked up the empty coffee pot.

"His name is Darren, I doubt he's Russian," I said.

She shrugged her shoulders. "Let me look again," she asked, holding out her hand.

I relented and handed it back to her. She placed the coffee pot back down.

"See this cross on his chest? Another Russian prison mark, the thieves' cross. And here, on his hand…Can you see the letter M, a reversed N, and then P? It means something like *only execution will correct me*," she said, quietly.

She handed back the piece of paper. "So sad, he seems so young and to be so indoctrinated."

"Into what?" I asked.

"The Russian mafia, Robert. They are rife here, you knew that, right? Heck, my father would have been right at the head had he not been on house arrest, or whatever they call it now."

Without another word, she picked up the empty coffee jug and left the office.

"The Russian mafia?" Rocco said. "Where the fuck did they come from?"

"Russia?" Travis mumbled.

"Her father would have been at the head of it, she said," I repeated. "Jesus fucking Christ."

"Is that significant?" Rocco asked.

"A proposal has been put forward by an agent to buy ten of my apartments for a little under ten mil, I think it is. Nothing unusual in that, except it's a Russian company instructing the agent, wants to pay cash, and a quick deal. I threw it out, of course, smacks of laundering to me, and I don't want that in Vassago. But, the most interesting thing, we can't find one thing on this company other than a name…"

"Let me guess, Katrina's father?" Rocco said, I nodded my head.

"Which means they wanted you to know if they made it that easy for you," he said.

"Yes. And now this kid is linked to the Russian mob," I said, staring at the image of Darren again.

"Do we think there could be a connection?" Travis asked.

"Maybe. We don't want to deal, they send in these kids to give us a message, maybe? Who knows," I said.

"Roberto, have you thought if this is connected to the photographs in any way?" Rocco asked.

"I don't see how it could be. Someone who knows your story and our connection with Matteo took those photos in Italy. It can't possibly be connected."

"Let's keep in mind there may be a connection," he said, as he poured us all a fresh coffee.

By the time I'd raised the cup to my lips, Mack walked through the door with Dean and Gary in tow.

"Anything?" I asked.

"Not sure you're going to like this," he said. He held up a large see-through plastic bag full of what looked like junk.

"Let me guess, Russian connection?" I asked.

"How the fuck...?"

"Darren has tattoos specific to the Russian mafia, prison tats, according to Katrina," Travis said, pride laced his voice.

"So what did you find?" I asked.

"The silly fuck left his cell at home. There's a text message he hasn't deleted, the number is one I found linked with Global Properties. It stood out because it's an overseas number." Mack handed the phone to Travis, he'd be able to extract any deleted messages easily enough.

"Do we have any idea where he went?"

"Nothing. His mom didn't seem to know, or care, as long as he was gone. She seemed pretty decent. She actually said she'd call if he returned. She thinks I'm with the Bureau," he said with a laugh.

"Any vehicle details?" I asked.

"I'm doing a check for CCTV as we speak," Travis said.

He had printed out a map of the area, we knew the direction he'd taken off in, but that stretch of road could have taken him anywhere and since it was pretty rural, I doubted Travis would find very many cameras at all. All we could hope was he'd be able to link in to any domestic security systems that might have cameras facing the road.

It was a couple of hours later that Mack, Gary, and Dean left. Travis, Rocco, and I walked from the office. Brooke and Evelyn were sitting at the breakfast bar, both looked exhausted.

"Hey," I said gently, as I walked toward her.

She shifted on her stool so as I stood in front of her, my legs were either side of hers.

"How are you doing?" I asked.

"Okay, still a little shaken," she said.

I nodded. "It's all sorted now," I said.

"Is it?"

"In as much as we know who and why. It's nothing for you to worry about," I said.

I saw her jaw clench and her eyes darken. "It never is, until it is," she said.

She placed her hand on my chest and gently pushed me to one side.

"I think I'll go and check on Gerry, Katrina brought him back over a little while ago," she said.

"And I think it's way past my bedtime," Evelyn added, frowning at me, obviously, like Brooke, not satisfied with my explanation.

Rocco escorted Evelyn home and Travis soon followed. I sat at the breakfast bar, expecting Brooke to return. When she didn't, I walked down to the bedroom. The light was off and she was tucked up in bed. I sat on the edge and ran my hand down the side of her face. She wasn't asleep but kept her eyes closed.

"Talk to me, baby," I whispered.

She opened her eyes but didn't look at me.

"You've changed, Robert. In the past month I've watched you harden, you're more distant, your lies are more obvious," she said.

"My lies?"

"Wrong word choice, your…evasive words, is that better?" Anger had started to lace her voice.

"I'm not sure what you're expecting of me right now. Two kids shot out the windows of a building I own. It appears those two kids had a message to send to me, hence, *you* have nothing to worry about. I'm not worried about them."

"Really?" she shuffled up the bed until she was in a sitting position. "Because I'm not so sure that's the truth."

"Brooke, where is this coming from? No, I'm not worried. I'm curious and I believe I know what it's about. It's no fucking secret, but it is my business."

"And not mine?"

"No, not yours. Do you want to know, Brooke? It's really not as interesting as you think."

She didn't answer.

"An agent approached us to buy some of my apartments. They represent a company in Moscow. No details, want to pay cash, and want a quick deal. What does that tell you?"

"That something isn't right," she replied.

"Exactly. So I turned down their offer. Two kids shoot out the windows of a restaurant; one of those kids has some prison tattoos that are relevant to the Russian mafia. I don't want their money, they want to send me a message. Like I said, nothing I'm particularly worried about."

"The Russian mafia?"

"Yeah, so is this company a front for the Russian mob? Who knows? I do know, Katrina's father is involved. Now you know, are you still worried?"

"Yes, Robert. So should you be."

"I have way more things to worry about than that. Would Katrina's father be involved in something that has potential to harm the man his daughter is about to marry?"

She sighed. "I guess not."

"Can we now let it go, for tonight?"

She crawled closer. "I'm sorry, I can just see how unsettled you are, and it scares me a little. We both have to adjust, I guess," she said.

"Don't be. Yes, I'm unsettled and it's for me to work through. I will, baby, I promise you."

I stood and she kneeled up on the bed. I pushed her hair behind her ears and held her face. I kissed her. I took her mouth, the air from within, and I reclaimed what was mine. I needed to reconnect and there was only one way for me to do that. I gently pushed her back and as she unfurled her legs, I undid my belt, lowered the zipper of my pants, and let them slide to the floor. I stepped out of them.

I stood back long enough just to pull my shirt over my head.

"You have too many clothes on, Brooke," I said. She wore panties and a tank.

She reached and slowly lifted her tank over her head. She lay back on the bed and raised her hips, lowering her panties at the same time. I didn't want slow and seductive, I wanted raw and passionate. I pulled her hands away and ripped the fucking panties from her body. Her thighs reddened where the material had stretched across her skin before it tore.

She sucked in a deep breath. I grabbed her ankles and pulled her across the bed. I wanted her close, I wanted to smell her arousal, see her pupils dilate, and feel her breath on my skin.

I needed to know, see, feel, and smell every sensation that I could produce in her.

Her reaction proved I was worthy of her. The fact she desired me, with all my faults, gave me confidence in our relationship. She could tell me until she was out of air, how much she wanted me. But words meant nothing. Her scent, her swollen labia, her dilated pupils, her wetness around my fingers, my tongue, or my cock, were more powerful than her words.

I ran my nose over her clitoris, inhaling that affirmation. I licked, tasting her desire for me. I splayed my hand on her stomach as her muscles tightened, feeling that want she had for me.

She gripped my hair, pulling hard at the nape of my neck. I felt her nails scrape against my skin. Gentle pain rippled through me, it excited me. That pain traveled all the way to my cock, causing it to pulse. I wrapped my hand around it, feeling the silky skin and the hardness in my palm. With each nail that dug into my skin, firing off synapses in my brain, so my hand tightened around my cock.

Her moans were the sweetest sound, they drowned out all the shit in my head. It was a sound I needed to hear, and more often.

I raised my head, my tongue trailed up her skin, darting into her navel before I took her skin between my teeth.

I marked her.

The compulsion to mark her wasn't something I'd thought up, it just happened. I wanted her skin to break, I wanted for her to feel the scratch, soreness, for days after as a reminder of our fucking and me.

She raised her hips, her hands tightened in my hair. She raised her head from the bed and looked at me. Her cheeks had started to flush, redness crept over her chest. I took a nipple between my lips, my tongue darting over the hardened nub. At the same time, I placed the tip of my cock at her wet entrance. I rubbed gently but Brooke was impatient for me. She wrapped her legs around my thighs. I chuckled as she thrust down the bed. I bit down on her nipple as I slammed my cock inside her.

Her tightness, her wetness, and heat consumed me. I was home. In that position, I was safe, secure, comfortable, it was indescribable. As her body tightened around me, as if I was born to be inside her, I felt complete. I doubted that she had any real clue of what she did for, and to, me.

I lost myself in her, in her sounds and her body. In my head, I lost all my troubles and myself. I fucked her hard; I fucked her for as long as my body could endure. And when I'd done that, when the rawness and the animalistic desire was spent, I made love to my wife.

# Robert - Chapter Eleven

I wasn't sure what it was that disturbed me. I swung my legs over the edge of the bed and sat up. I stared out of the window to the wooded area behind. I could see out, no one could see in. I saw nothing but blackness, no security lights that would have illuminated had they been tripped. I listened, wondering if Gerry had called out in his sleep, but the house gave up only the normal sounds of creaks or ticking clocks.

I stood and walked to the bathroom. I pulled the door behind me before I turned on the light and stood by the toilet to piss. As I stood, a shiver ran over me. My stomach knotted. I finished my piss and washed my hands, rushing to dry them before returning to the bedroom. I dragged my jeans over my hips and threw on a T-shirt. I stumbled as I grabbed some sneakers.

"What's wrong?" Brooke asked, as she sat up and rubbed at her eyes.

"I don't know, something is though. Stay here."

"Huh? Did you hear something? Is it Gerry?" she said, as she swung her legs over the side of the bed.

"No, I don't know what it is, just something in here," I said, pointing to my stomach.

She stood and I sighed. There was no point in telling her to stay put. I walked to the door and pulled it ajar as she dressed. I couldn't hear anything that would make me suspicious. I walked into the hallway and to the front door. As I opened it, Brooke walked up behind me.

"The lights are all on," she whispered.

The lights lining the driveway were blazing and as I saw someone run across the lawn. I pulled open the door. Gary stopped dead when he saw me, he pointed. I followed his arm. The doors to the pool house were open enough for steam to begin to escape. I ran, he ran, and we collided at the entrance. What I saw had me skidding to a halt, and a sound that started in the pit of my stomach, traveled with precision through my chest, exploding from my mouth.

Floating face down, arms outstretched, and hair fanned was a woman. A woman who had been my mother.

I jumped into the pool, I was aware I was shouting, I was spluttering as I inhaled water until I got to her. I grabbed her and turned her over.

Evelyn lay in my arms. Her eyes wide open, unseeing. Water ran from her open mouth as I moved her the edge of the pool.

I heard Brooke's screams, I heard footsteps and sounds and cries, but I blocked out what I could and dragged Evelyn and myself out of the pool.

"Rocco?" I heard. I looked up to see the grief-stricken face of Travis.

"Go and find him," I said.

I lay Evelyn on her back, as I did I placed my hands on her chest. I pushed down forcing her heart to beat. I screamed her name, over and over, until the word seemed lodged in my brain and my larynx didn't need to vibrate, my lips didn't need to move. Her name was a permanent scream.

Gary kneeled beside me. He cupped her chin, forcing her head back, and opening her airway. He breathed for her as I forced her beautiful heart to restart.

We did that until the tears blurred my vision, until Travis returned to say that Rocco was missing. I forced that heart to pump oxygen to her brain until the muscles in my arms shook with exertion. After what seemed an age, blue flashing lights lit up the whole area outside. Paramedics dragged me away. I didn't hear what they said; I had no idea of instructions or words. I just heard me screaming out her name.

I didn't feel Brooke when she wrapped her arms around me.

I didn't feel her hot tears as she rested her head next to mine.

I didn't feel Travis pull on my arms to move me out of the way.

I didn't feel.

I watched as she was worked on, I watched as they stopped working on her.

I saw the twenty-year-old that had found Travis and me. I remembered the words as she sent me for medicine. I tasted the coffee and the hot pie she'd brought for us. I heard the laughter and I saw the sadness. Then I saw her dead body, and it was all gone to be replaced by white noise and static and pain. So much pain.

I doubled over. I threw up. I physically hurt. I was paralyzed as Evelyn was lifted onto a gurney and taken to a waiting ambulance. Again, I screamed out her name, I punched the tiled floor; I watched blood from my knuckles mix with the pool water that dripped from my body and sick.

I pushed Brooke away and I clambered to my feet. I swayed, unsteady, and I walked out to an empty driveway. She was gone.

I raised my face to the sky and I screamed until my throat felt like it had been cut. Not even Brooke's cries could distract me from my pain. Not even Travis wrapping his arms around me could take away the hurt.

My mother, the only one I knew, the woman who had rescued me from the streets, from the predators, from the grime, was dead.

I wasn't sure how long I'd stood. Cars arrived, the family was gathering, and I was still standing in wet clothes in the middle of the night.

Something triggered in my brain. My eyes came back into focus and I looked around.

"Bro, fuck...Bro?" Travis said, his voice cracking on every letter, let alone word.

I clenched my jaw tight as I walked toward Gary, I reached forward quickly and pulled the revolver from his holster. I turned and strode to the security office at the gate. Gary ran after me, he got in front, running backward as fast as I was walking. He held out his palms.

"No one has come through here, Robert. No one," he said, over and over.

I raised the gun and I fired over his shoulder.

"You fucking cunts. You didn't protect her!" I shouted.

"Robert! No one has come through here!" Gary yelled and he ducked under my raised arm.

In my state of heightened adrenalin, of absolute devastation, he was nowhere near strong enough to lower my arm. In my peripheral vision I saw Jonathan not understanding why he was there.

"Rob, put the gun down," he said. His voice was soft and it reminded me of years gone by.

"Rob, put the gun down, son," he said, again.

I looked at him. I dropped the gun, I fell to my knees, and I sobbed.

---

I sat on the sofa and for the first couple of hours—I could do nothing. The police came and went, I listened, I watched, but I offered nothing and I wanted no one. Brooke tried to sit with me and I moved away. I needed to be left alone, just for a little while.

I had been told that Evelyn's apartment was torn apart for clues. There was nothing out of place. CCTV was checked, and although it had recorded, the door to the pool house had been opened from the inside, and no one crossed the drive. She had to have entered from the rear. There was a small door not covered by CCTV that hadn't been used in years. It had access into the pump room and then the pool house. She would have had to walk around my house, past my bedroom window. That was the noise that had disturbed me.

I stood cursing myself for not being more alert.

"You've called Rocco's cell?" I asked, finally finding my voice.

The guys stopped their talking and looked at me.

"Yes, the cell is in the apartment."

"Call Mario, tell him that Rocco is missing and we want everyone to help find him," I said.

"Robert," I heard in a broken and strangled voice.

I turned to see Brooke. She held both hands over her mouth, her body shook and the tear tracks had stained her face. I pulled her into my arms.

"I'm going to find who did this, Brooke. I'm going to tear them limb from limb as painfully and as slowly as I can. I will torture, and I will hurt them. Only when it's over, can I be the Robert you know. Until then, I need to be me, the real me. Do you understand?" I looked at the confusion that crossed her face. She scanned our friends.

"Do you understand?" I asked again, gentler that time.

She placed her hand on the side of my face. "Can you promise me one thing? Can you promise me that *my* Robert will return?"

I couldn't answer her, but I did take hold of her hand and kissed her palm.

"Look after our son, Brooke," I said, and then I walked away.

I heard her calling me as I walked toward the stairs. I called for my men to follow me. I left the house and walked over to Evelyn's apartment. It might have already been turned over, but I was going through it again myself.

"Rob?" Jonathan said gently to gain my attention. I held up my hand for silence.

He walked over to me and placed his hand on my shoulder.

"Rob," he repeated.

"The time to mourn is after blood has been shed, Jon. Until then, all my effort will be spent finding Rocco and the cunt that did this," I said. I took a deep breath, and I shut down. I refused to allow myself to feel.

For the second time in my life, I was happily numb.

My frustration grew at the knowledge there was nothing out of place in the apartment, nothing to give us the slightest clue as to why Evelyn would walk to the pool house in the middle of the night. She wore her pj's and slippers, she hadn't placed a coat around her shoulders, which suggested she was in a rush.

I walked to the discreet button beside the front door. Not one panic button had been pushed and I wanted to know why?

"He took a call from a foreign number," I heard.

I turned to see Travis with Rocco's cell linked via a cable to his laptop.

"Do you know from where?"

"Italy, but...hold on."

Travis' fingers worked the keyboard as he delved further into whatever he was looking at. His hacking ability had grown to epic proportions over the years. He couldn't read a book, but he could find his way around the dark net as if he'd invented it.

"He took a call from a cell registered in Italy. The call bounced to Italy before coming back to the U.S."

"Back?"

"Yeah, whoever owns the cell is here."

"What does that mean?" Jonathan asked. "Beside the obvious," he added when Travis looked over to him.

"An Italian called Rocco at just before midnight. That call originated from the U.S. but because his cell service provider is still in Italy, the call goes back to 'home' before being forwarded on."

"Why not change providers?" Richard asked.

"Maybe he isn't intending on staying long," I said. One of the first things I did when I landed on Italian soil was to switch phones to a local provider.

We spent some time putting the apartment back together. I could see the pain that flashed through the faces of the guys as they handled her things, as they remembered, and as they tried their hardest to contain their grief.

"Jon, if you want to go home, get some sleep for a little while…"

"No, Rob. She was as important to me, to all of us, as she was to you and Travis. We stay here, we find who did this, and we find Rocco."

I nodded as I looked around the men. Each had known her longer than I had and, in my pain, I had forgotten that. I slumped onto the sofa. I cradled my face in the palms of my hands.

"We need to think," I whispered.

"Okay, I have a number," I heard. I jumped up and walked to where Travis sat.

Flashing on the screen was a cell number. We stared at it for a while.

"Who does it belong to?"

"Not registered, a burner probably," he said. It wasn't what I wanted to hear.

I picked up Rocco's cell and my fingers hovered over the keypad.

"Wait," Travis said. A couple of pages flashed up on his screen. The last one was a continuous circle.

I looked over to him. As he looked back at me, I could see the tearstains on his cheeks.

"Rocco had a conversation with this caller for no more than four minutes, earlier this evening. That person then called back just before midnight. What time were you disturbed?"

"About then, I think, I don't know, I didn't check," I answered.

The continuous circle stopped and coordinates flashed across a map. Travis looked back to his laptop and enlarged a map.

"Fucking hell," he said, as he leaped up from his chair.

"That call came in from here, Rob. Somewhere in these grounds."

"The chapel," I said. I was already running for the door as I spoke.

I didn't know why the chapel was the place that came to mind, but it did seem an obvious choice. There were some buildings in the grounds, but that was the only one that didn't have a lock on the door.

"Rob, wait!" I heard as I got to the bottom of the stairs in the garage.

I turned and waited for Travis. Mack was pulling some keys from his pocket.

"We are not going in there until we have a plan, for fuck's sake," Mack said.

"Jon, Richard, wait here with the girls," I said.

All the lights were blazing in the house and I hadn't been back in there for hours.

"We can't do any recon, Rob," Mack said.

"I know that. But there is one way in and only one way out. We have the advantage. And Rocco has been missing for what? Four hours already? I doubt they're still there."

I started the walk toward the gun room; Mack already had his keys ready to open the door. Gary stood beside it, a semi-automatic across his chest. I filled him in with what we knew so far.

"There's no one at the chapel, we've scoured these grounds," he said.

"Did you go inside?" I asked.

"Not all the way, but you know we'd see if someone was there."

I nodded, he was right, but there might be a clue that had been left. When Mack had the door open, we piled in. I selected a revolver and placed it in the waistband of my pants.

As we left the room, all of us fully armed, we started to walk toward the chapel.

"Robert?" I heard from behind.

I sighed. I gave a nod to the guys to continue to the chapel, and I turned back to Brooke.

"Robert, where have you been? Gerry is inconsolable, we need you," she said, placing her hands on my chest.

I pulled her into my embrace.

"Just this once, Brooke, I need you to cover for me, okay? I need you tell Gerry that I love him so much, and I'm sorry I can't be with him right now. Just give me another hour or so, please?"

She went to speak and maybe thought better of it. I didn't know what prompted her silence, but I saw the abject pain and hurt in her eyes and there was nothing I could do. Any other time I could react, but right then, I had nothing to give her. I just needed another hour, or maybe a little more, and I could only hope both she and Gerry would forgive me for abandoning them in their time of need.

"I..." She didn't finish her sentence and I watched a tear run down her cheek.

"Brooke, I have nothing to give you right at this moment. When this passes, and I know it will, I'll be back. Just another hour, please," I stressed.

She mouthed the word Gerry and I wanted my heart to break, I really did. I wanted tears to roll down my cheeks, like they had earlier, but they wouldn't. I willed them, I truly did. I had nothing to give but anger and hatred, and I needed to expunge myself of those before I could find that love again.

She stepped back, her face was white and her eyes wide with fear. She sobbed as she turned and ran; I closed my eyes. I could hear her cries all the way back to the house.

I didn't know if it was an hour or longer that I'd need. I just knew I had to murder and I had to do it quickly. The urge to kill, to take revenge, was like a pressure cooker. I was boiling inside.

As Brooke got to the front door, an almighty explosion occurred. For a moment, I was stunned into paralysis. A small fireball rose in the air from the security hut, piercing alarms wailed into the air, and the smell of motor oil confused me. I looked toward the hut and I could see a body of flames fall to the ground, I had no idea of the other occupants.

"Fucking hell," I heard. I turned to see Gary. That motion, that sound, activated whatever it was that had kept me standing.

"Get everyone in the gun room," I said as I ran for the house.

Gary ran alongside me, we met Dean at the front door. As I kicked it open, I found Brooke cradling a screaming Gerry to her chest, both were shaking.

"Brooke, the gun room, now," I said. I was thankful she acted on instinct, or training.

She grabbed Gerry by the arm as Patricia and Susie ran down from upstairs. They were followed by Richard and Jonathan, and then Katrina, who was holding the hand of Harley.

"Gun room," I shouted as they filed past me.

The gun room was plenty big enough to house them all. It acted like a panic room in one way. The walls were solid stone and over two feet thick. The door was constructed of metal and it would take an explosion twice, three times, the size of the one at the gate to buckle it. There were crates of water, a satellite phone, and a monitor linking to the CCTV. More importantly, there was a trapdoor to a tunnel and a way out.

*Get to Ted*, I shouted in my head, knowing my wife would follow any previous escape instructions to the letter.

I locked Dean in with the others.

Just beyond the gates, we could see headlights approaching the buckled gates. That vehicle had the rumble of something way larger than an average car, and when the floodlights on top of the roof illuminated the drive; we knew it was some sort of military vehicle. It plowed through the crumpled gates.

"Head toward the chapel," Mack said, he had his cell to his ear and was calling for reinforcements.

We ran through the woods until we were at the chapel. We had no idea at that point who was at the gate, or how many. I had no clue who had survived the blast to the security hut. We were too isolated for neighbors to have seen or heard anything, and our alarm and CCTV system were linked to my own security team. They would be a good twenty minutes away.

As we got closer, I heard my name being called. The guys ran on to open the second set of gates. I came to an abrupt halt. The chapel door was open and standing there was Rocco with a younger man slightly behind him, his son, Marco.

"What the fuck is going on?" I shouted. Gunshots could be heard in the distance, I assumed from any survivors at the security hut.

"Get inside, then we can talk," he said.

Marco nodded to me as he was ushered past and into the chapel. It was as the door slammed and I heard the door lock, I realized my fucking mistake. I stopped my ascent up the aisle and chuckled. I looked up at the angel in the window; even she mocked my stupidity. I slowly turned to see Marco with a gun in his hand.

"Evelyn's dead, Rocco," I said.

"What! What did you say? How...When..." His level of confusion and disbelief was genuine. He spun around to see Marco's gun leveled at his head.

"I don't understand," he said, his voice shaking with emotion. "Roberto?"

Marco didn't speak, but he turned his head to look at me. Outside gunfire came closer, more rapid. I looked at my angel; her mocking stare had somehow changed to solidarity.

*You care for my family, leave this one to me,* I thought, and if I were religious, I'd have sent that up as a prayer as well.

There came a pounding on the chapel door, and my cell vibrated in my pocket.

I took a deep breath in and slowly released it. My pupils dilated, I knew that because my vision changed. What I saw was brighter as more light was allowed to pass through my eyes. My senses heightened. The smell of polished oak and dust particles fought with the thirst for blood. Hairs stood on my arms and my heart beat a little quicker. I felt my muscles tense, ready for action, the adrenalin flooding my system, allowing a surge of oxygen to enter my bloodstream and lungs. I was ready for the *fight* instinct I carried.

Marco, however, wasn't. I watched his eyes dart between the door and me; I watched the very slight shake to his hand and the sweat bead on his forehead, despite the cold.

"I found Evelyn in the pool, Rocco. She was drowned. The coroner took her away a while ago. We didn't know where you were."

"I was with Marco. He called me, needed to speak with me urgently…" He turned to look back and his younger son.

"What did you do?" he whispered as realization set in.

"I didn't do anything, Papa," he said. It was the first time I'd heard him speak.

Marco's accent was so strong that, although he spoke in English, it wasn't easy to fully understand him.

"If you did nothing, why are you standing there holding a gun to your father's head?" I asked. I started to take a step closer to him.

Marco took a step back and that gun swung between Rocco and me.

"I didn't know they would do that, okay?"

"Who are they?"

"Volkov's team. They just wanted to continue with our arrangement but, unfortunately, you caused them problems," he said, looking at me.

"How did I cause problems?" My voice became lower and lower, I needed his undivided attention before I could seize my moment.

"You divided up Papa's business. For years, we've had a good thing going and now you've cut off that money route. They blame me for that."

Rocco turned to me. "Roberto, what the fuck is he talking about?"

Before anyone could answer the side window to the chapel blew in. I threw myself down between two pews as shattered glass flew through the air. Someone was firing through the window; the wall behind me was peppered with bullets, dust, and stone chips added to the glass littering the floor. It seemed like an age, but in reality was just mere seconds, before that assault was halted. I could only hope one of my guys had taken out the shooter.

When I rose, Rocco was kneeling, he clutched his side, and I saw the blood drip through his fingers. Marco had moved toward the door. I assumed he wanted out at that point, but that wasn't going to happen. I finally reached for my gun and fired. I had the perfect shot and as blood and bone erupted from his wrist, he dropped his gun. It bounced across the floor, closer to Rocco.

"Start talking, you fucking prick," I said, as I walked toward him. I stood next to Rocco.

"They sent me the money, I cleaned that through one of Papa's companies. Then you came along and it got fucking complicated."

"And what happened then?" I asked, knowing the answer.

"I wanted for you to leave Italy and then I could have fucking sorted it."

"Did you send me Dominic?" I asked. He didn't reply.

"Did you think just three photographs would have scared me off enough to back away from *my* businesses? It makes sense now. You knew your father's life, you also knew what we did to Matteo, which is why you used that name, wasn't it? You thought you'd what…Confuse me? Scare me?" I shouted. I wanted to fucking laugh.

My cell vibrated in my pocket again. I pulled it out and answered it.

"Mack, Rocco is here, he's hurt. Marco is here, too. He's about to be hurt."

"Getting contained out here, but can't get to you yet," he replied. It was all I needed to know. I disconnected the call.

"What's happening?" Rocco asked.

"His friends are all but slaughtered. Now it's just you and me, Marco," I said, lowering my voice again.

Rocco tried to stand, he reached out for my help, and without lowering my gun, or removing my gaze from Marco, I held onto his arm to assist him. He gritted his teeth, and I heard the gush of air from between them as pain must have ripped through him.

"Why Evelyn, Marco, why? You know what she meant to me," he said, his sentence interrupted by winces.

"I don't make the decisions, I just follow the orders," he said. He had backed himself beside the door, thinking that I hadn't noticed.

"Let's get this clear. You laundered Volkov's money through your father's businesses. I took over, closed down that route, so you decided to, what? Frighten me to leave Italy?" I asked.

"You left," he said.

I had, and it was only because of Travis and Brooke that I had.

"Volkov tried to purchase some of my properties, I refused. So that's why you're here?"

"I don't know about that. I just follow fucking orders, it's all I've ever done," he replied, anger lacing his voice. I was riling him.

I nodded. "So Evelyn died because Volkov can't launder his money through my companies, and you came here, for what?"

"He came here to ask for my help, Roberto. He's my son," Rocco's voice was strained. I wasn't sure if it was the injury or the emotional pain he must have been in.

"What help did you require?" I asked.

"Papa needed to change your mind, but I guess Volkov got impatient."

His lack of empathy or concern for the death of the only woman his father had loved, or the fact that his father stood in front of him bleeding was all I needed to see. I strode toward him and placed the barrel of the gun at his forehead.

"Roberto, please?" Rocco said, his voice weak.

"He is responsible for Evelyn's death, Rocco."

"You can't know that," Rocco said. "Who is this Volkov?"

"I do know that, let me tell you how I know that. The minute this piece of shit got onto my property, that also allowed Volkov's, or Marco's, *friends* to gain access. He asked you to let him in those gates, didn't he?" I nodded my head toward the door of the chapel, indicating the gates beyond.

"Is that correct?" I asked Marco. He didn't reply. "Who let you in?" I asked.

He looked to Rocco. We all fell silent for a moment.

"I...I didn't know," Rocco said. "He's my son. He's your brother, Roberto," he whispered.

"And she was my mother." I pulled the trigger.

Blood, brain matter, and bone splattered against the white stone wall behind him, some splashed forward, and I felt hot liquid hit my face.

I turned to Rocco, he was back on his knees. He looked up at me and reached out. I kneeled before him. He placed his hand on my cheek and gave a ghost of a smile. It was only when he took his hand from his side that I saw the large circle of blood, his coat had concealed just how hurt he had been.

I reached out for him, I wanted for him to lay and let me try to stem the blood. He shook his head.

"She's dead?" he whispered.

I nodded my head. His hand shook as he removed his palm from my face; I shuffled closer.

"I wish...I wish I'd known you longer, my son," he said. I could see his body slumping.

"Hold on, Rocco, help is on its way," I said reaching for my cell.

He shook his head. "I don't want help, I just want her. She's all I ever wanted, I need to be with her."

He collapsed into my arms; he bled out over my knees as I cradled him to my chest.

"Papa?" my voice croaked.

"Papa!" I screamed, my voice bounced off the walls and my angel stared at me. If she could have, she would have cried with me, I was sure.

A pounding started again on the chapel door. My cell vibrated and I heard a noise from the broken window. I watched as Travis climbed through. He halted halfway down the aisle when he saw me.

"Is he...?"

I nodded and laid my father down on the stone floor. I touched my lips with my fingertips, and I transferred that kiss to him. I hadn't known him long, but just the short time I had, he had transformed me. He had awoken the Italian in me and given me everything I could have ever wanted—History—Destiny—Heritage.

I stood and Travis ran to the door, he stepped over Marco and unlocked it. I walked out to a sun fighting to brighten up the winter morning. I looked up to see large gray clouds threaten rain, and I wished for it. I wished for the elements to whip into a frenzy around me. I still held the gun in my hand as I walked round to the graves. I saw a line of men on their knees, their palms on their heads. I saw Gary, Dean, and Mack holding semi-automatic weapons.

I walked to Dean and took one from him. I walked to the first man kneeling.

"Where is Volkov?" I asked.

He shrugged his shoulder, spoke in Russian. I looked up at Gary. "Move," I said.

It took me raising the semi-automatic before Gary understood and dived out the way, just before I unleashed hundreds of bullets into the bodies that were once lined up neatly as perfect targets. I kept firing until faces were unrecognizable, teeth shattered beyond identification, until limbs were severed from torsos. I shot up hands until fingertips were no more than mush and fingerprints obliterated. When I was done, I was laughing, manically.

The smell, the ringing in my ears, the hands on my biceps trying to pull me away were, for a moment, all that I felt. That and the vision of my father, of Evelyn.

I felt the tears track down my cheeks and I didn't care who saw.

"How many?" I asked. I hadn't looked at anyone until that point. Dean's face was ashen, Gary looked distraught.

"Of ours?" Mack asked. I nodded.

"Four, one badly burned. Rob, we're going have the police swarming all over us at some point," he said.

"The girls?"

"They got out, they're at Ted's."

"That is where I need to be," I said, slinging the semi over my shoulder. I checked the revolver's clip and started to walk back to the house.

"Rob. Rob!" Mack shouted.

I stopped but didn't turn. "We can't get out that way."

I turned and was met by Travis and Gary. We left Dean by the chapel, I think his time with us was done, I doubt he'd recover from what he'd just witnessed. It was a shame because rumor had it he'd taken a shine to Petra, Mack's daughter. Why that thought came to mind, I had no fucking idea.

Outside the gates by the chapel was one of my Range Rovers. I climbed in as Travis opened the driver's door. Mack joined me in the back; Gary rode up front. He made a call to the security team we had left to start a cleanup. I pitied those guys and hoped they had the stomach for what they were about to witness.

For a while we drove in silence. I looked as my brother caught my eye every now and again. I knew he, and Mack, were busting to ask me questions, to comfort me in the only way they knew how, but I also knew that they understood to stay quiet. I needed to process.

As we drew close to the home, I pulled my cell from my pocket; I sent a text to Mack. Although he was sitting beside me, I needed him to know something.

I watched as he retrieved it, as his mouth opened as if to speak but then shut quickly. He looked over at me and I swear it was tears I saw in his eyes. I'm sure whatever it was, it mirrored mine.

Our lives had been irrevocably altered that night and it was about to get worse.

Michael stood at the gates to the home. He was a good lad and had been groomed to take over from Ted. Judging by the sight of Ted, that looked to be sooner than I imagined.

"The girls are in the lounge, kids are asleep. Jon and Richard are out back," he said as he met me on the drive.

Brooke hadn't come out to greet me and there was a part of me pleased about that. I needed her distance for just a little longer.

I walked around the property to the deck that ran the length of the house. Jonathan and Richard stood to greet me.

"What happened?" Jonathan asked.

I filled them in as best I could, trying my hardest not let any emotion creep in. I wanted my soul as black as could be, I wanted that heartlessness I knew had always been inside me. I needed it. I also told them what I needed to do.

"No, Rob…I…" Jonathan had no advice to give me.

Richard just covered his face with his hands and let his shoulders slump down.

Mack handed me a silencer and I screwed it to the end of my revolver. I adjusted it in the palm of my hand, getting used to the slight weight difference. Then I walked into the house. I kept the gun down by my side.

I walked into the lounge. Brooke stood and started to run toward me, she hesitated and I guessed the aura I was giving off was to blame for the lowering of the temperature in the room. I saw Susie visibly shiver.

"What happened? Are you okay?" Brooke asked, she took a tentative step toward me.

"I need you outside, Susie and Patricia, maybe you'd like to head home?"

It wasn't necessarily a question, and although Susie looked at Patricia who was staring at me, they responded without question. Both rose and walked through the room to the kitchen, I guessed to find their men.

"Robert?" Brooke asked. I looked over her shoulder.

"Time we left," I said.

"Okay, I'll just go and get…" Brooke paused her sentence when she realized I wasn't talking to her.

Katrina stood and smiled at me. Silently, she brushed down the front of her top and let her hands pause over her pregnant stomach, or was she? I wasn't so sure.

"What's going on, Robert?" Brooke asked.

Finally I looked at her.

"One more hour, Brooke," I said. I ran my fingers down her cheek and felt the quiver to her flesh as fear started to set in.

"I don't recognize you," she whispered.

I leaned down close to her ear. "No, and I'm glad. I don't want you to recognize me right now."

I grabbed Katrina by the arm and dragged her from the room. Brooke stifled her scream, and I saw her reach out but pull back at the last minute. I wasn't sure if she was reaching out for Katrina or me.

Outside stood my car with the rear door open. Beside it stood Travis, a gun held to his head just in case he decided to stop me, or hurt her, I'd never know how he would have reacted. I pushed her into the back of the car, she didn't even fucking glance at him. I turned to him before I joined her.

"Bro…" I started.

He held up his hand and shook his head. He kept his gaze over my shoulder as he cried silently, keeping his shoulders back, and his chest puffed out. Finally he looked at me. He gave me one nod of his head.

We drove the short distance to the bistro. Joseph opened the door and, without question, took Katrina by the arm and escorted her through to the kitchen and then out the back. I started to follow and then paused.

"You know what to do, yeah?" I asked.

Mack nodded. We stared at each other just for a moment longer.

"I'm sorry, Rob," he said before he pulled me into a hug. It was the one and only time we'd embraced.

"Take care of everything," I said. I left him standing on the sidewalk.

"So," I said as I reached Katrina. "Volkov?"

Katrina was on her knees in the backyard. The same yard that had seen many killings over our years as a family.

She shrugged her shoulders. I smiled at her. "I give you your due, Katrina, you fooled me. And you would have continued to had your father not tried to make contact. I guess he was trying to warn me, wasn't he?"

She shrugged her shoulders again.

"Will he be upset to hear of your death?" I raised my gun.

She stared me straight in the eyes and smiled.

"Robert, my employer had a good arrangement with your father. It was a disappointment to see that come to an end."

"A disappointment? Well, I'd sure like to see how your employer would respond if they were seriously fucked off," I replied with a bitter laugh.

She raised her eyebrows and pursed her lips. "I'm not the decision maker," she said.

"I don't care if you are or not. I do want to know when it started. You worked in my home, was that all fake?"

"Oh no, I am very well qualified, you must know that. This…well, this is just a little something on the side," she said.

"Exactly what is *a little something on the side*?" I asked.

"A murder here, a problem solved there," she replied.

"So you were sent to solve a problem. That problem being your employer's inability to continue to launder money through my business?"

Her timeline didn't make sense. She had worked at my home for two years; she had been fucking Travis for as long.

"No, I was genuinely working here. I was genuinely fucking your brother," she said, as if she could read my mind.

"So what is all this?" I asked.

"This? I was handed over as a child, Robert, in payment of a debt my father owed. I've been highly trained and I'd lain dormant for years. I get called upon by my government to solve a problem when required. I slowly repay that debt by being in service to my government…until now, that is. I'm glad, Robert, I'm tired of being owned."

"A sleeper?"

"A sleeper."

I laughed. I didn't think they existed beyond the movies.

"I guess I ought to feel honored your government deems my family of such importance to *wake you up*."

"I did love him," she said quietly, throwing me a little.

"Are you pregnant, Katrina?"

"Would it make a difference to the outcome?"

I thought for a moment. "No. Your actions killed the only mother I've ever known and my father. I cannot let that go unpunished."

"Then my answer really doesn't matter does it? Will you allow me to ask one thing of you?"

I didn't answer but as I raised my gun, I nodded.

"Do it quick." She raised her head but kept her eyes closed.

"There's just one thing that has been bothering me, Katrina. Why do you smell of chlorine, as if you've just been in a swimming pool?"

She didn't speak, she didn't open her eyes, but as a tear tracked down my face at the memory of Evelyn, she smirked.

"How did you lure her over?" I asked.

"I called and told her that I was bleeding and that I didn't want Travis because he'd panic. She thought I was using the hot tub to relax. She didn't struggle after I'd told her Rocco was gone, she wanted to be with him," she said it so matter-of-fact, bile rose to my throat.

I fired my gun and watched a small hole appear in the center of her forehead. A trickle of blood ran down her nose between two blue eyes still staring. After a few seconds, she slumped forward. I handed my gun to Joseph who had stood silently to one side.

"Good luck, Robert," he said. I nodded in response then turned to walk away.

My stomach knotted as I climbed back in the Range Rover. Mack turned in his seat and stared at me.

"It's done. She was a sleeper. She killed Evelyn and was sent to take us out because we didn't comply. Joseph can fill you in," I said. "And she wasn't pregnant."

Mack didn't respond but started the car and we drove back to the house.

---

The drive was littered with cars, blue and red lights flashed from roofs. Suited men stood to one side, arguing with the local police over who had jurisdiction. I climbed from the car and walked toward a group of men. Brooke ran from the house and straight to me. That time, I embraced her.

"Please, tell me, what's going on?" she asked.

"I'm about to get arrested and you just have to trust me," I whispered.

She opened her mouth to speak, or scream, I wasn't sure. I covered it with my own. I felt her tears as they ran down her cheek, wetting mine, washing the blood and grime from my skin, cleansing my flesh with her purity.

"Trust me," I said, as I was pulled away from her.

My hands were twisted behind my back, metal cuffs bit into skin with a deliberate tightness. I wasn't cautioned at all, I didn't expect to be. The FBI had spent years trying to pin any little misdemeanor on me. Regardless of what went down, they had no idea of my level of involvement, but they had RICO Laws on their side. I was patted down and my cell removed.

Just before I was ushered into a car, I watched Travis arrive with Mack. He stared at me, a broken man, before he wrapped Brooke in his arms. No matter his feelings toward me at that moment, I knew he'd take care of my wife; he'd loved her once.

I hadn't asked where Gerry was and I was glad that he hadn't seen me. I couldn't bear to see the disappointment, hate, or pain in his eyes. I had deserted my family when they needed me, but with good cause. All I could hope was that, one day, they'd forgive me for that.

We drove for a while until we arrived at a secure location. I wasn't given the address, in fact I wasn't spoken to at all as we drove into an underground parking lot and I was bundled from the car. I was forcibly walked through security doors, corridors until we eventually entered a room with no windows. I was left cuffed and on my own.

Having never been picked up by the FBI before, I wasn't sure of procedure, but I was sure that this wasn't it. I smiled up at the camera in the corner.

Maybe an hour later, the door opened, and a suited man holding a folder under one arm, two coffees, one in each hand, and pencil in his mouth, walked backward into the room. He'd used his ass to open the door. He placed the coffees on the table, sliding one to me. I pulled my arms as much as I could to one side. He pulled the pencil from his mouth and laughed.

"Sorry, they should have taken those off a while ago," he said, waving his hand for me to stand.

I wasn't sure what was funny, but I stood and turned. He uncuffed me. I rubbed at the broken skin around my wrists.

"My lawyer on his way?" I asked.

"No idea. I doubt he'll know where we are," he said.

"Where are we?" I asked.

He smiled and tapped the side of his nose. I sighed.

"Okay, so, C-4 blew up your security team. A military jeep was found abandoned on your grounds. The only dead are your gate people. Everyone else is missing. Want to tell me anything about that?" he said.

I placed my palms around the mug of coffee. I raised it, sniffing the black liquid and raised my eyebrows. I tasted.

"That is surprisingly good," I said.

"I know, this isn't a local office, Robert, I'm sure you know that. We get the good stuff here."

I wasn't sure he meant the coffee or the crimes.

"Tell me about Katrina Volkov," he said.

"Tell me how I contact my lawyer, what you are holding me for, and where the fuck I am," I replied.

"Okay, you're not under arrest, you're not even helping me with my inquiries because I don't know if we have any inquiries to answer to yet. As for where you are, not far from your offices, funnily enough. No one knows you're here, Robert, only that the FBI took you away."

"What do you want?"

"Honestly? Just some answers about Katrina. Robert, I don't fucking care what went down at your house. It took all my men's brilliance at lying and stealing suspects, namely you. Answer my questions and you're free to go. Where? I don't know. Those fuckwits at the local police force want your blood, or maybe they're just a little fed up of being paid to turn the other cheek, I don't know," he said, shrugging his shoulder.

"I have no idea what the fuck you are talking about, and if you have any evidence that I've paid the local police force, I suggest you fucking do something about it," I said, also shrugging my shoulders.

"Look, Rob, can I call you Rob?"

"No."

"Robert. I have a problem with Katrina. I know her father, why he's under house arrest, and the fact that his company is trying to buy some of your apartments. I know all that, and I know that you knocked him back. Did you know why he was trying to do that? Did you ever come across her brother?"

"Her brother?"

"Yes, Dominic, I think his *current* name is. He's a nice guy, not involved with his sister at all. He was working with us for a little while doing surveillance, but he's gone off grid as well. We think someone has gotten to him, maybe one of your associates?"

I shook my head, trying to work out why we thought he was Northern Italian. He spoke Italian, fluently, or had he? He couldn't have, as Travis had understood him. My head was spinning with how much I'd fucked up.

"Her father was trying to send me a message, James. You have now interrupted me finding out why," I said.

I'd stunned him. He blinked rapidly, unease crossed his face. Not once had he introduced himself but I knew him.

"I don't recall…"

"Giving me your name? No, you didn't. How is your brother, James? Donnie and I go back a long way. How's his wife, Sally? Is she over her illness now?"

Sally had breast cancer some time ago. Donnie didn't have the necessary insurance to cover her fees. Donnie worked for the local police force and at no time had I ever asked for the money I'd paid to the hospital to be paid back. At no time, until that moment, had I ever asked for that to be repaid at all.

James stared at me. He picked up his coffee and sipped, he picked up his pencil and tapped it against his teeth.

"Okay, truth time. You're not supposed to be here. The police are supposed to have you first for questioning. They want to know why someone blew up your gates and killed some of your men. We hoodwinked them into thinking there was a bigger crime and we were on it."

He laughed and I began to think he was some kind of imbecile. Idiots in power were often the most dangerous. I decided to tread carefully.

"And what are the police after me for?" I asked.

"Murder, of course. Then you're to be handed back over to the FBI because we have RICO to fall back on, if we need to," he said, not even trying to disguise the threat.

"Murder? Well, that's a new one. Who have I murdered? Is your brother involved in that?"

"I doubt it, although I will call him and find out. As for who, I'm sure they can find some corpse somewhere and put your fingerprints on it," he said.

"I'd suggest you do call him, I'll wait here. Oh, I want my cell so I can call my lawyer," I laughed.

"No can do, I'm afraid. You have some damning evidence on that cell."

He left the room. If there hadn't been a camera in that room I would have sunk my head into my hands and fucking cursed myself. There was damning evidence on that cell. I needed to think smart and quick.

Ten minutes or so, James was back.

"Okay, my superior is not happy with me. My brother is not happy with me, but I've a job to do, Robert. I have been watching that fucking woman for years, and now she appears to have disappeared. I know all about her working for you, I know all about her soon-to-be wedding to Travis. I need to know where the fuck she is, and more importantly, what she was."

"Why were you watching a woman when you had no idea *what she was?*" I said, emphazing his words.

I saw him quickly glance at his watch. I was guessing either I was supposed to be someplace else, or he was about to get in trouble for holding me.

"I don't give a shit what happened at your house. But my *project* is fucking missing and you know where she is."

I leaned back in my seat and finished my coffee.

"I don't know where she is. You've seen my text, so you know why I went after her. She's a sleeper for the Russian government, James. She's been here since she was a teenager, but all I know was that she was sold to the program to pay off her father's debt. I don't know what that debt is. I don't know what she's done. I do know that she was driven to the airport immediately after she confessed to me. The only reason she was given her freedom, James, is because she is carrying my brother's child."

He looked like he was about fit to burst with that information.

"I knew it. I fucking knew it," he said, with a smile that reached his ears.

"She problem solved, so she said. Now, you have that information and I have the resources to actually find out where she is. But I won't be doing it from here, and I won't be doing it from the local police station, either," I said.

The door to the room opened. "Unfortunately, they want me to hand you over to my buddies in Organized Crime," he said.

"Mr. Stone, would you like to accompany me?" I heard.

No names were offered, no badges shown. I rose and followed him. He walked me to the parking lot and to a waiting car. He opened the rear door and I slid in. The car reversed from the bay and drove slowly from the parking lot. Instead of the left turn I was expecting, which would take us to Great Falls, we turned right.

I was unsure as to what was going on, where I was being taken. I assumed, if I really was in the company of the Organized Crime Unit, I was being taken to a second secure location.

We drove for a half hour until we pulled through the gates of a private airstrip. Finally, I smiled and relaxed. The driver looked in the rearview mirror, he smiled back at me.

He exited the car and opened the rear door for me.

"Mr. Stone," he said. I patted his arm.

"Thank you," I replied.

"Your cell," he said, holding out his hand.

"Did James retrieve what he needed?" I asked.

He shook his head. "He saw the text message but it was deleted before he could get a copy downloaded."

"It doesn't matter, I told him what he wanted to know anyway."

A car approached and Mack climbed from the driver's seat.

"What happened?" he asked.

"I actually have no idea. All he wanted to know was about Katrina. I gave him some information, didn't seem to be any reason to withhold it. He's Donnie's brother, if you want to follow up on that," I said.

"Okay, they want to arrest you for the murder of one of the security guys.

Another, Peter, has told them that you freaked out when you found Evelyn and ran at them firing your gun. I've made sure there is no evidence of that at all. They have Peter but I'll deal with that. We have the lawyers on it, and the best thing is that you were last seen being taken away by the FBI, who denies any knowledge of having you. It's all so fucking perfect at the moment," Mack said.

"Brooke?" It actually hurt to say her name.

"Angry, hurt, you know. You must have expected this," he said, gently. I nodded.

This had always been a plan should the shit hit the proverbial. It was made easier with Italy, and even easier with the FBI taking me in for questioning. Right then, I needed to disappear for a while.

"Travis?" I asked as the plane door began to open.

"Mr. Stone, welcome back. Any luggage?" I heard, interrupting Mack from answering, initially.

Gary stepped from the vehicle. I guessed he was giving Mack and me some time alone. He walked to the rear of the car and popped the trunk where he retrieved a small carry-on. It would contain my passport, or rather, a passport, money, and a change of clothes. And, boy, did I need a change of clothes. I stunk of blood and sweat.

Gary handed the bag to the male steward and I turned back to Mack.

"How is Travis?" I repeated.

He sighed. "He understands, but..." was all he said.

"Look after them, Mack," I asked as I started to climb the steps.

I turned. "Katrina had a brother, Dominic. Seems he worked for the Bureau for a while but went off grid, they wonder if one of *our* associates had him,"

He nodded. "Her brother died of cancer. Are you sure he wasn't fucking with you?"

I shrugged my shoulders. I wasn't sure of anything at that moment.

"I'll check that out, if someone has him in hiding, it won't be hard to find out. I'll be in touch tomorrow, let you get settled," Mack added.

I didn't look back; I couldn't if the truth were known. I walked into the plush jet and settled in a seat. I buckled up and downed the whiskey that was handed to me. I leaned back, closed my eyes, and when I opened them again, we were in the air and over the ocean.

I placed my palm on the window and looked out. America was long gone; I'd slept for five hours and knew I'd soon be on the descent.

I unbuckled myself and strode to the bathroom at the rear of the cabin.

"Mr. Stone, you missed dinner. I didn't want to disturb you. While you shower, is there anything I can get you?" I heard.

"I'm starving, so anything you have going will be great," I said.

I stepped into the bathroom, stripped off my dirty clothes, and stepped under the small shower. Only then did I allow myself to think, and to start to feel.

A physical pain ripped through my chest, I placed my hands on the tiled wall, and while the hot water ran over my body, washing my sins away, I cried. I whispered Brooke's name over and over.

---

"Roberto," I heard.

I looked up to see Mario standing beside a Mercedes car. I descended the steps of the jet and the warmth of Italy enveloped me, calmed me.

I heard my name called again. When I looked over the hood of the car, I watched Franco emerge from the passenger side.

"Franco, Mario. It's good to be home," I said, reverting to Italian.

"My condolences, Roberto, I...I don't know what to say," Franco said. I watched the old man rub at his eyes.

"Thank you. I was with my father when he died, which is more than I can say for Evelyn. She died alone, Franco."

"You took out Volkov?" Mario asked as we climbed into the car.

"I did, but she's just a small part of all this. Marco was involved with the Russians, and whoever gave the command to take on my fucking family is still at large, for now. I believe I can get that information from Dimitri Volkov if I can speak with him, though. I'm not sure how possible that is."

"It's possible, Roberto. We have contacts in Russia," Mario said.

I leaned back into the leather seat and closed my eyes. "That's exactly what I wanted to hear," I said.

I inhaled the scent of Italy; I absorbed the language being spoken between Mario and Franco, and then the driver. I allowed the view of Rome as it slipped past, the countryside as it emerged, to soothe my broken soul. It was as my village, and it was *my* village, came into view and the welcoming committee stood, that I knew I had come home.

We stopped for a short while in the square. I climbed from the car to be greeted by the villagers. Some cried, and some hugged me. All passed on their condolences for the loss of my father, Evelyn.

"We'll bring Rocco home, and I'm convinced Evelyn would want to be with him," I said to Franco.

He nodded, "I'll make the arrangements."

"I need to get home," I said, walking back to the car.

We drove the short distance to the villa. Vinny waited in the courtyard, Elvira stood by the door. She looked as if she'd been crying and Vinny was, for once, quiet and respectful.

I wanted no one other than Mario and Franco with me. We walked into the house and I wallowed in the coolness of the central hall.

"When can I make a call?" I asked.

"Not yet, Rob. You're still officially missing," Franco said.

I needed to hear my wife's voice, knowing the hurt would tear me apart. I needed to be torn apart, I needed to feel her pain of abandonment to add to my own. But I also needed to keep her out of harm's way, and my location a secret.

"Make sure that you get her a message, Franco. Tell her…Just say, *Did I tell you that I loved you today?* She'll understand."

Elvira brought a bottle of wine and glasses; she placed them on a table on the terrace. As the night drew in, the scent of earth, of lemon groves, and olive vines wafted up. The sounds of the village below floated around and the colored lights strung between lampposts glowed. I sipped on my wine, and I told Mario and Franco all that had happened the past few days.

We talked, we planned, and I missed my wife more as the night drew in, knowing I was about to climb into an empty bed. Something I hadn't done in five years. After Mario and Franco left, I continued to sit. Elvira had plated some food and left it in the kitchen. I didn't want to walk in there. It would remind me of Evelyn. I sipped on my wine and I thought of her.

I thought back to the day I stole her purse and the sadness I'd seen in her eyes. I thought to the day I knew Rocco was alive, and how pained I was that she didn't know. I remembered her meeting him in the cemetery, just a short distance away, and I recalled her smile as she thanked me for bringing them back together.

It hurt.

It hurt so bad that I wanted my wife to wrap her arms around me and take that pain away.

It hurt so bad that I wanted my son to give me a smile that would melt it away in an instant.

A familiar feeling washed over me, I both welcomed and was repulsed by it. I looked up at the sky as a shooting star blazed against the blackness.

I felt lonely.

I felt broken.

I felt like that small boy, who had just lost his best friend.

I felt like that preteen, who sat under a bridge to shelter from the night.

I heard the sound of a telephone ringing. I placed my glass on the table and walked into the hallway. I picked up the receiver.

"She said, you didn't, but you can if you want to," Franco said, and then he cut off the call before I could respond.

"I'll her when I see her," I said, to no one in particular.

*Letter from Robert*

*I spent most of my life without a biological family, and the ones that became my family in their absence meant more than any blood relative could. Which is why it was so easy for me to kill my brother. Which is why I can ignore a sister that wants nothing to do with me, ever. Which is why I could kill Katrina.*

*The pain I feel at the loss of Evelyn, the only mother I really knew, and my father, Rocco, is still acute. I doubt it will ever leave but that's okay. It reminds me that I am capable of feeling—for a little while back then—I thought I'd lost that.*

*Today I drive to the airport and I collect my wife and son. I haven't seen either for a month, although we have spoken. We've cried, we've screamed at each other, we've slammed phones down, and we've dialed back. She assures me she still loves me, my son loves me, and both have forgiven me for abandoning them when they needed me. It was yet another testament to the character of my wife. We were bound way more than husband and wife; we were soul mates.*

*She took care of my son in my absence, she took care of my family, and she took care of my brother. She put him back together. He, and Harley, are flying out with her. Apparently, there was a little brunette in the village that had taken his fancy when he'd been out here last. It was a lie, of course, but it was his way of coping with losing someone he loved, and someone who had betrayed not only him, but also his family. Would he ever truly forgive me? I think so; I hope so. He is my brother, he, Brooke, and our children are all I need to heal—and I still have a lot of healing to do.*

*I would tell Travis that Katrina did love him, she'd confessed that. I would also tell him she wasn't pregnant. Call me a coward, but she was always going to die, I'd just prefer that he didn't know I'd killed his child as well. That was something that would haunt me forever. When I made that decision, I became more like the 'fathers' that I had. Both Joe and Rocco took secrets to their grave, as would I.*

*Many days I walked to the cemetery. Evelyn and Rocco had been laid to rest with just myself, Mario, Franco, and a few villagers in attendance. A* memorial would be held when the rest of my family arrived a week after Brooke and Travis.

There had been an extradition threat, of course, but so far, no charges were filed, and according to my lawyers, they'd never make anything stick anyway. Especially since Peter was no longer a witness. With my position in Italy, they'd be hard-pressed to get an extradition order executed anyway. That meant I was free to return, but I wasn't ready to. Travis, Mack, Richard, and Jonathon, who had come out of semi-retirement, were doing great in my absence. Things were running smoothly. Business was good and very profitable, still. Gary and Pat had moved into Evelyn's apartment, and I was glad not to have seen that. Although I sanctioned it, it pained but comforted me at the same time. Gary would protect Brooke and Gerry as if his life depended on it.

It was my life in Italy that was different.

Here, I was Roberto, head of a very powerful organization, the 'Ndràngheta.

Here, I sat in charge of the Commission on a regular basis. I was feared and I was admired in equal measure.

Here, I finally spoke to Dimitri Volkov. He commended me on my business acumen; I told him that I would kill him. He welcomed that, like his daughter, he was tired of being a 'State Puppet'. He told me he had now lost both his children, and I believed him when he'd said that. It wasn't probable that Dominic would be allowed to live, and he told me that Marco had dealt with him long before he went to America. To avenge his son, he gave me all the information I needed on the family in America that Marco had been laundering money for. He confirmed he'd tried to warn me when he realized his daughter had been 'woken'—he just hadn't tried hard enough or in a way anyone understood. I guess I was supposed to contact him and not walk away from a property deal. How different would things have been had I done that—that thought broke me further.

Here, I plotted the downfall of a Russian mafia family in America, and I sat back and watched the carnage from my terrace, sipping my wine, tending to my olive groves, and listening to the music that was Italy in the daytime, Italy in the evening.

Here, I was finally me. I was the man I was destined to be, and I could *only hope I could convince my wife, my son, my brother, to accept this version and to maybe spend a little time deciding where home was.*

*Here, or Washington, D.C.*

*I knew where my heart lay...Italy, it was my birthright.*


*Is this the end? I doubt it.*

*Robert Sartorri*

# ABOUT THE AUTHOR

Tracie Podger currently lives in Kent, UK with her husband and a rather obnoxious cat called George. She's a Padi Scuba Diving Instructor with a passion for writing. Tracie has been fortunate to have dived some of the wonderful oceans of the world where she can indulge in another hobby, underwater photography. She likes getting up close and personal with sharks.

Tracie likes to write in different genres. Her Fallen Angel series and its accompanying books are mafia romance and full of suspense. A Virtual Affair, Letters to Lincoln and Jackson are angsty, contemporary romance, and Gabriel, A Deadly Sin and Harlot are thriller/suspense. The Facilitator is erotic romance.

*Stalker Links*
www.TraciePodger.com
author@TraciePodger.com

# BOOKS BY TRACIE PODGER

25495955R00172

Printed in Poland
by Amazon Fulfillment
Poland Sp. z o.o., Wrocław